Jewels of Darkover
Darkover® Anthology 20

Edited by

Deborah J. Ross

The Marion Zimmer Bradley Literary Works Trust
PO Box 193473
San Francisco, CA 94119
www.mzbworks.com

CONTENTS

INTRODUCTION

by Deborah J. Ross

When asked which fantasy world they'd like to live in, many readers say, "Darkover!" I'm not surprised by their enthusiasm. For over 70 years, fans have treasured this amazing, rich world so much that it feels like a real place. If it isn't, they say, it ought to be. Now, more than ever before, we all look to the places of our dreams.

I think part of this loyalty is due to the way Marion Zimmer Bradley depicted Darkover, from the early Ace short novels (*The Planet Savers*, 1958) and juveniles (*Star of Danger*, 1965) to the more complex *The Heritage of Hastur* (1975) and *Stormqueen* (1978). The world, its history, and its characters unfolded more deeply with each new adventure. The Friends of Darkover formed a community through "Relays" newsletters, fanzines like "Starstones" and other publications, and even Darkover-centered conventions.

A second factor is how Marion encouraged loyal fans to write Darkover stories, much of them of professional quality. These stories filled in the gaps between the novels, explored regions off the map, created new characters, elaborated on nonhuman races, and delved into the nuances and ethics of *laran*. The first Darkover anthology, *The Keeper's Price*, came out from DAW in 1980. This current volume is the twentieth. These anthologies allowed fans to make Darkover truly their own, weaving together their imaginations, their literary skills, and the landscapes they had come to love. Over the years, Darkover anthologies have included stories by many authors who were encouraged and first published by Marion, as well as those who fell in love with Darkover and went on to notable while retaining a special place in their hearts for the world of the Bloody Sun.

When I sit down to edit a Darkover anthology, I look for stories that are compelling but also true to the spirit of Darkover.

Each author brings their own experience of Darkover to the creation of their stories. A skilled equestrian might write from their own experience about the fabled Alton black horses, or a musician about a performance of "The Ballad of Hastur and Cassilda."

It is a curious principle that reading a story involves several layers of translation. A writer sits down at the keyboard with a concept, akin to a film that only they can see. They use words to communicate that story, but in the process of setting it down, some things are gained as well as lost. Written language imposes its limitations but it also adds the connotations of word choice, pacing, and diction. When a reader picks up the story, a second translation takes place. Instead of being inserted verbatim from the text into the mind of the reader, a good story *evokes* associations and memories. The reader is not a blank slate but a person with their own emotional reactions, history, tastes, and so forth. In this way, no two people read exactly the same story.

Just so, no two writers depict the same world, even one as well-established as Darkover. As the editor, I look for a Darkover sensibility, a "feel" of the world that goes beyond a great red sun, breathtaking snow-covered peaks, starstones, Towers, and the aristocratic Comyn. Or the cultural clash between a world that has developed the sciences of the mind and one that relies on machines. I especially want stories that could not take place in any other world but Darkover.

I'm intrigued by where writers get their ideas, especially the inspirations for Darkover stories. Therefore, in preparing this anthology, I asked the authors to write a little about the origins of their stories. You'll find these in a separate section at the end of the anthology. I hope you enjoy these insights into the creative process as much as I do!

GOLDEN EYES

by *Marella Sands*

When not writing, Marella Sands spends her time watching superhero movies and scanning Etsy for more craft materials to buy. She escapes her keyboard to bake and make jelly. She was fortunate to be able to teach in Tashkent, Uzbekistan, for the spring semester 2022. While there, she was able to stand in the ruins of a city built by Alexander the Great, ride a Bactrian camel, and tour the bazaars of Samarkand. In her stateside classes, Marella watches students teach each other skills such as origami and improv, and referees debates on whether Steve Rogers is a utilitarian or a deontologist (for the record, he's a deontologist).

Marella currently has three series out: her Tales from the Angels' Share, about a bartender who encounters the supernatural and gets tossed into the conflict head-first; Escaping Normal, a non-fiction series about the paranormal; and her alternate history series, which is being reissued by Untreed Reads. That series follows the adventures of two federal agents in an alternate United States. She has a story coming out in the anthology Merciless Mermaids, edited by Kevin J. Anderson.

"Shay! What have you got there?" Gerardo called from farther down the slope.

Shay looked up from the ground, where she had been studying a small hole. Every so often she thought she saw something moving in the hole, but she couldn't tell for sure. Whatever it was, it would have to be small, perhaps only the size of her thumb.

"I don't know," she said with some irritation. She hadn't wanted this trip to include Gerardo, but the elders of the newly-founded settlement of Iona had insisted Shay and Liria bring Gerardo once he'd volunteered to come. Ungenerously, Shay thought the elders had been glad to see the last of the young man for a few days.

Gerardo strode up the hill, shoulders back, dark brown hair billowing out from his head almost like a crown. He was, according to all the girls Shay's age, the handsomest young man in the settlement. Her friend, Valentina, had been struck low with jealousy hearing that it was Gerardo who had been chosen to go with Shay and Liria, when, if he'd stayed at the settlement, he could have been attending the dance the young women were planning at the end of the tenday. Shay wished he were back at the settlement, too, dancing with Valentina. That was preferable to spending several nights in the Kilghard Hills with him. At the very least, she hoped Liria's presence might help Gerardo keep his calm. He had always seemed reluctant to engage Liria in conversation and avoided her whenever possible.

Shay looked back at the hole. For a moment, she thought she saw two golden sparks, but then those sparks retreated and the hole looked empty. A strange feeling suffused her mind for a moment, but she dismissed it. She sometimes had that reaction to the hills and had no idea why. She merely accepted it as part of loving the hills and wanting to walk them whenever possible. Nothing made her happier than to be in Liria's company or exploring the hills, or both.

Gerardo knelt beside her. He laid a heavy hand on her knee, and she fought the urge to lean away from him. He had approached her last summer with the idea of becoming a couple, perhaps even marrying, but she hadn't been interested. He was too hot-headed for her, and he didn't like Liria. Everyone liked Liria! As far as Shay was concerned, his dismissal of her best friend was simply one more reason Gerardo was not for her.

Liria came down the slope from above. She had been looking for plants the settlement had not yet cataloged. In the century since their great-grandparents' arrival on this planet, many such expeditions had been made to catalog the flora and fauna of this world. Much of the native flora was beneficial to the settlement, but some could be dangerous. It was best to find out as much as they could.

Gerardo glanced over at Liria, then looked away. He seemed unnerved by her tall, slim frame, pale eyes, and long white hair. She had six fingers on each hand, as many did who were descended from Lori Lovat. Most of them weren't as odd-looking as Liria, but then, her mother had produced Liria when she claimed never to have shared her bed with a man.

In fact, the identity of Liria's father was a mystery everyone liked to speculate about, especially in the depths of winter, when there was little to do except try to stay warm. Gossip was rife at any time, but in winter, it was worse. Now that spring had burst forth, and the flowers and cloudless morning skies promised summer, everyone was far too occupied building, farming, or repairing things broken by winter storms to worry about such things. Still, the attention Liria's birth had garnered had been too much for her mother; two years ago, she had walked off into the mountains and no one had heard from her again. Liria had not seemed distressed at her mother's fate; according to her, her mother was "well enough and happy." Since she had some odd way of knowing things she couldn't possibly know but always later turned out to be correct, no one worried about her mother after that.

"Anything?" asked Liria. Her widely-spaced eyes were ice blue and framed by stark white lashes. She was, in Shay's opinion, the most beautiful woman in Iona, maybe in all the settlements that had popped up around the original settlement of New Skye. Shay never tired of being near her or looking at her, which Liria found amusing. Shay never minded being the butt of Liria's amusement, because she knew there was no malice in it. As far as Shay knew, Liria was never angry at anyone or disliked anyone, not even Gerardo.

"Maybe. There's something in this hole." Shay continued to stare at the darkness of the hole. *Come on out, little one. I won't harm you.*

"Dig it out," said Gerardo. "Stick it in a bag, and we'll take it back with us."

Shay didn't even look at him. "Perhaps it doesn't want to be dug out and turned into a dead specimen on a table." She got up and shook the dirt off her pants.

"More reason to do it," said Gerardo. He picked up a stick and plunged it down the hole.

"Stop it," said Shay angrily. Really, did he have to be cruel to even the smallest creature? "I'll collect what I think's important. You're here as a *guardian* to keep Liria and me safe. We'll decide what we take and what we leave. You keep an eye out for danger."

That didn't sit well with Gerardo, but what could he say? Let him fume about whatever little thing was in the ground, but let him leave it to its own devices. Shay despised those who were intentionally cruel; although she regretted the necessity of killing animals to eat, she appreciated that those who culled the herds tried their best to be as kind as possible when doing the actual deed. The animal was destined to die to be on the dinner table, yes, but that didn't mean it had to suffer or be afraid. The psi powers that had developed in most people in the colony were diverse, with some being able to put animals into a calm stupor to make them more biddable.

Shay climbed up the slope, Liria easily keeping up with her. Shay was slightly above average in height for the women in the settlement, but Liria towered at least eight inches over her. Liria was the tallest person in Iona now, more so even than MacAran. Shay liked the way Liria's white hair floated about her head like the seed tassels of spring flowers that swirled away from their parent flower on the barest hint of a breeze. Being with Liria on this beautiful day with the heavy perfume of a dozen flower species drifting through the air made the day perfect. Not even Gerardo's presence could ruin it.

"Did you spot anything new up here?" asked Shay.

"No," said Liria, "or, I don't think so. There's some tiny purple flowers up here that I think I've seen before, but I can't put a name to them. Perhaps you can."

"You don't know if you've seen them before," said Gerardo from behind them. "I thought you were some kind of fantastic botanist we all had to be impressed by."

"Really, Gerardo," said Shay. "Are you *always* such a boor?"

That silenced him, at least for now. Shay knew Gerardo too
well to think he'd be silent for long.

Shay and Liria continued up the slope as the red sun began
descending toward the horizon.

"Just up ahead," said Liria. She pointed at a stand of tall,
straight trees. The three of them walked to the trees and, sure
enough, there were tiny purple flowers playing peek-a-boo with
them through the stalks of grass.

"Oh, they're lovely," said Shay. She knelt and plucked a
single flower. "Are these the ones the catalog calls Purple Spring
Bells? I'll take this as a sample." Quickly, she stashed the flower
in her carry-all. She got out her notebook and not only drew a
small copy of the flower, but she noted its elevation, the plants it
was found growing near, and the side of the slope it appeared to
prefer. She also took one of the small, round leaves that sprang
out from the base of the plant and put it in the bag with the
flower.

"We should go back down the slope," said Gerardo. "The
sun's getting low and it's likely to snow up here."

"It won't snow tonight," said Liria lazily. Then she gave a
small laugh. "The slopes will be rioting with flowers as soon as
the sun sets." Liria was always delighted by flowers, any
flowers. During summer, she almost always had one tucked
behind her ear, and when decorating her head, the flowers
seemed to stay fresh and beautiful far longer than a plucked
flower should. It was as if even the flowers tried to enhance her
beauty.

Gerardo frowned at Liria's announcement and possibly at her
good humor, but said nothing. When Liria made pronouncements
about the weather, everyone knew to listen to her. If she said it
wouldn't snow, then it wouldn't snow. Liria herself had never
claimed to understand how she knew these things; she just *knew*.

"We should get down the slope, anyway," said Shay. Whether
it snowed or not, late spring evenings in the hills could be frigid.
Winter did not like to lessen its grasp on the landscape. Shay's
grandmother had told her that *her* grandmother had claimed to
have grown up in a place where it was always hot and never

rained, let alone snowed. Shay had been unable to imagine it. "No snow means a Ghost Wind, more than likely."

Liria nodded, and they began walking down the slope. Liria wasn't afraid of the Ghost Wind; it never seemed to affect her. Shay had been exposed a few times, and it had only made her giddy. Few people were truly made ill by it, but the doctors theorized that everyone was mostly desensitized these days. Not like in the early days of the settlement, when people completely lost their senses, at least for a few hours.

Gerardo ranged on ahead, perhaps feeling he should be the one to pick their campsite. Let him. One spot was as good as another, as long as it was near water.

Liria pointed at the ground they walked on. "Look. More of those little holes."

Shay looked around as they walked. Liria was right; the holes were everywhere. In some of them, she spotted two golden sparks. Those had to be eyes. Each hole must be the home of one or more of the creatures.

"I don't recall anyone on previous expeditions mentioning them," said Liria. Her low voice was comforting and warm; Shay loved listening to her.

"Maybe no one was looking so closely at the ground," said Gerardo, who had stopped just short of a stand of trees. "They probably had something more important to be doing."

Liria said nothing; in fact, her face, which was generally impassive, was as unmoved as usual. Shay frowned, though. Gerardo was often unpleasant, but he seemed even more so today. "You volunteered to come," Shay said. "But all you've done is complain."

"I volunteered to protect you, not be interested in some stupid holes. Why aren't you looking for new sources of protein, or something we can use to build larger structures that can take more snow load in the winters? You know, something the settlement actually *needs*."

"I don't know that *you* are the expert on what the settlement needs," said Shay. She knew what Gerardo's complaint was really about: some of the residents of New Skye had recently been finding new ways to use the mysterious blue stones. Recently, several people had figured out how to use the stones to link their minds together to see what was under the ground: metal, building stone, more crystals. So far, what they had seen with the stones turned out to be an accurate catalog of what was underneath their feet. Soon, New Skye would have an abundance of materials that had been difficult to locate up to now.

The only downside seemed to be that the ones linked mentally were always exhausted after a few minutes. So far, no one had figured out how to link minds for longer than that. Shay's cousin, Darren, had said he slept for three to four days after every five-minute session.

Yet their need for metals was so great, even those five minutes were precious.

Shay hoped she could figure out something equally as precious. She had a rivalry with Darren, though her competition with him was good-natured and full of comradeship and love. Gerardo's desire to rival Darren and the others was of a darker nature. She knew he hunted the creeks and valleys around the settlement for a blue stone of his own, but so far, hadn't found one.

Shay did not want one. Touching one, even once, seemed to be enough to open the floodgates of telepathic or empathic ability in many people. Her older sister had touched one and had suddenly been able to hear the thoughts of the herd animals. She'd sobbed inconsolably every time an animal was killed for food or when one froze to death in the midst of winter. Eventually, she had become so lost in the animal minds that she'd stopped responding to people entirely. Then she'd stopped eating.

Now she was in a grave.

So, Shay was not overly interested in these blue stones. If hearing the thoughts of animals were bad, then surely being privy to the thoughts of other people was even worse! She couldn't imagine doing something like Darren did: having one's mind and thoughts open to others, and them being open to you. That was an intimacy too much for Shay to even contemplate.

"Here," said Gerardo. He threw down a few branches he'd collected on the way down the slope, apparently claiming that spot for a fire. "Let's camp here. The stream is just past those trees, but this is a nice, sheltered place in case it snows."

Shay said nothing, and neither did Liria. Let Gerardo deny Liria's ability to predict the weather; he knew as well as Shay that Liria was never wrong. It would not snow tonight.

Liria cocked her head. "I think I see some grass over there that I don't recall seeing in the samples back at Iona, or even at New Skye." She pointed to the north and slightly downslope. "I'll take a look and be right back."

Shay couldn't see anything unusual, but maybe Liria just wanted to get away from Gerardo for a few minutes. She sighed and began pulling out the ingredients she had brought for their dinner. Much of what she had was dried fruit and meat. The meat was a bit tough but tasty, and the fruit was tart and flavorful even in its dried state. They might be away from the settlement for a couple of nights, but they'd eat well. She glanced back at the retreating form of Liria, wishing it had been Gerardo who had walked off.

"Why do you watch her like that?" he asked while fanning the fire. He had been careful not to use too much wood or allow the flames to get too high; the resin of the trees in the area was too flammable for carelessness. At least, Gerardo was taking this part of the journey seriously. Though, of course, the strictures concerning fire, its creation, and maintenance, were well-schooled into every child by the time they were five. Fire was important, but it was also far too dangerous to take for granted.

"Watch her like what?" asked Shay wearily.

"You moon over her like a lover," said Gerardo. He seemed almost sad, which struck Shay as odd. Why should he care how she looked at another person? "She's just some weird human-alien half-breed. She's not like us."

"I saw you dancing with Arianna last winter," said Shay. "She's descended from Lori Lovat, too. If you have something against Liria's parentage, why not Arianna's?"

"That was generations ago. We don't know who Liria's *father* was, and anyway, Arianna and the rest of her cousins don't have the extra fingers and weird coloring. She just looks...different. She talks oddly and the way she meets your eyes..."

Gerardo shut up. Shay glanced at him, surprised to hear the fear in his voice, and now to see it on his face. "The way she *meets your eyes*?" she prompted.

Gerardo just shook his head. "She should never have been allowed to be born. She should never have been *conceived*. It's wrong. She's all wrong."

"There's nothing wrong with her, and she's a lovely person," said Shay. She couldn't feel angry at Gerardo right now for the ignorant things he was saying; she wasn't even shocked he'd suggested terminating a pregnancy. To the settlers, any pregnancy was precious. An illness or especially harsh winter could still wipe them out; their existence was that precarious. Not one pregnancy could be treated lightly. "There are a dozen other new settlements that would take you in. Go to one of them if Liria's presence bothers you so much."

Gerardo cast her an odd hopeless glance and went back to tending the fire. Shay dismissed the conversation from her mind and just tried to enjoy the spring weather. A balmy evening after a harsh winter was not only a relief but a joy to experience. She stretched and let the cool air fill her lungs and her mind with peace.

Gerardo finished with the fire and came around to kneel beside Shay. He sorted through the meat and vegetables and took them back to the fire, where he spitted the food and placed it near the flames. They had not carried pots, and the food was already cooked, anyway, but it would taste better warmed. Already, Shay could see her breath, and she could spot the first few ice crystals of the evening glittering in the grass nearby and in the pine needles overhead. The night would get far colder still, but at least they would have warm food to fill their bellies. Plus, the cold of spring was nothing like the cold of winter. This was heavenly weather, the sort nearly everyone in the settlement loved and which was often the subject of their winter poetry contests. Flowers, green leaves, and a few snowflakes were the defining images of spring.

Tonight, she not only loved the weather, she felt as if she were being born anew after a lengthy time of bracing against the harshness of winter. Just thinking about spring almost made her flesh tremble with ecstasy.

Gerardo looked up from the spits he was tending. "There's no reason for me to go to a different settlement. Why can't *she* go?"

It took Shay a moment to remember where their conversation had ended; she was too distracted by the weather, the odd thrumming in the back of her head, and the overwhelming excitement of the night.

"Why don't both you and Valentina go?" Shay asked through her almost transcendental joy. "She'd go anywhere you asked."

Gerardo's lips curled up in a confused *who?* before he realized who Shay was talking about. He shrugged. "I'm not interested in her."

Shay felt a moment of sympathy for the rejected Valentina. She was just looking for a mate, like anyone else. But her eyes had landed on a man who literally couldn't remember her name and face. That was sad, but not enough to crack the shell of joy that Shay felt surrounding her. She sighed and let the happiness drift around her like a fog.

Liria wandered back to the fire as Gerardo was taking the warmed food off the spits. He handed the food to both Shay and Liria, giving Shay an odd look and not even glancing in Liria's direction. Shay noticed the slant of his jaw, the delicacy of his fingers, and the length of his neck. Gerardo was certainly a beautiful man—on the outside, at least. If he could just handle his emotions, he would be a good companion, even a good husband. He certainly had enough survival skills and strength of character to provide for a family.

The three of them ate in silence. Shay continued to enjoy the cool night air as the hillside became carpeted with the spring flowers that sent out their pollen to form the Ghost Wind. Shay smiled at the thought. The Ghost Wind was nothing to fear, and only a niggling voice at the back of her head wondered if the odd emotions she felt were connected to it in any way. How could that be? No one was as sensitive to the Ghost Wind now as their ancestors had been a hundred years ago.

After the meal, Shay leaned back against a tree and let the happiness wash over her without worrying about what it was or where it had come from. It was enough that she felt it now, with Liria nearby, the beautiful stars overhead, and the slope so gorgeous with its thick carpet of white, gold, and purple petals.

Gerardo glanced over, "Going to sleep already? You're generally the one joining in the fun after dinner."

Shay just shrugged. Gerardo's comments weren't going to cut through her joy at the night. At home, people were nearly desperate for something to do in the quiet dark of the post-dinner evening, especially in winter when they were trapped inside. Shay's grandmother had told her that, in the early days of the settlement, people had tried games that had required skills like bluffing or lying, but with half the settlement being populated with people who could sense lies, those games had died out. Shay's favorite thing to do on long cold winter days was to engage in poetry contests where each person made up a line, and the next person had to make up the next line while following arcane rules of rhyme, rhythm, or topic. Gerardo liked that game as well, and he was at his most pleasant while competing.

Most people got more aggressive when losing a game they enjoyed, but Gerardo, who could be so difficult to be around most days, was actually easier to endure once winter came and he could make poetry for much of the day.

At last, Gerardo banked the fire and wrapped his own blanket around him. Liria did the same. Shay stayed leaning against her tree, contemplating the night and watching the stars shimmer in the frosted sky.

Gerardo and Liria appeared to be asleep, but sleep was going to be a stranger to Shay tonight. She could tell. The feeling in her head had suffused her whole body. She felt as if she needed to get up, to run through the grass and embrace the flowers. This was her night, her one night, to fulfill her destiny.

She got up and began walking back up the hill. Three of the moons were out, so it wasn't difficult to navigate the grassy slope. When she reached a small rock outcropping, she sat down. The feeling now seemed to be coming from all around. It was close and familiar.

Slowly, she observed a multitude of the twin yellow sparks she had spied earlier in the holes. Only now they were in the grass. Shay slid off the rock and sat down in the midst of the grass and waited.

One pair of sparks inched closer, and now Shay could see the sparks were the eyes of a small multi-legged creature that was strange to her. The body was black, and it had some kind of antennae on its head. The legs ended in tiny hooks. How did those tiny feet make holes in the tough soil?

More of the creatures came forward. None were bigger than Shay's thumb. She reached down and held out her hand. One, apparently more bold than the others, walked resolutely onto the palm of her hand.

As soon as the tiny feet touched her skin, she felt the life of the creature in the marrow of her bones. Despite the fact they were of different worlds, different body plans, and different minds, she could still feel the forces that powered this tiny creature as much as she could hear the pounding of her own heart. It was their joy she had been feeling. Their happiness.

More of the creatures came forward. Some had stripes on their backs, but most were black. Perhaps that differentiated between males and females? She wouldn't know without taking some back to the lab with her, but at the moment, she couldn't bear the thought of harming any of these creatures, not even for study.

More crawled on her, some in her lap. Others unfurled wings and clumsily flew to her shoulders and on top of her head. The scratchiness in her mind evolved into dim feelings of affection and purpose.

Shay laughed. She'd never had a single moment of psi powers before, and now, she was feeling the primitive emotions of her tiny friends. They had emerged to fly and mate and lay their eggs in the ground. Though these concepts were not conveyed by thoughts, but rather by emotions, Shay understood. The creatures were so ephemeral, emerging from the ground for just this one night. But not every year. She could feel the patience they had had, waiting and waiting, through cold winters that drove them to the depths of their deep holes, and through previous summers when they could dig new tunnels and shore up the old ones before the next winter. And now, they had put aside their old skins, the large, scoop-shaped feet they had previously had in order to dig, and they were prepared to stretch out their new shimmering wings and fly under the light of the moons and sing their joy at the sight of a new world, of mates and mating, and of laying the eggs that would hatch the next generation of tunnel-dwellers. Until, sometime in the distant future, they would emerge again in winged form, and take to the skies.

Shay was covered in them now but didn't care. A few that had crawled to the top of her head launched themselves into the sky with such energy, it was almost as if they intended to fly right to the moons. This would be their first, and only, flight, and it would be completed by dawn. That was the cycle of their lives. But they weren't sad to be at an ending, they were joyous at the thought of the skies and mates and eggs. Death held no terror. This night was theirs.

"What are you doing?" That sounded like Liria. Her voice was full of fear.

Shay laughed again and turned to Liria, holding out her hands now covered in the small creatures. "Look at them! Aren't they beautiful!" she exclaimed.

Liria's face went from concerned to beatific. She reached out her own hand. "You can feel them in your head," she said bluntly. It wasn't a question.

"Yes yes yes," said Shay. She wanted to dance and sing. A desire to fly away, mate, and fall spent onto the ground at dawn seemed to suffuse her every nerve.

"Be careful," said Liria. "Remember your sister."

But why remember someone who was dead? Her sister was gone and in the ground, but Shay stood in the midst of *life*. The tiny creatures were so *alive*, so vibrant. They sang to her. Shay wanted nothing more than to listen to their thoughts and ride their joy for the rest of her life.

"What is going on here?" That was Gerardo. His face was flushed even in the pale light of the moons.

Shay laughed. "Come, see what was in the holes. They are the tiny sparks of life that emerge after ages underground and fly through the night sky for just a few hours. I can hear them; I can feel them!"

Shay was weighed down by the little creatures, small enough on their own, but now hundreds sat on her head, her shoulders, her ears. Combined, they were heavy, but she didn't mind. The weight was comforting, like a living blanket. The creatures covered her arms and legs as they crawled upward. Those that reached her head launched themselves into the star-blotted inky expanse above. Shay's mind rose upward with them until it seemed she was looking at herself from above through the lenses of a thousand eyes.

Gerardo uttered an animalistic growl and leaped forward. Liria jumped in between him and Shay.

"Stop," said Liria without raising her voice or her hands. "Leave her be."

Gerardo swung his head from side to side and clenched his fists. "Get...away...you...thing..."

He shoved Liria aside. Or he tried, but the willowy girl was stronger than she appeared. She stood her ground and punched Gerardo in the face. Surprised, he fell backward onto the grass. "What, why?"

"You know about the Ghost Wind," said Liria. "Get control of yourself; you should be able to shake off a lot of the effects."

But Gerardo wasn't listening. Shay watched from above, but dispassionately; her heart and mind were still with the little creatures and their joyous flight. The two arguing beneath her did not interest her. Only the open skies and the call to mate were important.

Gerardo's face was a mask of fury and terror. He climbed to his feet and grabbed at Liria. Liria evaded his grasp.

Shay's joy at being part of the creatures' mating flights was shattered as she watched her friend try to defend herself from the man.

The creatures were so tied into her thoughts that some of them were distracted as well. They flew clumsily toward Gerardo and Liria. Some landed on Gerardo's shoulders. He screamed and pushed them off. A few of those he flung aside climbed awkwardly back into the air, but others were too injured to fly again. They lay on the ground, their one chance at reproducing taken from them. Their joy had turned to despair, and Shay felt it to her core.

"Why are you so cruel?" Shay screamed. She leaped forward and pushed Gerardo down. He was strong and leaped right back up. He raised his fist to strike Shay, but suddenly Liria was in the way. She took the punch to the jaw and went down with an "oof."

Shay darted forward and smacked Gerardo on the face, terrified that he'd hurt Liria. But the other woman was already climbing to her feet.

The creatures on Shay had now begun covering Gerardo and Liria. Liria ignored them, but Gerardo screamed, "Get them off of me!" In terror, he fell to the ground and covered his face as the creatures walked all over him, their tiny hook-like feet holding fast to his shirt and his hair.

Shay's anger had turned to fury. "Don't you dare hurt them!"

Gerardo's hands slipped slightly, and Shay saw the terror in his eyes slowly leach from them to be replaced by wonderment and awe. "I feel them," he said in a whisper. His entire body shook. "I feel them."

Liria shook her head. "There's something going on…I feel it."

"Yes," said Shay as the little creatures kept emerging from their holes and taking to the air. "Something is happening. We need to record this for the settlement." She sat down heavily on the cold ground and watched the creatures spin and whirl through the night sky.

"No, something else," said Liria. Suddenly, she clutched her head and ran down the slope.

"Liria!" shouted Shay. She was alarmed but couldn't follow. The creatures had too much of her mind for her to be able to do much besides let her thoughts join them in their maiden flights.

She heard crying. That couldn't be right. Who could feel grief on such a glorious night? A tugging at the back of her head told her she should be worried about Liria, but how could *worry* overpower the joy within her?

Gerardo's face was covered in tears. Shay cocked her head, curious as to how he could feel so wretched at such a time. Suddenly, he climbed to his feet and ran back to their camp. Shay watched him go, content to be alone with the creatures, until Gerardo returned with a flaming brand from the fire.

"No!" Shay shouted. He waved the torch overhead, dangerously near the pine needles that would go up in moments. If Gerardo weren't careful, he'd burn acres of land, including himself and Shay. The explosive resin in the surrounding trees would send flying splinters, as well as flaming needles, everywhere. The slopes would be enveloped in fire before Shay could flee.

The creatures that had not yet taken to the skies reacted with alarm. They had survived previous fires while being safe underground but now they were vulnerable. Their instinct to hide underground had faded, to be replaced by the urgency of mating and protection of the next generation. If the slopes were afire, no eggs could be laid before morning. An entire generation would be lost.

Their focus suddenly became Gerardo rather than the skies. *Danger! Fire! Protect!*

As one, the thousands of creatures began swarming the young man. They batted against his face and flung themselves into the torch's flame as if they could put out the fire with the wetness of their small bodies. Some would never fly to mate, but by protecting the rest of their broodmates, they could secure the future of their kind. If only they could put out the flames.

Gerardo swung the torch around. Shay ran forward in alarm and grabbed at it. "No! Gerardo! Get a hold of yourself!"

Now more of the creatures came and flew to Gerardo. They landed on him *en masse* until he could no longer hold up his arm. Shay took the opportunity to grab the torch and stomp on it until it was nothing but ash.

But the swarm continued. Gerardo collapsed on the ground, covered by so many creatures, he couldn't stand. They would crush him.

Shay's heart leaped at that. She held up her own arms and begged the creatures. "Stop! Don't hurt him anymore. The fire's out!"

But their instinct to protect the next generation was too strong. More and more creatures came to land on him. Many of them were males who had just mated and were now doomed to die before dawn. If nothing else, they could help the eggs their mates would lay in this one way: they could make sure Gerardo never had the opportunity to bring fire to the slopes again.

Shay's mind broke free of the creatures' emotions. She had to save Gerardo. He was a boor, true, but he was still a member of the settlement. She waded through the heaps of dead males until she reached the lump that was Gerardo. She plunged her hands into the mass of creatures until she felt an arm. She latched her hand around it and pulled.

Slowly, Gerardo's arm emerged from the dunes of dead and dying creatures. Shay pulled on him but he was too heavy with the creatures on him. She began scooping the thousands of their lifeless bodies aside until she found Gerardo's head. He wasn't moving. Was he even breathing? She couldn't tell. Desperately, she grabbed his wrist and pulled his upper body out of the pile.

He didn't seem to be breathing. In terror, Shay knelt down and shoved her fingers into his mouth. It was crammed with dead creatures. She pulled out as many as she could and hoped they had not managed to also fill his throat and lungs.

Shay was rewarded for her efforts by a sudden deep whoop of a breath from Gerardo, followed by coughing. After a few moments, he weakly pushed a few of the creatures off his body and head and struggled to sit.

"What happened?" he asked.

"You tried to destroy them," said Shay, equally angry and relieved that he was all right. "They tried to destroy you in return."

"But not you."

Shay shrugged, though she realized Gerardo probably wouldn't notice the gesture in the dark. *You're an idiot!* she wanted to scream at him. She took a deep breath and pushed aside her own grief and anger, which seemed to hang like a splinter over her heart, just waiting to pierce it. Her own emotions were tangled up with what she had felt from the creatures; it would take her some time to understand it all. For now, she simply tried to hold it in her heart in such a way that it hurt the least. In time, the splinter would soften and its ability to hurt her would diminish, even disappear. But would these feelings ever come again? What was really going on in her mind? She didn't know. Maybe someone back at the settlement could help her, one of those who had more experience dealing with psi powers.

Shay had tried to stay away from those with psi powers when she could. Now she'd be seeking them out. Life had a strange way of surprising you no matter how set you thought you had made everything.

She rubbed her eyes and took a deep breath. The feeling of the creatures in her mind had faded. Most were dead now. The males had fallen to the ground, exhausted and spent, and had died. The females had ripped off their wings so that they could squeeze themselves back into the holes. They had retreated underground to lay their eggs and die. Their bodies were to be their brood's first meal.

The Ghost Wind still tugged at her emotions, but she was able to cope with it now that the creatures were no longer sharing their feelings with her. She stretched her mind over the slopes but felt almost nothing. The few remaining females who were still returning from their mating flights had no thought except the driving necessity of laying their eggs and ceasing to be, content in the knowledge they had produced, and safeguarded the next generation.

"They were so beautiful," said Gerardo softly.

"Then why did you try to set them ablaze?" asked Shay with some asperity, a bit annoyed that Gerardo had distracted her from her last attachment with the creatures. She abandoned her efforts to reconnect with them; even the last few females were fading into oblivion now.

"Because...because they rejected me!" shouted Gerardo.

Shay turned to him in surprise. "Rejected? How?"

"I felt them. I felt their joy. I wanted to join in like you seemed to be able to, but then suddenly there was nothing. As if they had shut me out."

Shay shook her head. "I don't think they had that power. It's you. You must have some small bit of psi talent that the creatures helped you tap into, but only barely. You should go to New Skye and have their council test you. They might help you understand what power you have, if any. I need to go, too, so I can deal with whatever happened here tonight. Too bad there's no schools where this could be taught or places for people to practice their new-found skills safely."

"There will be, one day," said Gerardo dreamily. "Great towers will be built, where our children's children will sit in silence and yet be able to stretch their minds out over the entire planet. They will be able to reach into the very DNA of their cells and into the roots of the mountains. They will converse with each other across the continent and bring about a new age of power and glory."

Shay stared at him, amazed by his words. Something in the back of her mind whispered *he's right.* Whose voice was that? It sounded like her own, but that couldn't be.

Gerardo suddenly jerked. "What did I just say? What's happening?"

Shay leaned forward and grabbed his cold hands, her mind and heart reaching out to him in pity and sympathy. "It's all right. I think you're developing some kind of talent. Maybe...seeing the future?"

Gerardo sobbed. "I don't want to see the future. It's...big. It's frightening. There's...there's fire and dreadful weapons. People dying of embers burning into their flesh to cook their bones while they live. I don't want to see it!"

Shay squeezed his hands. "I'm here. I'll help you."

Gerardo looked at her with his tear-streaked face reflecting the light of the moons, which were only now beginning to descend toward the horizon. "But what about you? You could feel these creatures' minds. You'll need help, too."

Shay sighed. "Yes, I think you're right. What else do you see of my future?"

Gerardo said, "Why did I say that? I can't know the future."

"Maybe you can," said Shay as gently as she could.

He made a sound halfway between a groan and a sob. "I've always been able to," he said with some resignation. "At least, that's what I think, now that's it's so strong inside me. But I've always had these weird glimpses of things I couldn't have known. I didn't know what to make of it. I'd hoped it would make me special, different. Instead, it only brought me nightmares and terror. I couldn't understand what was happening to me. I hoped, if I could find a stone, I'd find a way to control it. It was always worse around Liria."

"Is that why you don't like her?"

Gerardo closed his eyes. "Her face isn't right. When I see her in my head, she's different. I don't understand why she affects me so. I don't know what's going on." His voice broke off as another sob ripped through him.

"Perhaps this face is one you recognize, then?" a deep voice asked.

Shay looked up to see Liria, or someone who strongly resembled Liria, standing a few feet away. The figure had the same eyes, the same white hair, and the same six-fingered hands. It was even wearing Liria's clothes, but they were now too tight. The figure was undoubtedly male, with a much stronger jaw, and broader shoulders than Liria had ever had.

"What...what happened?" asked Shay.

The figure shook its...his...head. "I don't know. I felt something inside me change. I'm still Liria. But now..." Liria brushed her...his...hands across the squareness of his chest, the narrowness of his new pelvis. "I think I need to go find my father. He can explain all this to me."

Shay's confusion melted into grief. Liria couldn't leave her! "But you can't go! I'll miss you so much."

Liria smiled sadly. "I'll miss you, too. But I must understand myself. I need to know what's happening to me. Then, maybe, I can return." The figure leaned down and kissed Shay gently on the forehead. "Farewell. For now."

"But do you even know where to go? You have no supplies," said Shay, desperately trying to find a way to delay Liria's departure.

Liria smiled, his eyes locked onto the mountains in the distance. "I've always known where my father is, I think. It's been something inside of me since I was a child. My mother is with him. I will go to them directly. It's not so hard. Think well of me if I do not return." He strode off.

Shay watched the lithe figure go, her heart threatening to seize and stop beating from the succession of shocks.

Gerardo took her hand. "That's the face I've seen in my mind ever since I first saw Liria. He will find his father and return again to you. And, maybe, to me." Suddenly, Gerardo sounded shy, nothing like the braggart he was most of the time.

Shay turned back to him and wiped the tears from his cheeks. Her own grief still threatened to overwhelm her, but she took comfort in Gerardo's pronouncement that she would see Liria again. "We'll go to New Skye and speak with them about you. And me. And Liria. And we can return to Iona or go to a different settlement and start a new life together while we wait for him to come back to us."

Gerardo smiled; it was the first time Shay could recall him smiling for months, not since he'd won the poetry contest at Midwinter.

"Yes," he said. "Let's go home."

LITTLE MOUSE

by *Shariann Lewitt*

Shariann Lewitt would like to say that she has traveled to Africa and Antarctica, gone scuba diving in the caldera of an ancient volcano, and been awakened by a jaguar in her tent in Costa Rica's Osa jungle. She would also like you to believe that she studied algebra in graduate school, did evolutionary biology (and ended up doing mostly computation because she hated field work) because she didn't want anyone to see her faint in the lab, and spent several years demonstrating against anything she didn't like in the streets of her native Manhattan.

Shariann is the author of nine science fiction novels under two names but has written another eight under three other names that span genres including fantasy and YA. Her short fiction has been published under only three names and in two genres, science fiction and fantasy, and even she isn't sure how many stores over fifty she has sold. She is sure, though, that the story "Fieldwork" (editor's note: *Not* the story by Margaret and Les Carter in this anthology) appeared in the *Thirty-Fourth Best Science Fiction of the Year*, edited by Gardner Dozois. That story was inspired by her personal preference for doing science in a nice clean lab building with climate control and indoor plumbing.

When she's not off adventuring, either in her head while seated in a coffee shop in greater Boston or somewhere remote in the physical world, she impersonates faculty at MIT. She'd like to tell you what she does in her spare time, but she doesn't have any.

First she heard the fracas and then her mother screamed. Jonil put down her *ryll*, not able to make out what was going on.

"Put him there," her mother said as if she were talking about a dish of nuts, though Jonil could sense the terror that lay under the command in her voice. "Darna, hot water from kitchens. Now, girl."

"Will he live?" one of her mother's ladies asked in a low voice. If Jonil hadn't been concentrating, she wouldn't have caught it.

"If we had someone Tower trained," the other replied, and that's when Jonil couldn't remain in the corner. She stood and held out her hand. "Take me," she said to whomever was nearby.

Although she was blind, Jonil could usually get around her mother's solar without help. She could feel the sun from the large banks of windows where the ladies' embroidery frames were grouped. She could feel the worn place in the carpet where everyone walked from the door over to those windows, and she knew the route from the entrance to her own little alcove where she played the *ryll* while the ladies did their needlework.

Now, though, it was all in disarray. She could hear people moving around, the heavy boots of armed men, and the chatter as unfamiliar voices decided precisely where he should be laid. A rough hand landed on her shoulder. "Jonil, you're blocking things up. Let's leave."

She knew that voice: Samel, her cousin, always so sure of himself. Now he tried to pull her out of the room as if she were a small child. "You're only in the way here," he said as he steered her away from the emergency.

"Who is it?" she asked.

"Lorenzo. Now get out and let the people who can do something help him," Samel replied.

"I am a *leronis* of Arilinn," she announced, the sound of her voice cutting through the confusion around her. "Lead me to my brother and let me see where I can help."

"You can't help," this time her father answered, and he was angry. "You're just the blind girl, useless. Samel, take her out."

"My eyes may not work, but my *laran* is more than sufficient," she replied and walked confidently toward where Lorenzo lay on an improvised stretcher right before their mother's huge embroidery frame. She'd seen the room through the eyes of one of her little friends, a small mouse that had scurried across the floor and back into the fireplace, empty in the summer heat.

Ever since she had been a child the mice had seen for her. As a strong empath, the mice, all the animals, really, readily allowed her into their senses and permitted her to use their eyes. For her part, Jonil tried not to abuse their generosity and always gave something in return, bread and cheese from the kitchen for the mice and oats and carrots to the horses and chervines whose minds she slipped into so easily.

Two small brown mice entered the room and ran to her, rubbing up under her skirts and against her stockinged ankles. They were worried. She calmed them, and in return, they both opened to her like flowers, and suddenly the darkness around her resolved and she could see. As the mice did so, the colors were muted and scents enhanced, but that was when she saw her mother bent over Lorenzo's head with her embroidery silk and finest needle, stitching together his flesh.

"Let me try."

No one answered. No one even turned or paid attention, no matter that Jonil was known to be one of the strongest *leroni* to come out of Arilinn for a generation, with rumors of more potential should she choose to stay. She might be able to do something for her elder brother, if anything remained to be done. If he were not already dead of blood loss or the wound that had caused it.

Jonil breathed deeply and steadied herself. She needed Lorenzo alive and well and heir to Aldaran. She wasn't going to get out of her marriage to Samel without him, even if she hadn't loved him for himself, for him just being Lorenzo. For being the only member of the household who thought she was fine just as she was. She could not imagine life without him, her laughing, bright-haired brother.

Her father brushed her away, pulled her mother up, and started to shake her. "You can't do better than that? Take care of him, make him well. Do it, woman."

Jonil flinched even as her mother did. While her mother, who had little *laran*, could do no more than she was already doing, applying herbs to fight infection and stitching the wound closed with her embroidery silks, Jonil might be more successful. If they let her. If it wasn't too late.

She reached out a single hand to touch Lorenzo's bare wrist; she needed only the smallest touch to read him. Yes, he was alive—but he wouldn't be for long. She knew the signs well. Little blood circulated to his heart and she could not make more, not enough to push it through his veins and arteries, not in time to save him. *Please, please*, she thought at him, trying to draw material from anywhere, from her own body, to raise the pressure in his although she already knew it was useless.

If only she had gotten there faster! If only she had had the support of actual healers.

Which was all a lie, to herself more than anyone. No one could have saved him. She felt his soul retreating from this world, pulling away from them all. Already more than halfway to the veil in the Overworld that separated the living from the dead.

"Brother," she whispered. "Lorenzo. Come back."

She tried to reach out to him with her *laran*, but again she was too far behind. As she entered the gray Overworld, he approached the barrier between the living and the dead, the division that she could not cross. He gave her a look that was far too mature for the years he had lived, and he shook his head firmly. Then he departed past the veil and he was gone.

Dead.

"Where is Samel?" her father yelled.

"He was right here," one of the grooms said from his post at the wall. "He tried to talk Lorenzo out of taking Rilly to Bramble Creek, but Lorenzo was dead set. For Rilly's training, he said the youngster was ready."

"What was Lorenzo doing riding Rilly, I'd like to know," her father said, but no one answered. That didn't matter, not now when Lorenzo was no longer alive. "And where in all nine hells was Samel when Lorenzo was out on that high-strung piece of horseflesh?"

"In the kitchen, eating honeycakes hot out of the oven," Darna whispered from her place by the door. "And drinking all the fresh *jaco*."

Without rapport with anyone, not even the mice, whom she had to release to try to help Lorenzo, Jonil was truly blind. She pushed herself backward toward the wall and used it to guide her around the crowd. She could hear them murmur, smell the perfumes that covered the sweat of horse and hard work, hear the susurrus of the women's skirts. With her memory of the scene and her knowledge of the room, it was enough for her to make her way back to the niche where she had left her *ryll* on the window seat.

Only when she found her place there she found she was not alone.

"Ah, little mouse, what a terrible time for us all," Samel's whisper carried none of the emotion that his words expressed. "That Lorenzo would be injured riding, I don't think anyone ever thought it could happen."

She hated when he called her *little mouse*. When Lorenzo had done so, his voice had been warm and teasing, full of the love that ran between them. From Samel, it only meant humiliation. He hated mice; he had made that clear often enough before.

"I shall escort you to your chamber," he said. "I expect that you would prefer to be alone at this time."

"No, Samel, I would prefer to remain with my family," Jonil had trouble keeping her voice steady. She could feel his hand on her arm, ready to drag her out the door and down the stairs. He had done so before, as if he could simply dispose of her when he found her presence inconvenient. No wonder he was willing to marry a blind girl when he thought that because she could not see when she was without rapport, she was unaware and unable to understand what was happening.

"I really think it would be better if you weren't exposed…"

"Leave me, please." At least, she managed the polite word if not the tone. "I expect that Mother will have need of me to help with the women in preparing the funeral feast."

He snorted. "How could you help? You couldn't see if anyone put too much spice in a dish or overcooked the gravy. You should be where you can't get in the way."

He tried to pull her up, and Jonil resisted and fought him with her nails, long and strong from playing a stringed instrument. Samel pulled back. "I'll assume that your reason is affected by your grief," he said stiffly.

But he left. She could hear his boots on the flagstone flooring. At least, he knew not to walk with his riding boots on the fine carpet. She did not know if she were safe enough to try to make her way down to the kitchen where she would have duties to perform. For all that Samel thought her useless in the kitchen, Jonil could smell and taste perfectly well, could hear the gravy bubble and touch the dough. In fact, her bread was the best in the household because she could tell the texture as she worked it with her hands to where it was just perfect.

And she would much rather be busy doing something than crying over Lorenzo. Or herself.

Lorenzo had promised to intervene with their father against the marriage with Samel. Her brother knew—had known, she corrected herself—just how their cousin saw her. And Lorenzo had valued her. Lorenzo had known, more than most, how strongly she could enter into rapport with any species she encountered. Lorenzo also knew—had known—that she had more *laran* than anyone else in the family had displayed in four generations.

He had known about the mice, how she could call them when she needed eyes. He had been impressed, for she had even learned to read using their ability. They could not understand what they saw, but she did. And Lorenzo knew what she could do.

He had tried to explain this to their family, but their father hadn't listened and their mother cared only for what Jonil could command as a wife. Or rather, her fear of Jonil's shortcomings as a chatelaine.

The fact that Jonil had no desire to be anyone's wife, let alone Samel's, did not matter. Not even when the Keeper of Arilinn had told them that Jonil was meant only to have a short visit home before taking up more involved duties in the circle. Her father had used the "short visit" to draw up the betrothal and force Samel on her, and her mother couldn't understand why she would rather return to the Tower than stay at home "where everyone will take care of you."

Because her father needed Samel, or so he believed. After Lorenzo, he was the next in line to inherit Aldaran. Now, with Lorenzo's death, he was the heir. All the more reason to rush the marriage and make certain her future was assured.

Only she knew that their father had finally given Lorenzo permission to marry Bethanyi. Her brother had not been able to stop whistling this morning at breakfast before he had gone out to ride Rilly, which was quite unlike him so early. Of course, she had to ask why he was so cheerful when the sun was barely up and he couldn't contain his good news.

At least, they were alone for a while yet. Lord Aldaran had already eaten and was out talking to the groom about the mare who was due to drop her foal any moment now and wouldn't return to the house until he had checked in with the overseer and the estate agent. Their mother was still abed, as was her habit. Only Marga, the head cook, was about, scuttling around the kitchen between the kettle for the cups of morning *jaco*, sliced cold meat, and warm fresh bread that the family and workers alike took as they went about their early chores.

"But how did you convince him?" Jonil had asked, for Lorenzo and Bethanyi had been freemates for years and he had sworn he would marry no one else.

"You must promise to tell no one," Lorenzo swore her to silence. "On your starstone."

She pulled out the pouch that held her starstone around her neck and held it in her hands. "I promise. No one."

"Bethanyi is expecting. A boy. Father could hardly turn down my heir."

Jonil had laughed with him in pure joy. "That's wonderful news." She had thrown her arms around him as she had when she was a girl and the two of them embraced. Touching, Jonil could feel Lorenzo's joy course through her. Everything he had wanted for so long, and a reason to get rid of Samel as well...

"When shall you announce the happy event?"

"I sent a message to Bethanyi at once, and she should be here tonight. So tonight at dinner. I already told Marga to make it a special one." Then he had kissed her cheek and run out, having barely touched his food.

Only a few hours ago. And now the world was bleaker than ever.

With Lorenzo gone, her misery was assured, Jonil thought as she kneaded the dough for her nutbread, the finest served in the Domain.

After Lorenzo had left, the morning had turned strange, now that she thought of it. She could feel the mice reach out to her from the barn, afraid. She'd taken her mug of *jaco* and a slice of the cold roast chervine and had gone over. Lorenzo had already left, but the mice swarmed around her legs and jumped from the beams onto her shoulders and arms. She entered rapport with them easily and she could see—strange things. Not the plain old barn with a few of the older horses in their stalls, a few younger stable boys mucking out the dirt as she had noticed when she had entered.

No, with the mouse vision she saw swirls and movements and smelled a grain bucket that at first enticed and then turned sickly sweet. She heard all kinds of noises, footsteps and boots, Lorenzo's laugh and something that sounded like Samel greeting him, only Samel was rarely up this early, and then Samel hiding in a corner of a stall? Then it all mixed around again and the noise became too strong, the movement too fierce.

She sent wave on wave of calm through them, reassuring them that all was as it should be, but they were not convinced. The sounds, the movements, did not dissipate for all her comfort. She let them gather around her skirt, even climb up onto her lap and shoulder, as she sat in the kitchen garden, enjoying the sun on her face and the warm *jaco* in her mug. And she wondered why all the mice were seeing things that weren't there, were so hypersensitive, and were so terribly frightened of things that they normally found ordinary.

That had only been this morning when Lorenzo had still been alive. Now she had to bake for the funeral feast. Slamming the dough onto the board, she imagined slamming Samel's head into a rock. She was stronger than he imagined. Playing the *ryll* and kneading bread made strong arms and back. She was not some lady who could pick up nothing heavier than her needle.

But the fact remained that no matter what now, Samel stood to inherit. Either through her or on his own, and because of her father, both. If Bethanyi and Lorenzo had already married or at least had announced their intention and their coming child, at least the child would be protected. But now...

Samel was sure to challenge the child. Or, if not, he would certainly challenge Bethanyi's right to raise him and would say that he and Jonil should raise the boy as their own. And then...Jonil knew her nephew wouldn't live very long. Children are susceptible to so many diseases, and if nothing else, he would perish of terrible threshold sickness.

Because while Bethanyi was no Comyn, her mother was the *nedestra* daughter of a Comyn lord and had passed on more than an adequate share of telepathic talent to her daughter. More than Lorenzo and certainly far more than Samel had ever had. In fact, Samel was nearly mind-blind.

Better to be eye blind than mind-blind, she thought, as tears ran down her face.

"Careful, *Damisela* Jonil, or you'll break the bread board," one of the cooks called out. It brought no laughter, not now.

"Stop crying into the dough, or you'll make it too salty," Marga said to her. Meant kindly, to take her mind from the worst of her pain.

And then the bread was in the oven, the meats rested, ready to be carved, her mother pronounced herself satisfied and told Jonil to go upstairs and change her clothes. And take a bath as she had flour all over.

At least her mother knew perfectly well that Jonil could make it to her own chamber without help. Still, a maid trailed after her with a large bucket of warm water so that she could wash, as she would serve any Comyn lady. When they got to her room, the girl not only poured the water into her small tub but also provided soap and held the towel until she was ready. A luxury, really. At Arilinn she didn't have anyone to serve her a warmed towel and hot water or to help choose a gown.

Of course, at Arilinn she wore the same blue robe every day. Well, she had three of them, one to wear, one to wash, and one for best with red edging to proclaim the rank that she had not yet announced to her family.

Now she didn't wear the blue of a matrix monitor. For her brother's death, she instructed the girl to take out the pale golden gown her mother had stitched with a deep hem and cuffs of leaves and vines, and a cascade of *kiriseth* blossoms falling from the neckline, the one her mother and her ladies had made for her betrothal and wedding.

"Oh, no, *damisela*, not that one," the maid moaned, as Jonil ran her fingers lightly over the rich fabric. Then, with the sharp knife she carried in her belt, she began to rend the gorgeous dress into rags.

"He was my brother," she said firmly, defying the servant to interfere with her destruction of the gown. "And it can be mended."

When she deemed it sufficiently shredded she had the girl help her into it, and then re-dress her thick damp hair with a wooden butterfly clasp instead of the copper one she had worn earlier. Although she left enough hair to gather modestly at the nape of her neck, she also teased out strands around her face and cut some of them off at uneven angles.

Perhaps Samel would find her less attractive with her hair ruined and wearing rags. Though he, and her parents, had made it clear that, because of the scars around her eyes she could never be beautiful, her hair was heavy and thick and fell past her hips in a deep copper curtain. If it wouldn't be brazen, she would just cut it all off. That would make Samel think twice about marriage.

But then, Samel had no interest in her other than the Domain she could secure for him. Perhaps he would care about an heir, though he would use her for duty and not pleasure. For that, he would look elsewhere and she would, no doubt, know every detail. He would make sure to tell her.

There was the final threat, of course. But she had already tried that with her father and failed. He had simply refused to believe that it was too late.

"No one has told me that you are training to be a Keeper so don't get above yourself, girl. You're here now and that's final."

But she had thought she would be safe, at least from the marriage. Samel didn't want her, and as long as Lorenzo lived, their cousin couldn't inherit. Once Lorenzo produced an heir, Samel would be well out of it. She had only had to protect her brother that long and she had failed and now she refused to pay that price.

"Lorenzo," she screamed, willing him with all the power in her to return to the body which even now was being washed and dressed in his finest. If she could see she would be with the women at these final ministrations, but yet again she was left aside.

Instead, she paced her room, seventeen steps from the door to the single small, high, window, six from the window to the bed, along the bed, and then twenty from the far wall back to the door again. She walked briskly, knowing the position of even the smallest detail in her room. Her water glass and pitcher on the nightstand were always in exactly the same place, her comb and toiletries laid out on the dressing table so that she could place her hands on whatever she needed. In the top left drawer of her dressing table, she could find her jewelry collection. Her fingers located the butterfly clasps for her hair, a brooch that had been her grandmother's, and a fine copper chain for her hair with a green stone that hung on her forehead, that her mother forbade her to wear because it called attention to her useless eyes.

And, like every other bed chamber, she had a lantern on the table and a candle next to the bed. Why these remained in her room she found puzzling, but let it go. Perhaps the extra light was useful to the servants on dark days.

Bethanyi was due this evening and now she would be greeted by a nightmare. Jonil made her way from her room to the main hall and clapped sharply. One of the maids, trained to her signal, stopped and came over. "Yes, *damisela?*"

"When *Damisela* Bethanyi arrives, please have her brought to me directly," she instructed. And then she sat down to wait.

She had to assume that the maid, Wena by her voice, had made some gesture that showed her disapproval at the use of an honorific for Bethanyi, whose father was wealthy but was otherwise no rank different than she.

Jonil had heard the gossip when Lorenzo had stopped trying to hide his relationship with the girl. Mice hear very well through walls and she had listened in order to tell Lorenzo and Bethanyi what they might have to face. Lorenzo hadn't cared.

"There's enough trouble, you don't have to borrow more," she told herself. She started the breathing exercise she had learned in her first week at Arilinn, to calm her mind and center her thoughts. Bethanyi would come. All the pieces should fit and yet...still something was off, like a boot that had been cut just a little too tight or a singer who couldn't quite reach a note.

And yet...

Lorenzo wasn't supposed to die.

She could not figure it. If she were simple, she would suspect Samel. He certainly wanted to be Heir to the Domain, but Samel wasn't stupid. He would do better to wait until they had locked the marriage bracelets around their wrists and he knew it. That was the only reason he was willing to marry her and, if her father had his way, the ceremony was not far off. So why strike before he had taken that final step?

No, it made no sense for Samel to kill Lorenzo. Not yet.

She heard the scream from outside, she felt the wave of rage before the wall of grief hit her, and she knew Bethanyi had arrived. She rose and let the pure emotion guide her toward its source as she ran into the arms of her would-be sister-in-law.

"No," screamed Bethanyi. "Never. Lorenzo was too good a rider to have an accident like that. He wouldn't. He couldn't. No, someone else had a hand in this, I promise you."

Jonil just held her. Bethanyi was raving, but she agreed fully with the feeling. She felt that way herself, that if she fought and denied hard enough that the gods would have to realize that they had to undo this mistake immediately. Make it go back to the way it was when they woke this morning, to the way it was last night when everyone was drunk and singing late, after the older folks had gone to bed.

Holding Bethanyi now, she felt something, someone, else. Someone not quite aware of their own existence yet, like when she touched a butterfly's mind/emotions. It simply was, without any sense of selfhood. This was similar but vibrated with—potential.

"Bethanyi, the baby, I can feel him," Jonil said.

"The one thing I have left of him," Bethanyi sobbed. "If not for this little one I would kill myself now. But with him, I cannot."

And then everything came clear. "Bethanyi, we must hide you immediately. Samel can't know you are here," she said, pulling the shorter girl around and up the stairs. "You'll stay in my rooms for now and then we'll figure it out. I have a key and let no one in. No one, do you understand me?"

She felt Bethanyi nod against her shoulder as she pulled both of them into the room and locked the door behind them. "But why?" Bethanyi asked. "I must be there to say goodbye, I must."

"No, Bethanyi, listen. I think Samel knows about the baby. You say your child is a boy?"

Bethanyi managed a strangled "yes."

"Then your child is the true heir to Aldaran. Which is what Samel wants."

"Lorenzo said he would defy his father to marry me *di catenas*, even though I don't care. I know the heir to your house should have a Comyn bride and we could just wait," Bethanyi said.

"But he talked Father into the marriage because of the child. So Father knows. Which means Samel probably knows, too." Even though Lorenzo had sworn her to silence, he hadn't thought of what Samel might do.

"You don't really think Samel would kill me and an unborn babe?"

"I think it's possible. And I think he might have killed Lorenzo before the marriage could be announced so that everything could be denied. I don't know if Mother knows, but

I'm sure Lorenzo used it as leverage with Father." Jonil took a few deep breaths and sank onto the bed. "We must get you out of here, away from Samel. He can't leave for the next few days, so if you're away from the family he won't be able to follow and you'll be safe. Father knows about the child, and possibly Mother as well, so they will have to support you if they want anything of Lorenzo left. And I will claim that I witnessed your marriage myself and even forge the papers. For Lorenzo's heir, I think Father might even go along."

Then she almost laughed.

"But what about Samel?" Bethanyi asked.

"I will take care of Samel," Jonil said, her voice as cold as the steel in her knife. "Now we need to keep you hidden until we can get you out of here. Can you ride?"

Bethanyi snorted. "How do you think I got here?"

"You will have to leave during the funeral feast itself, during the toasts when Samel must stay in the hall."

"But doesn't he already know I'm here?"

"I'll think of something if he asks. You need to stay hidden for now. Do you know the way down the servant's stairs out the back to the stables? Can you get to your horse quietly?"

"Yes," Bethanyi said. "I used that route plenty of times when I stayed in this house before."

"Good. I need to go down now. Stay shielded and wait. I'll let you know somehow when it's time for you to leave. When I do, go. Don't hesitate, don't think about it, just head for the stables, get on your horse, and head home. Lock the door behind you and leave the key on top of the lintel. Can you do that? To save your child?"

"Yes," Bethanyi agreed in a small schoolgirl voice, but Jonil was already out the door and didn't hear her.

~o0o~

She had called them to her so she could see. All over the room rodents made themselves small and darted out for crumbs of her spilled bread. Samel, seated next to her, flinched as they ran up to her fingers to take their share.

"Can't you keep those filthy things away?" he hissed.

41

So she asked them to go around the room and she listened to the half-whispered exchanges down the tables. While she knew that Wena resented Bethanyi rising so high in rank, the other men and women from the stables and farms gathered at the far corners of the room did not appear to share her pretensions.

"She should be here, though, you think?" Ria Cossler said. "If it was me I'd be here."

"And be thrown out again? I'll bet you a new saddle that she's already been and gone and them not allowed her," Kazel O'Cormel said.

"Like you can afford any new saddle," someone else laughed, Kazel along with them.

"That's why the bet. I could use a new saddle and can't afford one, that's how sure I am of it."

"Yes, and saddled, it's us who'll be saddled now," said another of her father's retainers, someone she didn't immediately recognize. "Samel and that blind girl."

"That blind girl is Jonil Aldaran, and she is going to be a Keeper one day and not marry the stinking likes of Samel," Ria defended her. "He's a pig, that one is, and not fit to hold the stirrups of Lorenzo."

"Oh?" one of the men asked.

"Oh, all the girls know." That was Camilla, whose family made the best cheese in the area. "We try to stay as far away as possible, and if he's around you put mud on your face and in your hair."

Ria nodded. "Smelly mud if you can. He doesn't like things that smell bad so he'll look elsewhere. Camilla has it easier than me because she's always got turned milk nearby." That caused another laugh.

Jonil withdrew her attention. She had always known that Samel was free with women; she hadn't known that he pushed beyond acceptable limits. Her father would not take that well, but then he would say that the girls on the estate were overly sensitive and excuse his heir. Because Samel had been his only choice—until Bethanyi's son was born and acknowledged.

But the toasts were beginning, from lowest ranking up to

highest. By tradition members of the family must remain as everyone who wished remembered and praised the dead.

Jonil concentrated on the mouse that cowered near her skirts, that she had fed with bits of bread and cheese all evening. She had no appetite but had to pretend to eat, or at least move the food around on her plate. This mouse was more intelligent than many of her fellows and Jonil thought of her as a bit special. She thought very hard about sending the mouse to her room with a single message to the person there. "Run."

The rodent scampered off and Jonil returned to ignoring the ceremony swirling around her. She waited. After what seemed like far too long, the animal returned, anticipating a treat. Jonil fingered the servings on her plate and dropped two entire nutmeats as a reward. The creature's pleasure and satisfaction were not only for the special indulgence but for having done well. Jonil let her gratitude and approval wash through the mouse and added a few thing strips of dried meat to her bounty.

"Don't feed those things," Samel commanded her. "It only encourages them. And I don't want them around. Ever. They're disgusting."

It was done. It was up to Bethanyi now. As long as Samel didn't catch up with her later. And kill her.

~o0o~

By the time the toasts were finished, it was well into the darkest hours of the night. The mice stayed carefully inside the walls, for even stone walls have passages that they could navigate. Jonil had called them and asked them to rest in her room this night. She would need them.

She filled them with love and gratitude and her pockets with nuts and seeds and cheese before Samel came as she expected he would. "I will see you to your room," he announced. "To make sure you are safe."

He grabbed her above her left elbow, strongly enough that she expected it would bruise, and yanked her up. "Come now, time for you to go to bed."

She made no retort as he spoke to her as if she were a child and dragged her along as if she were a prisoner of war. He held her with his right hand and had a lantern in his left. Exactly as she had hoped, though it was the way he had acted most times before.

But this time he didn't leave her at the door. "Open it," he commanded. She took a deep breath in and started to grope on top of the lintel where she had told Bethanyi to leave the key. "What?" he asked.

"I put it up there so no one could take it from me if I got drunk tonight," she mumbled, playing as if she might have had a bit too much to drink.

Samel sighed heavily, reached up, fingered the lintel until he found the key, and unlocked the door. Then he shoved her inside and followed and locked the door behind him. He put the lantern on her dressing table and the key in his pocket.

While she saw what he did with the lantern and the key through the eyes of the mice who hid in the shadows of the room, she dared not let him know that she had seen.

"We need to have a little talk, you and I," he began. "Now that I am the sole heir, I no longer have any reason to marry you, except to appease your father, perhaps. But if I do, remember that I am taking care of you only out of pity and not because I have any need of you anymore."

Jonil said nothing. She wanted to lash out at him but knew that the longer she let him build his superiority in his own mind, the better for her plan.

Finally, she made her voice very small. "What do you plan to do with me, then? I could go back to Arilinn if you like."

"Hmm, that might be useful. But it might be useful to marry you, as well. I'll have to think about it. In the meantime…"

He laughed deep in his throat and studied her. "If it weren't for your eyes you'd actually be pretty, you know…"

That's when she leaned over and blew out the lantern.

It was dark. Deeply dark. Three of the moons had already set and Idriel was new and so shed almost no light through her one tiny window. A blind girl didn't need a decent window in her room, after all.

And she called the mice.

They were with her, the warm furry bodies, massing into her small room in numbers she had never sensed before. They filled the space with their warm soft bodies, their earthy smell. More and more of them darted under Samel's feet, nipping at his boots and scabbard, even jumping from the tall bedposts into his pale curls.

Samel howled and pulled out his sword, singing it wildly around the chamber. Jonil, with the help of the mice, backed out of the way of his uncoordinated blows. He screamed and tried to brush them away from his face as he continued to swipe uselessly with the sword. They ran down his tunic, two played with the feather in his hat, and one nipped at his fingers.

They swarmed to her call, enveloping him in their scent, their fur, their feet. He screamed and tried to brush them from his face to no avail.

Jonil sent the image of the key in his pocket. That's all she needed, that key. The mice felt the weight of it, smelled the iron, tasted it, and explored the soft fabric of the soft pocket under their feet. "You can't do this," he yelled at her. "Get them off of me."

But Jonil had already left the room and locked the door behind her.

~oOo~

She had to rouse her mother; she had no choice. A maiden of good family could not sleep just anywhere, unknown, while a man slept in her chamber. And so, even though she knew her mother had drunk deep and had likely taken a sleeping potion as well, she hammered on her mother's door until Darna, her personal maid, opened it.

"What do you mean, disturbing your mother at a time like this?" the maid asked, furious. "You go back to your room and leave her alone."

"Let her in, Darna. I can't sleep anyway," Lady Aldaran said.

Darna did not offer her arm to help Jonil navigate the room to her mother's side, but a few mice had followed her so she knew that her mother had pulled had pulled herself up to sitting in her large curtained bed. Jonil reached over to hug her mother but found herself pulled down so that she sat on the edge of the soft mattress, anchored by her mother's iron grip.

"You can't sleep either, Jonil?"

"No, Mother. And it's worse than that. I think, I think I know something awful. But you must promise not to be angry with me."

"Why would I be angry with you?"

"Because I believe that Samel killed Lorenzo," Jonil blurted out.

"Why would he do that?" her mother asked.

"Because he wants the Domain," Jonil began. "Did you know that Bethanyi is pregnant with a boy and that Father had given them permission to wed *di catenas* so that the child could be the true-born heir? The child has *laran*, I have felt it."

"But to go so far as to kill Lorenzo?" Her mother was clearly not convinced. "But he was not even riding when Lorenzo had his accident. He was nowhere around. So how could he have done it? Everyone knows that Rilly is high-strung and that there are snake nests near Bramble creek. Yes, Lorenzo had taken Rilly there before, but I can't believe it was anything but an accident."

"What if I could prove it?" Jonil asked.

"If you could, that would be different. But it's the middle of the night and you're having dreams. Maybe you should go back to bed?"

"I've just locked Samel in my room," Jonil replied. "He entered without my permission and locked us both in. The mice took the key from his pocket, and I locked him in on my way out. I have an idea of how he might have done it, but we would have to get Father."

"Oh, that's not going to be nice," her mother muttered. "Darna, get my dressing gown. And my shoes. We have to wake the Master."

~o0o~

They didn't have to wake anyone. Lord Aldaran was still at the table, deep in his cups and yet not truly drunk, when they arrived in the hall. He didn't seem so much angry as simply surprised to see them.

"I want to show you something, Father, if you will come with me," Jonil said, tugging at his sleeve as she had when she was little. He responded, rose shakily, and leaned on his wife's shoulder as Jonil led them to the stables. They had a slight delay as her father insisted on two lanterns as they left the house, but Jonil kept walking into the night.

"Look in his feed bucket," she said when she stopped them at Rilly's stall.

The young, high-strung horse did not like being disturbed in his sleep. He protested and a groom calmed him with a carrot while a half-asleep stableboy took out the bucket.

"Has it been refilled from this morning?" Jonil asked.

"No, Lady. He shouldn't eat that much grain, not good for 'im," the stableboy said. Then the boy looked at the bucket. "That's odd. Usually, he cleans it out but look, there's a decent bit left. Seems he didn't like his treat today."

The groom stared into the bucket and pulled up a fistful of the rich mixed grains. "No wonder. What's this?" He pointed out dried darker bits of something that was clearly not grain at all.

"I'll take that," Lord Aldaran said suddenly apparently awake and sober, took the bucket, and marched them back into the house.

When they reached the kitchen he immediately called for all the lanterns to be lit so they could have a clear view of whatever the horse had been fed. Darna got down a large serving platter and Dom Rafael spread the contents of the bucket on the platter so they could see every element.

"Most of it is grain," his wife said. "I recognize it."

"But what are these?" Lord Aldaran picked out the small dark bits that appeared solid and yet somewhat soft. He smelled them, rolled them in his fingers. "Maybe we should put them in water?"

"No, no, no my Lord!" Marga had appeared from the small chamber near the kitchen where she slept. "Get that out of my kitchen right now! All of it! Bad it is, that mushroom, although it looks like the good-flavored one you like with your gravy. No, that one makes people go crazy, see things that aren't there, be afraid for no reason. No, that's a bad one and no mistaking, get it out now!"

"How can you tell, Marga?" Darna asked.

"By the smell of it," the cook replied. "Smells a bit sweet, doesn't it? That's the sign alright, of something you don't even want to touch. Now get it out of here now."

Darna moved immediately to comply. "And mind you don't dump it in the garden or near the stables or barns," Marga yelled after her. "Dump it out in the Brambles. Or down the ash pit, there's the place for it."

~oOo~

"The horse was drugged," Dom Rafael said in front of the Comyn Council. "And so my cousin, Samel Delleray-Aldaran, stands accused of the pre-meditated murder of my son Lorenzo Aldaran by drugging the horse he was training. I ask you to approve Lorenzo's freemate's son as my heir to the Domain of Aldaran, as my daughter Jonil has decided to leave the Domain to take her place as Under Keeper at Arilinn."

"A very sad time for you," Regis Hastur said softly. "You are fortunate to have a grandson to inherit, and a daughter as brave and capable as Jonil of Arilinn."

"I am, indeed," he agreed.

Jonil couldn't see from her eyes, but she could weep as she observed from the gallery. Touching her mother's wrist on one side, and Bethanyi's on the other, she could not miss the look of pride that her father gave her as the Council gave their approval.

AVARRA'S SCION

by Evey Brett

Evey Brett says, "I live in a desert, I write stuff occasionally, and I have a collection of critters including a three-legged Carolina dog, a Lhasa Apso detained by the cops, a visually impaired cat, and an old cranky cat."

Only one moon was in the sky the night my mother abandoned me: Mormallor, shining like a cold white jewel.

My mother's face was equally pale though rimmed with a strange shadow I attributed to the moonlight. She was near to dropping with exhaustion when we entered the boundaries of the estate and were met by a dozen guardsmen. "My son and I wish to speak with the lord of Serrais," she said and shoved me before a half dozen mounted swordsmen.

I had no such desire. I was but five years old and stared at the guards, mute with fear.

"You appear exhausted, *mestra*. Perhaps we can offer you some rest and refreshment—"

"You will offer me nothing but the *vai dom's* presence."

The lead guard frowned but led us to the courtyard. "Wait here," he said, and the rest of his men remained with us.

It was some time before Lord Serrais appeared, dressed in clothes finer than any I'd seen. My own were ragged and threadbare; my mother's dress had been patched several times.

The moment he saw my mother, he froze. His expression was one of pure terror before he schooled it back into neutrality and waved his men to fall back as he strode straight to my mother. "You have no right to come here."

"It's your time to take him," my mother said. "We had an agreement."

"Never. Get him out of my sight."

"And what do you propose I do instead? Take him to the spacemen's orphanage?"

When she was angry, the very air around her grew frigid. I was used to it, but the *vai dom* shivered. "I asked you to leave, *mestra*. Take the child with you."

A wind whipped up, chill and cutting. "The boy will stay with his father, to be raised as a *Comyn* son should."

"Never."

She just smiled, a queer, small expression that meant anger boiled just beneath the surface. If I were home, I would have run for my hiding-place in the cupboard, but here I had no idea where safety might lie.

"You're clearly ill. We will give you shelter, and I will send for a *leronis*."

Her laugh was as bitter and wild as the winds of the Hellers from which we'd come. "It's too late for that."

"Then leave, and let me not set eyes on you or the boy again." Though as stiffly as he stood, I could tell that she still frightened him.

I confess, she terrified me.

The wind picked up. Dried leaves scraped across the ground. In the distance, a horse whinnied.

And so I ran, darting past startled guardsmen until I reached the stable and slipped into the first box I found. I huddled in the corner, grasping my one possession: a matrix stone, wrapped in silk and tucked into a leather pouch I kept around my neck. *You'll understand when you're older,* was all my mother told me, so I feared it, much like I did her.

I was not the only creature in the box. A tall, dappled stallion snorted and craned his head down to sniff me. When I didn't move, he went back to nibbling stray bits of hay.

Outside, a storm brewed. The stallion grew uneasy and snorted, pacing with ears pinned back. The light dimmed. Wind tore at the stable walls. Horses whickered and stamped.

And then it came; a strike of lightning so close that for a moment, the inside of the stable was as bright as day, followed by a deafening crack of thunder and a deep tearing within me, as if a hand had reached inside and ripped out my innards.

Mother!

There was no answering presence. Even so, I tried to find her. The stable faded and the world turned gray and shadowed, but the moment I attempted to move, there was a great *push* that kept me from leaving my body.

Not yet, child. Not for years yet.

It wasn't my mother's voice, but one I didn't recognize, stern yet compassionate.

I will be waiting.

I woke, sobbing at the stallion's feet. The noise caught the attention of the grooms that had swarmed through the stable to calm their beasts. One alerted a guardsman, who scooped me up and rushed back out to the courtyard, where the rain had turned to gentle snow.

My father waited. I went quiet when I saw him and focused on the snowflakes sticking to his dark coat.

He tucked a finger beneath my chin and bade me look at him. "You're as wild as she is, no doubt. Six fingers, eyes gray as a ghost. She's dead, you know. This storm took the last of her strength. And now what am I to do with you?"

I had no answer for him. All I had left was the stone I clutched in my hand. My mother had left me here, alone, just like Mormallor. Small. Distant. Cold.

~o0o~

My father saw to it that I received an education, of sorts, well-rounded if not befitting a *nedestro* son of a *Comyn* lord. From the guards, I learned swordplay, and from the grooms how to ride and care for the horses. The *coridom* saw to it that I learned to read and figure and showed me the details of running an estate. Yet I was passed off as a fosterling from the mountains, even to my father's wife and other children. None knew the truth save for my father's most loyal guards, who kept a wary eye on me as if I might turn into something monstrous. The distrust wore on me, but it was instinct to keep out of the way. In the few years I'd spent with my mother, we'd kept to ourselves, so outside my lessons I was left alone.

Cold, they called me. Cold and strange, and I did little to convince them otherwise.

My father spoke directly to me only once more, and that was when I lay feverish with threshold sickness. He'd been the only skilled telepath nearby when I'd fallen ill that terrible night.

The weather had turned sour, going from pleasantly warm to a hard, driving rain. The accompanying thunder made my head ache, so I'd pled fatigue and gone to bed early. It wasn't long before fever took me. Whether I experienced dreams or hallucinations, I couldn't tell. I drifted into what I later learned was the Overworld; a vast, gray expanse that seemed familiar, yet not. There were dozens, hundreds of forms, but they held little interest, engrossed as they were in their own activities. I wandered until a voice spoke to me.

There you are, at last.

Female, I thought, although it was nearly sexless. I wasn't sure what it was, other than not human. "Who are you?"

We've met before.

"I don't..." but I did remember. Cold Mormallor. Snow. The night my mother had left me. "Tell me who you are."

I am old beyond telling. I am the end...and the beginning. I am the comfort of the night, the stillness, the quiet of winter.

The explanation made no sense. Surely my illness had affected my mind and I was recalling some old tale of strange spirits and mixed it up with *laran* and matrix stones.

This is no fever dream, child. You are your father's son as well as mine.

"Mother?"

Yet I knew that wasn't the answer. Not quite.

Come.

So I traveled through the strange world, more by will than actual movement, until I came upon a strange shimmery wall. I tentatively raised my hand to touch it. "Are you behind this?"

Come and see, child. Or are you a coward?

I had no fear, but the chill seeped through my nonexistent bones. I was shivering, freezing, and overcome with a strange tingling. I couldn't move.

Felipe!

The shout came from a distance. It was a male this time, commanding and worried.

Felipe, come back. You've gone too far.

Come ahead before it's too late, said the female. *I will show you the truth of who you are.*

Longing mixed with fear. I didn't know where I was or who either voice belonged to. I was alone with no idea who to trust.

A moment later, the decision was seized from me. Pain lashed through my body; sudden, agonizing, and I came to, gasping and drenched in sweat. Thunder cracked, so loud that it sent another wave of torment through my skull.

"I'm sorry," said my father, who sat on a stool beside my bed. I was surprised to see him; never before had he taken an interest in my well-being. "You'd gone too far. I was afraid you wouldn't return."

My matrix stone sat on my chest partially unwrapped, and I realized he must have touched it in order to call me back. I hadn't looked at the stone before, but now that I did, I could see sparkling white lights deep within.

The sight increased my nausea, so I looked away and tried to focus on my breathing. A mistake; a shadow had grown around him

"Felipe? What's wrong?"

The thunder had receded to a low roll, as did the throbbing in my head. I was finally able to speak. "I saw things. I heard someone. She wasn't human. She said she'd tell me who I was. There was some sort of veil, but I couldn't see beyond it. It was cold. Freezing." I was rambling, still feverish, but I couldn't mistake the concern on his face, and now, with my newborn *laran,* I *knew* how worried he was.

And for a moment, we were in rapport; I *felt* his concern and guilt along with a modicum of affection. He was silent a moment before saying, "There are many strange things in the overworld, especially for one untrained. I was at Arilinn for a time, and there were always stories."

What about the shadow? I wanted to ask him but didn't. He picked it up anyway.

"It's the fever talking. I also saw oddities during my bout of threshold sickness."

So he was being evasive. I expected nothing else. At least he didn't despise me, as I'd feared. He'd kept his distance because I was a constant reminder of my mother.

"Yes, your mother," he said and sighed. "You should know the truth of your birth. Coward that I am, if I don't tell you now, I will probably never have the courage again."

A bolt of lightning struck, followed a moment later by another clap of thunder.

My father jumped. "Damn this storm. It reminds me of her. Too much. I met her one night when I was traveling through the Hellers on my way to Aldaran. There was a storm then, too. A bad one."

And, like the wind gusting through the trees, his memories emerged, potent and unbidden.

The horse had spooked; whether it had been because of a wolf or a banshee, he'd never know, but the mare had dumped him in the snow and fled, and by the time he'd gathered his wits his escort had disappeared in the blizzard. He was alone, and lost. He kept moving, but the cold and biting wind quickly sapped his strength. "Avarra have mercy," he said. "Don't let me die out here."

He had no idea how much time had passed before he saw lanternlight and a woman appeared like a spirit, draped in a cloak of fur, red hair blowing loose in the wind. She knelt beside him. "I've come to answer your prayer, Dom *Ridenow. What will you give me in exchange for your life?"*

"Anything."

"Then come."

The wind eased. He followed her to shelter where she provided warmth and food, and before long he was dazzled by the heat...her nearness...and within her, he sensed something wild, so unlike the restrictive Comyn *traditions he'd been born and raised to. Women like her were dangerous and forbidden, but he was too weak in mind and body to resist.*

"Merciful Avarra," were his last words before he gave in to her touch.

One of his guards found him a day later, wandering aimlessly, rambling about feral creatures in the mountains. He'd survived, but the price of that survival haunted him.

Rain pounded loudly against the window. So I, too, was a torment. The memory gutted me.

I'm sure he sensed my pain; the joining ended as abruptly as it had begun. I clutched at his hand, desperate for any sort of connection, but he drew back.

"I'm sorry. You deserve better." Obligation, more than any sort of affection, had brought him to my side this night, and I knew that shame and self-preservation would drive him away again. "I thought she was a dream until that night she came down from the mountains, and there you were. You've been a good, dutiful boy despite the way I've treated you. I was afraid you'd take after your mother; thank the gods you did not."

I took what small comfort I could from that. "Who was she?"

"It doesn't matter." But it did. From his pinched expression, he was worried. "Whoever—whatever that voice was, it isn't your friend. Don't go into the overworld again, Felipe, and don't tell anyone of your birth. Swear it."

It was strange; he'd never asked anything of me, and for him to do so gave the request a frightening weight. "I swear."

"Good. I'll send for a *leronis* to tend you. She'll teach you the use of your stone, and if she thinks it necessary I'll send you to a tower to train." At last, awkwardly, he patted my shoulder. "You'll not have the family name. I can't give you that, not when I have legitimate sons. But I will see that you have a chance to make something of yourself."

Outside, the storm waned. The wind gave way to a gentler, steadier rain that I found depressing rather than comforting. "Thank you, Father."

It was the first and last time I called him such. Not a month later, he slipped on an icy stair at Comyn Castle, broke his neck, and died.

~oOo~

It was raining the day I joined roll call for the Cadet Guards, a chill, steady drizzle that trickled down scalps and dribbled beneath collars to make us all miserable.

Only a few days before, my father's *coridom* had packed me up and sent me to join the cadets at Comyn Castle. "The *vai dom* left orders," he said and made sure I had adequate uniforms and supplies. The guardsmen pitched in and made sure I had little comforts to take with me, such as a new dagger and a pair of sturdy boots to grow into. They told me stories of their own years in the cadet corps, and so I believed I was prepared.

I was not.

By the time I arrived at Comyn Castle, my head ached from the emotions of so many strangers being pelted at me. I managed—just—to answer to my own name when called and stand at attention throughout the morning.

"Terrible weather, isn't it?" one of the cadets asked me after we'd been shown our room. His name was Isidor Lindir, and his smile was a welcome contrast to the cloudy skies and grumbling of our roommates. "Still, it's better than being at home. I couldn't wait to get away. Family, you know?"

I didn't answer. My family was either dead or ignorant of the fact that I was kin.

"Not much of a talker, are you? Doesn't matter. Where are you from again?"

"I was born in the Hellers."

"Ah. That explains your storm-gray eyes, no doubt. I don't know how anyone survives there. Give me the warmth of the dry towns over the snow any day." He smiled again, which eased my anxiety. "Come on, don't be so glum. The first day is the worst. The new cadets always get teased." When I didn't answer, he asked gently, "It's not just the teasing, is it? Didn't anyone teach you anything about *laran*?"

Ashamed, I shook my head.

"My sister is a technician at Arilinn. She taught me a few things. I'll show you."

The offer was tempting, especially because I had so little

control, I sensed Isidor's kindness and sympathy toward a fellow outcast. He, too, was lonely and seeking connection in a world turned awry, though he was not entirely candid. I brushed up against some dark piece of himself he kept locked away.

When he felt my touch, he gave me a cautious smile. "It's rude to pry, you know."

"I'm sorry. I..." I had to take a moment. Trusting a stranger was hard. I recalled my promise to my father, and I was afraid what would happen if any of the cadets found out the truth. It was shameful enough to be an unacknowledged bastard; having a witch for a mother would make things unaccountably worse. Yet I couldn't continue inadvertently sensing things I shouldn't. "I accept your offer. Please show me."

At that, he laughed. "You needn't be so afraid. You can trust me."

I hoped so. I was so used to the indifference of those at Serrais that outright kindness was hard to get used to. I liked him, though, so I took the risk. "I do."

"Good. I'm starving. Shall we find the mess hall?"

I latched on to his offer like a starving pup to marrow, and as we took the first, tentative steps toward friendship, the clouds parted and left the red sun to dry the cobbles.

~o0o~

The other cadets teased us. "Evanda and Avarra," they called us, and it wasn't hard to guess which was which. Isidor was tall with light, reddish-blond hair, always warm and likable, while I was short with darker hair and gave everyone the chilly reception they expected.

Yet however sociable Isidor acted, he had no other true friends, and I came to wonder if he preferred my company simply because I spoke little and asked him no questions.

The two blue moons, Liriel and Kyrrdis, shone like jewels one night as I climbed the stairs to our favorite parapet atop Comyn Castle. I came up here often with Isidor, since he liked to linger and watch the great Terran ships depart in a rush of wind and power.

We also passed secrets here, courtesy of a loose stone in the wall. I crouched, pulled it out, and reached into the hole to find a note: *Wait for me.*

That was all, but it was enough. I replaced the stone and leaned on the wall, gazing down at the people walking through the courtyard.

I knew, even at a distance, which was Isidor. To my surprise, he had company.

Female company.

He'd never had any visitors that I knew of, nor had he ever shown interest in women. My curiosity was piqued, but whoever she was, I would have to wait to find out.

At long last, Isidor climbed the last few stairs. I knew at once from his slouch and overall demeanor that he was unhappy, and I used just enough *laran* to sense the grief that lay upon him. I wanted to ask what had happened but didn't. It was an unspoken pact between us that we both got to keep our secrets.

Yet he leaned on the wall next to me and gazed up at the moons. "Pretty, aren't they?" he asked. "I wish I could go and see them for myself. Or, better yet, some other world. I'd give anything to leave Darkover and go where no one knew me. What do you think it's like where the Terrans come from?"

I had no answer for him. Neither of us had rank enough to do any sort of exchange program with the Terrans, nor did we have the wealth to travel. In a way, I was glad; I would have been heartbroken had he gone.

After a long silence, he said, "That was my sister, Isibel. She's a technician at Arilinn. You're lucky, having no family to answer to. I'm the second son. My brother got the title and the land—what's left of it—and my father had to scrape to buy my commission. I wanted a career in the guard. It was my chance to leave, and Isibel came to tell me…" There was pain in his voice when he spoke of his family, some deep hurt that had never healed. He wouldn't reveal it, though, not even to me.

At any rate, I had my own hurts, and luck was relative. I was a bastard, and while my father had kept his promise and purchased a cadet commission for me, I wouldn't have his name. Never that. "What about training in a Tower? You have *laran*."

"Not enough to be useful. The family Gift mostly passed me by, but Isibel has it in full." He made a wry face. "My only skill is swordplay, and I'm not even that good compared to the others."

That wasn't true, not completely. He'd never be able to beat the more privileged young *Comyn*, who were born and bred to such things, but it wasn't hard to envision him as Arms-Master one day, coaching the younger cadets the way he had me.

And while the other cadets believed him to be happy or at least content, I knew this darker side of him. Sometimes a foul mood would take hold, and all I could do was stay nearby and not pester him. Tonight was worse than usual, although I couldn't quite say why. He kept his mind closed against me.

"What about your future? There's so much more you could do and be. Mounted patrol, hawkmaster...hell, anything other than walking back and forth atop a wall night after night. Don't you want that?"

"No." I couldn't say that the reason I didn't leave was that I couldn't bear being away from him.

"I wish you would. I wish..." But whatever it was, he didn't finish. "We won't be cadets forever, and when it's over..."

"Don't." I didn't want to think about it.

"Felipe, I..." But words failed, replaced by a gentle touch of *laran*. He gazed at me with that sweet, tender smile he showed only to me.

I knew what he wanted, but I dared not give it to him. I sensed fear. Guilt. And a deep, aching torment that had something to do with me.

"Whatever you've done or think you've done, you can't keep it a secret forever. It'll eat you up inside."

I knew he was right, and I wished, more than anything, I dared tell him the truth.

The air around us grew chill. He shivered. "It's cold, *bredu*. So are you."

The observation stung. I cared for him, yet I could not open myself to him the way he wanted—the way he needed. "I'm sorry."

"You need to go to Arilinn. Speak with my sister. She can help you."

Unsaid was the reason he couldn't help me himself. I wanted to ask *why*, to pry at him with my *laran* until I dragged the answer from him, but I didn't. I gazed at him, hoping for some sign that he would explain, but he stared ahead with a distant look that meant he wasn't registering anything he saw.

At first, I thought the shadow around him was from the moons, but then it took on an eerie glow I both recognized and dreaded.

I shivered. "Isidor."

"You should go in. I'll stay up here for a while."

"I'll stay with—"

"No. Go to bed. I'll see you in the morning." There was an edge to his voice I'd rarely heard, and his barriers were up so tightly that I couldn't penetrate them. "Everything will be all right, Felipe. I promise."

I should have stayed with him. If I had, maybe I could have stopped him. Maybe I could have pried out his secrets and taken enough of his pain to spare him; maybe I could have finally shared mine.

But the shadows were enemies I did not know how to fight, and so I went to bed, uneasy, and found no sleep at all.

Not long before dawn, a wrenching pain tore through my chest. Thunder cracked overhead, and the lightning was so sharp, so close, that the hairs on my arms stood on end.

Someone raised an alarm that the armory roof had caught fire.

I knew, before they found him hanging inside, that Isidor was dead.

~oOo~

"Did you know what Cadet Lindir planned to do?" the Cadet-Master demanded when I arrived in his office after his summons.

I could only shake my head *no*. The Cadet-Master was kin to the Altons; if he tried, he could force rapport and find out whatever he wished. In truth, I would have welcomed the invasion if it meant finding any sort of answer.

The Arms-Master, Di Asturien, flanked the Cadet-Master on

his right, saddened, yet a far more sympathetic and comforting presence. "Please, son. Any idea at all?"

Tears stung my eyes, but I refused to let them fall. Not here. I settled into the cold numbness I used as a defense and shook my head again. "He spoke to his sister a little but gave no details. Whatever she said upset him, and he bade me leave him alone."

The Cadet-Master narrowed his eyes. "And you picked up nothing else with your *laran* last night? Don't look at me like that; of course, I know you two were *bredin*. It's my job to know. Just like I know you took his matrix stone."

The accusation shook me. Like any telepath, Isidor never parted with his stone. "Sir?"

"Don't lie to me, Cadet. It wasn't on him. Where is it?"

I could only stand there and stare.

"Damn it, cadet! Have you lost your mind as well as your tongue?"

"Enough," Di Asturien said. "The boy's in shock."

"He's a fool. Zandru's hells, cadet. Stop shaking. I know you're not lying, but gods help you if you've managed to hide anything. You've no idea of the mess you've made. Get out of my sight. The service will be in an hour; I don't want to see you before then."

Gods help me, indeed, although I had little hope of that.

"Come on, son." Di Asturien took pity on me and guided me out of the room, but not before I caught the Cadet-Master's parting shot: *I suppose that's what we get for accepting a nameless bastard into the cadet corps.* He was a strong enough telepath to be able to keep the thought from me; the fact that he made sure I heard it was a cruelty that drove me deeper inside myself.

"It's not your fault," Di Asturien said quietly as we walked through a steady rain toward the barracks. "Nothing like this ever is."

He meant well, and even let me feel his sympathy and sincerity, but I was too numb to accept. Yet if it weren't for him, I wouldn't have survived the day. He found my dress uniform, brushed it off, and helped me put it on. "Be strong. This will be over soon."

I had no such hope, but I let Di Asturien lead me out to the courtyard where cadets and officers alike lined up, all stone-faced despite the rain soaking their uniforms. At the end stood two women, one wearing the scarlet robe and veil of a Keeper, the other clad in black.

From her sorrowful eyes, I knew who the second *leronis* must be: Isibel. A new wave of anguish flooded through me. She was the instigator of this misery; whatever news she had brought had caused Isidor such despair he'd seen no other option, and I was desperate to know what she'd told him.

Now was not the time to ask. I took my place amongst my year-mates and fixedly stared at the ground rather than at the casket housing my friend. The Cadet-Master spoke a few words, as did Di Asturien and a few of the officers. Standing there at attention was a torment; my uniform was too damp, too itchy, too stifling, and my head ached from the stress of shutting everyone out.

"May that memory lighten grief," we all intoned as the Cadet-Master walked up and down our ranks. He paused in front of me, mercifully blocking my view of the casket. "Cadet. Do you wish to say a few words?"

I felt the gazes of my classmates upon me along with the intensity of their judgment. Thoughts leaked, pricking me like dozens of pins.

Why didn't he know?

Why didn't he do anything?

That icy little bastard has disgraced us all.

I had no answers. I had no words.

"Cadet." The Cadet-Master was sharper now, more impatient.

I stared at the sash across his chest. "Cadet Lindir was kind to me when I arrived. He was my—" I couldn't keep my voice from breaking. "—my friend."

When it was obvious I couldn't say anything more without shaming myself, the Cadet-Master spoke the ritual words. "May that memory lighten grief."

The cadets echoed him. Isibel spoke briefly and formally on

behalf of her family. Whatever else was said, I had no recall of. My only defense was to put up shields so tightly that I could sense nothing at all, not even the frigid air that had descended into the courtyard.

I was still standing there, staring at the casket, when Di Asturien led me back to the room I'd shared with Isidor. It stung to see the empty space where his bed had been. All his things, including his sword, had been removed.

"I'm sorry, son," Di Asturien said and helped me out of my wet uniform as if I was a child of five instead of a cadet of sixteen. "This isn't your fault."

The words rang hollow. I think he knew it; he just put me to bed, pulled the blanket over my shoulder, and left me alone where I lay for hours gazing at the emptiness. No one else came, but they didn't have to. I could feel their anger and disbelief stalking me like hungry wolves.

Why?

He should have known.

He should have done something.

The thoughts became oppressive. Intrusive.

Desperate for fresh air, I raced out of the room, down the hallway, and up the stairs that led to the parapet where Isidor and I had spent so many nights guarding the castle. The red moon, Idriel, was waning, fading like Isidor's presence.

Without much hope, I pulled out the stone in the wall and reached inside. There was no note, but I was surprised to feel a hard lump. I drew it out, shocked to see the leather pouch containing Isidor's starstone.

My first thought was to turn it over to the Cadet-Master, to spare myself any more dishonor or accusations. My second was the certainty that Isidor had left it there for me.

A message, perhaps? With a sudden burst of hope, I pried at the laces securing the pouch.

Then I thought better of it. I wasn't trained to handle another's starstone, and I'd heard the horror tales of such experiments gone awry. I should turn it over. If I didn't and the Cadet-Master discovered it somehow, I'd be dismissed from the

Cadets.

Yet I couldn't bear to part with the one memento I had left of my friend.

For one mad moment, I considered launching myself over the wall. After all, I had nowhere to go and only a vague hope of a career in the Guard as a livelihood. Everyone I'd cared for was gone, and I had nothing left save for guilt and sadness.

Then a breeze stroked my face with such tenderness that I ached. A voice carried with it: *No.*

"Isidor?"

There was no answer. I leaned farther over the wall, debating.

"Please don't, Felipe. My brother wouldn't want that."

The voice startled me into drawing back. I'd been so lost in myself that I'd neither heard nor seen Isibel Lindir climb the stairs to the parapet. I tucked Isidor's stone into my pocket, hoping she didn't notice. "Forgive me, *damisela*. I was not expecting company."

"I'm to bring you to Arilinn. The Lady Leondra wishes to speak with you. She's already made arrangements with the Cadet-Master."

She was blunt, giving none of her own feelings away. I wondered what the Keeper of Arilinn wanted with me; nothing good, I expected. "Is she angry with me, too?"

"Should she be?"

"I didn't stop him." No matter what Di Asturien had said, Isidor's death was my fault. Just two years after we'd met, he was gone, all our dreams dashed. Why hadn't I done anything? I'd seen the shadow, I'd known what it meant, and I hadn't stopped him from leaving.

There was a long, taut silence before she said, "I didn't, either."

I wasn't sure how to respond to that. Isidor had wanted me to meet with her, but even a shared grief couldn't erase my distrust of a stranger.

"Please, Felipe. We should go."

There it was, again; the expectation that I was to accompany her to the Tower. I didn't want to go. "What did you say to him last night?"

"Lady Leondra is expecting us."

I had no choice, then, if I wanted answers.

Mormallor had just started to rise when we walked through the castle gates and into Thendara, reminding me of just how cold and alone I was.

~oOo~

The days of travel blurred together in chilly unhappiness. At night, fog crept around us, tinted silver by the moon. I remembered little of the journey; when Isibel spoke, her voice seemed at a distance, giving me an unnerving sensation akin to being lost in the overworld. She bade me stop and sleep, and placed plates of food in front of me that I ate with the same dissociation. Whether it was her *laran* or my grief keeping me pliant, I didn't know, and I didn't care.

My mind cleared a little when we at last reached the tower of Arilinn, The arched entrance shone with an eerie blue light. The Veil. I felt a moment of nervousness, remembering a similar barrier in the overworld.

But I needn't be afraid. I had *laran*, and was *Comyn*-born, even if I'd never been acknowledged.

So I stepped through.

I trailed after Isibel, although I wasn't entirely sure how I managed to maneuver through twisting hallways and into a sitting room where a fire had been stoked. I could not feel the heat; I was too stunned, too exhausted, and only vaguely aware of Isibel announcing me to her Keeper and leaving.

The Lady Leondra was already seated and inspected me without compunction. "What misery have you brought to this tower, Cadet Felipe—ah, but in a fairer world, your name would be Ridenow, wouldn't it? What a pity your mother was a wild telepath and your father was too fickle to acknowledge you as he should."

I kept silent as shame rose to my cheeks. My parentage was no secret, but the reminder hurt.

"Are you going to stop fiddling with the weather now? I'm getting tired of unexpected rainstorms and fog. They disrupt our work in the tower."

I attributed my confusion to grief and fatigue. "Forgive me, *domna*, but I don't know what you mean."

There was a long, prickly silence. "I don't know what's worse, that your father kept you so woefully ignorant, or that a mere cadet thinks it wise to handle a matrix far beyond his ability."

Her disdain ignited a spark of anger. "I didn't touch Isidor's stone. I know better than that."

"No, you don't. Besides, that isn't the matrix I was speaking of," she said and made a resigned gesture. "Did anyone teach you even the basics of using a starstone?"

"Isidor did, a little. My father meant to send for a *leronis*, but—"

"He died with that promise unfulfilled, as he did so many others. Were you ever formally tested?"

"No."

She sighed. "So it's no wonder we have another wild telepath in our midst. Where did you get your matrix?"

"From my mother."

"Show me."

No.

The word came from deep inside me. I hesitated, wondering if I was so tired I was imagining voices.

"Now, Cadet!"

My hand trembled as I gingerly withdrew my stone from the leather pouch and tugged at the silken wrappings. I couldn't help but stare into its depths, where white light flickered like stars.

Like snow.

Silver sparked within, catching me. The chill of a blizzard sank into my bones. Blessed numbness. No more thinking, no more feeling, only…peace. I wondered if that was how Isidor felt, gone now into Avarra's mercy. I wished I could be there with him instead of here, grieving, alone.

Not alone. I'm here. I'm always here.

Cold wrapped me like a cloak.

"Felipe."

The Keeper's voice was muffled, distant, but it was enough to draw me reluctantly back into the room. I tore my gaze away from the stone and glanced at her. "You have a shadow."

There was a brief flare of unease before she collected herself. "As I feared, you're already keyed to it with no idea of the strength of what you wield. For your own safety, I must ask for your stone."

She lies.

The voice gave me chills. The Keeper eyed me as if she knew what I had heard. "Give it to me, Felipe."

Don't.

It was an order, one that went to my core. I stood, frozen.

"Right now." She held out her hand.

I tilted my hand, nearly enough to let my matrix fall into the Keeper's palm.

No.

I flinched. A moment later, madness overcame me. I shoved the Keeper's hand away and clutched my starstone to my chest, just over my pounding heart.

Her expression was a mixture of surprise and fury. Terror overcame me. I had done the unthinkable; I had not only assaulted a woman but a *Keeper*. I had forever sullied my name and ruined any chance of a future.

I would never be welcome in a Tower or in the company of any *leronis* again.

Run.

And so I did, out of the Tower and into a terrible storm. Lightning struck close enough to make my hair stand on end, followed immediately by a deafening crack of thunder. Rain stung my cheeks and all but blinded me as I ran through the streets of Arilinn, twisting and turning, driven by the presence that had lodged itself securely in my mind.

The rain followed me, lashing hard, drenching me clean through, yet I didn't care. The precipitation turned to hail, then sleet, then snow pelting into my cheeks and icing my wet hair. The chill seeped in, but I craved it.

Needed it.

I didn't know when the cold became too much and I stopped moving. Peace enveloped me at long last; there was no pain, no worry, only the icy stillness.

I had strength enough for one last prayer:

Avarra have mercy.

~oOo~

At first, there was only silence.

Then, slowly, awareness crept in. Shades, shadows, dreamers, all of them traveled in the overworld, and I was a stranger among them, once more in a place I did not belong.

Come.

So I did. Distance mattered little in this peculiar place where I was thought and energy; I simply followed the presence back to the veil I'd seen once before.

This time, I knew where it led, and I didn't hesitate. Isidor would be waiting. I reached out to feel a strange, electric tingling that made me grit my teeth in discomfort, yet I bore it and pushed through.

Isidor wasn't there.

She was.

Here you are at last.

I dropped to my knees, awed by the presence—or at least the manifestation—of a goddess. She was cold, but it was the beautiful chill of winter, the silence of new-fallen snow glowing silver under Mormallor's light. "Where is he?"

Gone, beyond your reach.

There were no tears here, only a stifled grief. "I want to be with him."

That isn't your fate.

"What is?" I had no name, and, now, with Isidor gone, no one to care.

You're not alone, child. I'm here. Always. She leaned down and placed a kiss on my forehead. *You are mine. You are blessed.*

I didn't feel blessed. Cold rolled through me, and I shivered. During the Ages of Chaos, it was said there were priestesses of

Avarra, cloistered on the Isle of Silence, but they were women, and dedicated to the healing arts.

Can there not be healing in death?

"I didn't help Isidor. I should have stayed with him. I should have…"

If it were not last night, it would have been another. You accepted him as he was. You brought him the peace he could not find at home.

"What good is that?" In an instant, I was angry. I couldn't understand why I'd been cursed with such strange *laran*. To see death, to know it was coming, yet be helpless against it. "My father died too. He despised me."

Did he? Didn't he unburden himself of his secrets before I called him to me?

"And my mother?"

At that, She had a strange, fey smile so reminiscent of my mother's that I trembled. *She served her purpose, and with that, she was content.*

And I knew; the foreknowledge of a weather witch had been purposefully tempered with the empathy of a Ridenow. I was no random bastard of the Hellers; I'd been bred for a reason. I was a scion of Avarra; bringer of cold and darkness, death….

…and rebirth.

~oOo~

When I opened my eyes, it was warmth, not cold, that greeted me. Fire crackled in the hearth, and the light sent shadows dancing in the corners.

"Felipe? There you are, thank the goddess." Isibel sat at my bedside, voice pinched with worry. "It's been two days since we found you in that blizzard. Lady Leondra wore herself out getting the storm to stop. She took your stone so it didn't happen again."

Automatically, I reached to my chest, seeking the pouch that always hung from my neck. It was gone. Worse, my hands felt strange. When I held them up, I saw the bandages wrapping them like thick mittens.

"Frostbite," she said. "You were so cold, we thought…"

"I was. For a while." If I closed my eyes, I could remember the cold. The peace. "Will she give me my stone back?"

"I don't know. Lady Leondra was afraid you'd try to hurt yourself again."

"I won't."

"Are you sure?"

Even if I wanted to, I knew I'd never be let past the veil again until it was my time. "I tried to find him. To be with him. I couldn't."

Her expression twisted, and I caught a pang of grief. "He's gone, Felipe."

"Tell me what you said to him. Please."

Raw as I was, her anguish and uncertainty were painful in my mind. I bore it, knowing she wanted someone to blame for her brother's death as much as I did. For a long time, she stared at her hands, lost in thought, before she collected herself enough to speak. "My brother was troubled from the time he was small. Even before his *laran* came, he was aware of too much too soon. Our father was often cruel; he would beat his children as well as his servants and blame everyone else for his ills. I got away; far better for his reputation to have a daughter be a *leronis* than to worry about finding a dowry. Isidor was a third son, but even so, our father had plans for him. He was promised to a distant cousin of ours before he went to the Cadet Guards. I'd only met her once. She had no *laran* but came with a dowry that would ease many of our father's debts. The agreement also stipulated that Isidor went to the Guards as befitted a *Comyn* son and became a man. Isidor was glad to go, and held onto the hope that the pact might fail, but it wasn't to be. Our father sent letters ordering him home at once to be married, but my brother refused to respond. I had to bring the message."

The revelation cut deeply. "He should have told me. We could have run away. We could have stowed away on a Terran ship and…" A thousand possibilities ran through my head, all of them too late. "I should have asked." Then came another, worse thought. "Did you know?"

"I knew he was troubled and unhappy. I did not know what he

planned. A telepath does not pry, but," she added with a quiet fierceness, "I wish I had."

I wished I had, too. *It's cold,* bredu, he'd said. *So are you.* I was at Arilinn, as he'd wanted, speaking to his sister, yet I felt as lost as ever. "I should have told you. He left me his..." Panic struck as I realized I wore nothing more than a nightshirt. "My jacket. Where—"

Isibel held out her hand. In her palm rested a familiar silken pouch. "You were holding it when we found you."

I wanted it back, but I lacked both the strength and the will to snatch it from her. I didn't deserve it, anyway. Isidor was dead. It was my fault.

Her *laran* brushed against mine, and, tired as I was, I didn't have the strength to fight her. *Don't blame yourself, Felipe. Please.*

Her presence was an odd sensation, more welcoming than I might have thought. Strange how I was so much more aware of Isibel's presence, how close her thoughts seemed to mine.

Then, with a pang, I realized I could have had this with Isidor, if only—

Don't. He's gone. You're here, with us. We can help you if you'll let us. Even Lady Leondra. She has a temper but she cares, even for the bastard son of a weather witch. It doesn't matter where you came from. Not here. It matters who you are. My brother loved you, and you are worthy of being loved.

I didn't feel like it. My parents had abandoned me; my friend had chosen death to avoid the pain of making a terrible choice.

There was one I could trust. The chill called to me, and yet...

Isibel's *laran* tugged at me, drawing me into rapport where she laid bare her love and sincerity. *Will you forever seek the company of a spirit or someone here in the flesh? Will you hide forever behind your own defenses?*

It would be easy, so easy, to retreat into the cold, into the comforting arms of my goddess, the bringer of cold and darkness, death....

...and rebirth. It was Isibel's mind-voice, fierce and determined.

And with her words, understanding dawned like the red sun rising in the morning, spreading light across the courtyard and nudging away the night's chill. The walls I'd kept tight around my mind crumbled. They served me no longer, if they ever had.

I was not merely my mother's child, a frightened, wild thing, nor only my father's, quiet and lonely. I was more than Isidor's friend, poor at it as I had been, and gone beyond what Avarra had created me for.

I was something new.

I was *me*.

And I desperately wanted the connection Isibel offered, for someone to truly understand my grief and confusion.

I do. Oh, Felipe, I do.

She gently guided me into rapport, where I felt the depths of her grief, her inability to help the only sibling she truly cared for. For the first time, I let go, pouring out my sadness and loneliness. She took it all without comment or judgment, and let me express years' worth of pent-up emotions. With them came the secret my father had bidden me keep, the one that had cost me the intimacy I'd craved with Isidor.

She didn't flinch when I told her about my turbulent childhood with my mother, how I was born of a liaison manufactured by Avarra Herself, and how my own father had known only guilt and fear when he thought of me.

I'm not afraid of you, even if you do wrap Arilinn in a blizzard, Isibel said, teasing yet sincere. *You're not a freak or a mere creature of the Hellers. You have value. We need you.* A moment later, she added, *I need you.*

That last gave me a relief so profound that the very last of my defenses dropped. I was safe. Cared for. Isibel was there, and I finally had someone I could trust with my life and secrets.

When the rapport faded, I was worn and breathing hard. Isibel looked pale, but I *knew*, somehow, she was tired but would be all right.

"It's like living with your skin off," Isibel said shakily. "That's what they say."

"Sounds about right. I never knew. Never could have

guessed."

"Thank you."

"For what?" I should have been thanking her for saving my life, amongst other things.

"You chose life. And friendship. And trust."

Her words touched me. "There hasn't been anyone else besides Isidor, and I..."

"I know."

So she did. For a moment I was shamed at being so open and vulnerable, but then I shoved it away. There was a freedom that came with disclosure, and I felt lighter than I had in years.

"One more thing."

She withdrew Isidor's stone and cradled it gently in both hands, gazing at it with that faraway look I recognized. I looked at the matrix, almost lifeless save for a swirl of blue light so faint I might have imagined it.

Then Isibel grasped my arm, and in a moment I was caught up in the stone's last vestiges of Isidor. Grief. Loss. Guilt. A fierce sense of honor. He could not run away and dishonor his family's name; neither could he bear a life with a woman he did not love and could not share rapport. Greatest of all was the love for Isibel...and me. He'd wanted us to meet, to look after each other.

At the last came a brief moment of peace before the inevitable. A shock hit me that had nothing to do with the stone. This, then.

This was Avarra's mercy.

Isibel drew back and said wearily, "That's all. He's truly gone, now."

The stone lay dead in her palm. I rolled over and wept.

~o0o~

All the *leroni* took turns attending to me. With my hands bandaged, I could not feed myself and had to sit patiently while being spoon-fed and had to put up with the assistance of tending to my other bodily needs. Yet never once did I feel like a burden; I was treated as a newcomer, a student, and, in a few cases, a friend.

"They're healing," Isibel said when she unwrapped my hands

to inspect my fingers. She gave me daily treatments, and along with them came lessons of a different sort. Gentle nudges of *laran*, getting used to the feel and using more than the rudimentary control Isidor had taught me. Simple tasks, like monitoring, before moving on to more complicated tasks such as working with a matrix.

Her patience still surprised me. She found my naïveté amusing, and let me know. We were friends, drawn together by our shared love for Isidor, and I valued every moment with her. We didn't need anything more from one another, and she even gave me a nudge when she caught me staring at a handsome male technician.

"Careful. He's a terrible flirt."

Heat rose to my cheeks, all the more hotly since the technician turned and gave me a slight, knowing smile. All the same, I felt at home here, and unafraid.

Even Lady Leondra seemed to have forgiven me for my misconduct. "There aren't many who can say they've seen the goddess Avarra and returned to speak about it," the Keeper said as she sipped a cup of tea.

We were in her sitting room one evening after the bandages had been removed from my hands. The skin was still tender and pink, but Isibel assured me I would have full use of them soon enough. "No, I suppose not. I owe my life to you and Isibel."

"She's told me of your progress, and seems to think you might be able to tame that wild *laran* of yours, but don't get your hopes up. You're starting later than most of my students, and by rights, I ought to lock that matrix of yours up where it can do no more harm."

My heart sank. I thought I'd been catching on to Isibel's teachings fairly quickly; I must have been wrong.

"Don't look so glum. I have no desire to anger your patroness, but if you want that matrix of yours back, you're going to have to earn it. No more storms. No more fires. And if you ever deliberately put anyone in this tower at risk again, I will make sure you never use your *laran* again. Is that understood?"

"Yes. Thank you, *domna*."

"Good. You'll continue your lessons with Isibel until you have the basics. Once you do, you'll come to me, and we'll see how you handle that matrix of yours."

At that, she dismissed me, and I sought out Isibel. We went out onto one of the tower's balconies, where I told her what Lady Leondra had said.

"She believes in you. It might not seem like it, but she does. Besides, your matrix intrigues her. She's always had a fancy for the strange and unusual." Isibel added lightly, "That includes you, you know."

I chuckled, relieved that I was no longer ashamed of my birth. No one at Arilinn cared. I was valued for who I was and what I could do, and I had hope for my future.

The wind picked up, depositing snowflakes on our cloaks. Being out here reminded me of those nights with Isidor, where we'd said nothing, comfortable in the silence and company of each other. I hadn't realized how truly lonely I'd been until that gap had been filled.

Below us, a few townspeople were out, hurrying on some errand or another. One of them had a strange glow about him. I didn't need my matrix to see the shadows after all.

A breeze tickled my cheek, and with it came a voice: *I'm here. Always.*

So She was, as a reminder of my duty to this world. Perhaps the man below would seek help from a *leronis*, and maybe I could help him find some peace before the inevitable.

I felt Isibel's curiosity. "He's dying. That one, in the gray cloak. I should go—"

"You should stay, and learn. Soon you'll have enough work to do."

She was right. I couldn't help anyone if I couldn't help myself, first.

We stayed outside until Mormallor was high in the sky, casting a bright glow on the falling snow. Beneath it, I was no longer lost but found.

FINDERS KEEPERS

by *Deborah Millitello*

Deborah Millitello published her first story in 1989 in *Marion Zimmer Bradley's Fantasy Magazine*. Since then, her stories have appeared various magazines such as *Dragon Magazine*; *MZB's Fantasy Magazine,* including the third-place Cauldron winner "Do Virgins Taste Better?"; *Science Fiction Age*; and anthologies such as *Aladdin Master of the Lamp; Witch Fantastic; Sword and Sorceress; Tale of Talislanta*, and *Bruce Coville's Book of Nightmares.* Her first book, *Thief's Luck*, a YA fantasy mystery, is out from Double Dragon Publishing, and a YA fantasy novel, *The Water Girl*, has been out since February 2015 from Word Posse. She also has a collection of her short stories, titled *Do Virgins Taste Better and Other Strange Tales. The Mourning Dove* and *The Wizard and the Warrior,* Books 1 & 2 of *The Baramayan Chronicles*, are also out from Word Posse. She spends her free time baking cookies, cakes, and pies, making gourmet jams such as strawberry lemonade jam, lemon blueberry jam, and tangerine marmalade, knitting and crocheting, and growing herbs, vegetables, berries and orchard fruit. A member of the Alternate Historians writers group since 1988, she lives in southern Illinois with her husband Carl (who has put up with her writing obsession for over fifty years), has three children and nine grandchildren, and one great-grandchild, and is retired.

Erendia was gathering wild flowers to sell at the Thendara market when she felt the charm in her necklace vibrate a warning. She dropped to her knees, then spread out prone, cringing from aching joints and hoping to hide from whatever danger threatened her. Peering over the tops of the two-foot-tall flowers, she scanned the surroundings for anything that she should hide from, but she saw nothing. Still, she could sense something or someone was nearby, and she was frightened, She was old, and she had no weapons.

She never knew why the pretty blue crystal sometimes seemed to give her warnings. She'd found the gem when she was a homeless orphan, twelve-years-old, in a cave she had hidden in to escape a gang of boys who constantly harassed and beat her when they could catch her. When she discovered the gem, partially covered with dirt in the cave wall, she'd dug it out, then began to shake as she held it. For several days she lay on the cave floor, drifting in and out of dreams and visions, her head feeling like it was on fire, unable to move or speak. When her fever had broken, she was weak, and her thoughts seemed scattered. But the blue gem gave her comfort.

Almost fifty years had passed since Erendia had found the gem, made it into a charm for a necklace that she always wore, and escaped the vicious gang in the small village where she'd been born. She'd fled to the nearby great city of Thendara and scavenged whatever she could to earn a living: firewood, honey, wild flowers, but her most profitable item was the blue matrix crystals she found and traded to the matrix tower in Thendara. Other scavengers had tried to find her secret source of gems, but she's always eluded the ruffians. Until now.

Erendia looked over the flower tops again and saw four scruffy men, spread out at the eastern edge of the meadow, searching the flowers with walking sticks as they approached her hiding place. She glanced at the woods that bordered the meadow on the north. Her riding *oudrakhi* was tied up out of sight there. If she could reach it without being seen, she could escape on it, but she was a long way from the woods. Wrapping bunches of flowers in a damp cloth to keep them from wilting and tying the bundle on her back, she pulled her greenish-brown hood over her thick white hair and began crawling slowly toward the trees, although her knees and hands ached with every movement.

When she reached the trees, she crawled behind a large tree and stood up, breathing fast, her knees popping. *I have to reach my mount*, she thought as she brushed dirt from her well-worn pants and hands. *Then I can make it safely back to Thendara.*

Peeking cautiously around the side of the tree, she saw that the men had turned south with their backs to her, so she ran as quietly as she could deeper into the woods to her *oudrakhi*. She quickly tied the bundle of flowers to her mount, then hurried to the nearby cave to retrieve the rest of her goods. Pulling a piece of leather and a small woven pouch from her greenish-brown shirt, she began picking up gems from a pile, one at a time, being very careful to touch each only with the leather. Just as she was about to put one in the pouch, she heard a low laugh. Spinning around, she saw the four men, all grinning at her.

"So this is your treasure trove," said the tallest man, his dark eyes gleaming hungrily at her. "Took me five years to finally catch you. Hand them all over, and maybe I'll let you live."

"You don't want to take these," Erendia said.

"Oh, but we do," he said, laughing again. "These will make my fortune."

"Our fortune," said the blond-haired man to his right.

The tall man scowled at the other man. "Yes, our fortune." He turned back to Erendia. "And now that we know where to find these, we'll be rich. So hand them over."

"No!" she said.

"Then we'll take them!"

The men leaped forward, each grabbing a crystal from the piece of leather, shoving Erendia and knocking her to the floor. For a moment, they held the gems up and laughed. Erendia clutched her charm and reached out toward the thieves. Suddenly, their faces contorted with pain, and they started screaming, Lightning snaked around their bodies as their hands turned black. Their clothes caught fire. They fell to the floor and rolled around, trying to put out the flames, but the flames just became more intense. The stench of burning flesh was so nauseating, Erendia covered her mouth and nose with a cloth, fled the cave, and vomited, her heart pounding in her chest. When the screaming finally stopped, she crept back into the cave.

Four blackened skeletons lay twisted on the floor, tendrils of smoke curling from them up to the roof. Holding the cloth over her nose, she cautiously picked up the gems with the leather, rubbed the soot off each one, and placed them in the woven pouch. She retrieved the rest of the crystals, then turned to leave the cave. Pausing at the cave's mouth, she turned back to look at the dead.

"Finders, keepers," she said, then she turned and walked back to her mount.

A COLD, BLEAK DAY IN THE HELLERS

by Barb Caffrey

Barb Caffrey is a writer, editor, musician, and composer from Wisconsin. She's written three novels, *An Elfy on the Loose, A Little Elfy in Big Trouble,* and *Changing Faces.* The first two are set in her Elfyverse, an urban fantasy with multiple universes and magical beings, and the latter has been called "Freaky Friday on acid." (She's not sure if that was being complimentary, but she's going with it anyway.) She has at least twenty short stories to her credit and hopes to have a story collection set in her Elfyverse out by the end of the year. She's also the co-writer of her late husband Michael B. Caffrey's "Adventures of Joey Maverick" series—she needs to get that third installment written!—and has a YA military adventure in progress set in his Atlantean Union universe.

"Dammit! My father wrote to me again!" Cynthia MacDougal had just finished up swordsmanship practice with the rest of the Sisterhood of the Swords, and she was in no mood to read yet another missive from her father pleading for her to come home.

Her friend, Dori, patted Cynthia on the shoulder. "It can't be that bad."

"Oh, yes it can," Cynthia said grimly. "He's wanted me to come home now for months. After saying ten years ago that I could join the Sisterhood with his compliments, because he knew I'd be as fit in a sewing circle as a black thumb—"

"Careful, you're mixing your metaphors again," Dori warned.

Cynthia rolled her eyes, happy that only she and Dori remained outside. Everyone else had run for the jacks, especially as they'd camped in a place with hot springs to soothe their aches and pains. Cynthia liked hot springs the same as any other woman, but she needed to get this out, first.

"Dori, he wants me to come home and get married. I always said it would be a cold, bleak day in the Hellers before I did that, but..."

Dori fixed her with a glare. "That's what's upset you so much? You know he can't do that. You're a Sword Sister. You can only marry at your time, your place...you can't get married *di catenas* at all, even by dispensation, unless you're the last member of your family..."

At that, Cynthia's head bowed. "I am," she admitted, lowly. "It's Father, and me. That's it. We're all that's left of the MacDougals. That's what all these letters are about. The family's in trouble, and all our dependents—"

Duty, honor, family. That's what she'd been taught. Now she had to do her duty again, even if she hated it. And so she told Dori.

Dori let out a long sigh. "I see why you're so upset."

Together, they made a plan to speak with the head of the Sisterhood of Swords, Camilla d'Aron. Later, after the baths, of course...as it did not do to appear in front of Sister Camilla unless one was neat, clean, and scrubbed to a fare-thee-well.

~oOo~

Later, they both went to Sister Camilla. Cynthia had been touched when she realized Dori would muster out to go along with her...their friendship meant that much. (Dori had said, "I'm your *breda*. You're not going alone.")

Camilla took one look at their faces and let out a long sigh. She then turned to Cynthia and said, "It's your father, isn't it? The MacDougal?"

"How did you know?"

"Come, child. All the letters with the royal seals of the MacDougals were seen before they were sent to you. There wouldn't be so many unless they're attempting to call you home. And you wouldn't care as much about it, or them, if you didn't feel a remaining obligation to the family that raised you."

"That's just it," Cynthia told her. "It's not my own family, really. It's the smaller families that are dependent on us that I'm so worried about. We've banded together to keep bandits out of our part of the Hellers for years. But now, there are others coming, looking for new territory, or so my father says." Then, biting her lip, she added, "He said I must marry, too."

"Not *di catenas*," Camilla said swiftly. "We can spare you that. Marry as a freemate. In case the marriage does not work, you will always have a place here." Camilla left unsaid the level of disaster it would probably take for Cynthia and her sworn-sister Dori to return to the Sisterhood of Swords.

"I hope the man in question—I've never met him, but his name is Donal of Rockraven—will understand."

"He will," Camilla said.

Dori added, "If he doesn't, I'll find a way to…explain it to him…somehow." She massaged the hilt of her short sword like a lover until Cynthia chuckled.

Within two days, Cynthia and Dori were on the road, swords in hand. They'd been paid, given food, extra horses for the trail, even a few blankets.

Until all that happened, Cynthia had had no idea how much her sword sisters had appreciated her and Dori.

Dori just shook her head, and said, "I told you so."

Sometimes, Cynthia wished Dori would just shut up. But she'd not say that, because they were *bredas*, after all. And for all Cynthia knew, in the past maybe Dori had wanted to tell Cynthia off but hadn't for the same reason.

~oOo~

Donal of Rockraven scowled when he received the latest missive from his mother. He'd been a scholar at Nevarsin for the last fifteen years. He was not a *cristoforo*, though he believed many aspects of that faith had merit, and sometimes he believed the Holy Bearer of Burdens was real.

And despite what his mother believed about scholars, Donal was not a lover of men, either.

No, Donal liked women just fine. He liked scholarship more, though. Being at Nevarsin, in the company of other scholars, had made him feel settled. He'd never fit in, at home, considering his scholarly instincts.

Mind you, if the nascent system of judges he'd read so much

about had reached his part of the Hellers before he left, he probably would've become a judge, but...that option hadn't been open to him fifteen years ago.

So, he'd sworn off women. Gone to Nevarsin. Studied to his heart's content. And he was happy...except his mother's missives had been growing dangerously shrill, lately.

His three brothers had all died in rockslides in the past three years, saving other families that looked to Rockraven. His two sisters had married out, long ago; one was on the plains of Valeron somewhere, married to the Hastur heir...the other had been sent close to Temora to cement some long-lost alliance, while one of the daughters had come to marry his brother Bard. Unfortunately, Bard's wife had died in childbirth three full years ago; their twins had been stillborn.

He still remembered Sherilla, his sister, complaining that she "did not want to be a fishwife." But she had no choice. Their parents said she had to go, so off she went.

He'd tried to keep up correspondence with Sherilla, of course, as Sherilla was literate. (His other sister, Dierdre, hadn't bothered to learn. Then again, they'd never had much in common, anyway.) But three or four years ago, Sherilla's letters had stopped...he'd thought about making a pilgrimage to Temora, but he'd stayed instead, safely ensconced at Nevarsin.

Maybe that had been a mistake, but he couldn't undo it now.

He opened the letter, sealed with the various Rockraven runes, and scanned it. His mother was commanding him to come home, right now, as he'd been arranged a marriage with the last remaining MacDougal to save both of their Houses from extinction.

Wasn't she one of those Sword Sisters or something? Why would she agree to marry him?

The letter said it would not be a *di catenas* marriage, just a marriage of freemates. That made him feel a little better. Men who married *di catenas* could not study at Nevarsin, not until their spouses were dead and buried. So, maybe, if the marriage didn't work, he and his intended bride—Cynthia MacDougal— would be able to dissolve their marriage and then return to their old lives.

But something inside him said it would not be that easy.

~o0o~

Cynthia and Dori had spent days on the road now. It was fall, nearing winter, and there was at least a light snow every night. Cynthia knew as they got closer to her homeland that there would be colder temperatures and far more snow, so she may as well accept it.

Still, she hated the cold.

Tonight, they'd found shelter in a deserted cave that wasn't all that far from a small stream that hadn't completely iced over. This meant they could keep their horses close by, which pleased them. They'd used their shovels to make a temporary jacks out of the freezing dirt far enough from the stream that their own waste shouldn't pollute it and had relieved themselves. After that, they'd performed their usual tasks: Cynthia made dinner, as Dori burned everything she touched, while Dori set out their bedrolls.

After a simple meal of beans and bread, they got to talking. They'd mostly swapped jokes at night, to keep themselves amused. While they were literate and loved to read, it was too dark for either of them to finish their books. Cynthia in particular couldn't wait to finish her latest book-obsession: "Chronicles of a Scholar, Sailor, Lover, and Spy," by Rodrigo d'Asturien.

Dori just chuckled when Cynthia had told her about the book. "It sounds like something you'd love. Though how was this guy all four of those things? I thought scholars spent their whole lives at Nevarsin, not touching women, not wanting to touch women... Hellfire, I thought they were all as meek as those *cristoforos*!"

"Well, being a scholar can save the day," Cynthia pointed out. "There are also so many things to learn. Life is all about learning, isn't it? Even as a Sword Sister, we learned all sorts of things...including to not get on Sister Camilla's bad side. Oh, and that Mistress Loren made the very best honeycakes, whenever we stopped by her inn near the plains of Valeron."

"Weird place to put an inn, but her cooking is divine," Dori agreed. "And she never looked down at us for being Sword

Sisters, either."

"Well, why should she?" Cynthia never had understood why some women hadn't appreciated them. After all, without Sword Sisters fighting along with various other forces, innocent women and children would've died. Men too old to take up sword or spear would've also died, of course, but Cynthia never had expected one word of praise to ever come from a man's lips.

Very few of them wanted to be partners with a Sword Sister.

Of course, quite a few men she'd met automatically assumed she was a lover of women. That was absurd. Dori was her sworn sister, yes, and her good friend. But lover? By Zandru's Hells, no!

Dori just gave Cynthia *that* look. "You know most women hate us. They're afraid we'll take their daughters and teach them how to fight."

"A man who beats his wife is no kind of man," Cynthia said shortly.

"Agreed. But..." Dori sighed and turned her palms up. "I hope Donal, whoever he is, will be kind to you, *breda*."

"Me, too," was all Cynthia could think to say, before they banked their small fire and headed into the cave to rest.

~oOo~

Donal had also spent several days on the road, riding his trusty steed, Charger. For the most part, he'd been left alone, as he was obviously a member of the *Hali'imyn,* lack of *laran* notwithstanding. Only once had a few ruffians had thought to steal from him one morning as he broke his fast, but Donal just used his stout staff and clouted them both over the head.

Problem solved.

He mounted Charger and galloped away.

Those...cretins, he supposed was the best word...would've been upset, though. He didn't have much in the way of money. His cloak was well-tailored, but it also was quite plain. He didn't have any of the Rockraven colors with him, as he'd never thought he'd needed them. It was possible that no one would ever know what had happened to him if he died before he got home.

He was not about to allow that. He would survive, meet this Lady Cynthia of the MacDougals, and they would take the vows of marriage as freemates.

He turned his mind to other things, especially scholarly ones. (As one of his colleagues at Nevarsin had put it, "You can take the scholar out of Nevarsin. But you can never take Nevarsin from the scholar.") What he did have were manuscripts, including d'Asturien's latest missive discussing his career as a sailor and spy. He'd not yet had time to finish it, but as he'd made the copy himself from the book sent by d'Asturien's family while he was still at Nevarsin, he had no problems taking the book home with him.

He hoped Cynthia MacDougal, whoever she was, was literate. That would make things so much easier.

He sighed. She was a fighter. He was a scholar.

How could they possibly be happy together?

Yet, this was the only way to save not just his family, but hers, if his mother was correct. (And as his mother Namia loved to meddle, and also loved finding out whatever her heart desired, it was vanishingly unlikely she was wrong.)

They had small holders depending on them to keep ruffians like the ones he'd brained out of their part of the Hellers. And those small holders had dependents, who also needed to grow up safely, and maybe a few of them would be inclined to learn their letters.

That cheered him, a bit anyway. If he could pass literacy along, that would be a blessing.

But as he and Charger continued to ascend toward Rockraven, he had a hard time believing anything good would—or could—come to pass.

~o0o~

Cynthia and Dori had made it to the hereditary MacDougal lands and had been greeted sedately by Cynthia's father, Adanis. (It was a hereditary name, and her father didn't like it much, so he mostly just went by "the MacDougal" as was proper.) There'd been a feast where she'd been reintroduced to their smallholders (who all agreed to look to her for support and defense when it came to the family if the MacDougal himself was inclined to do the same), which had included rather inferior honeycakes and some gamy strips of wild chervine along with whatever small game birds had been able to be brought down—and they'd bedded down for the night before the MacDougal would discuss any business with them.

Dori had sighed. "Politics. It's always, always politics, isn't it?" She looked at her sword, now sheathed and wearing peace-strings, and shook her head. "This is why my family wanted me nowhere near our seat of power."

"Where does your family live, anyway? You've never said," Cynthia put in as she attempted to find a decent place on her overly soft bed to rest upon.

"Close to Arilinn, if you can believe that," Dori replied.

Cynthia knew her friend would not lie, and she murmured exactly that.

"It wasn't easy to get my family's permission to join the Sisterhood, just as I know it wasn't easy for you, *breda*," Dori continued. "After I'd walloped our swordmaster for the fourteenth time in a row, though, my parents found the wisdom in sending me away. Especially as I told them that if they tried to marry me off without my consent, such as I am, my promised husband would end up singing soprano all of his days."

"Fourteen times? Compared to that, my way of leaving was far easier. All I had to do was tell my father how unhappy I was, except when I swung a sword."

"Helping your father's small-holders—what are their names again?—in that fight with the Sain Scarp raiders certainly had to help," Dori murmured.

"Both the Aldriks and the Carolas look to us. Small clans, but mighty ones…so we've always thought."

"Yes. That makes sense." Dori sighed, turned away from Cynthia on the overly soft and much-too-large bed, and went to sleep.

Maybe that last was why her father had called Cynthia home, rather than take a new wife himself. Especially as the only woman he'd ever loved—besides her own mother, of course—

was Namia of Rockraven. Cynthia wondered how she was related to Donal; would her father get a chance to renew his acquaintanceship with the wedding ceremonies to be held soon on the borders of their two countries?

Stranger things had happened, after all. And a double wedding might be even better to allay fears in both kingdoms (really homesteads, but the Highlanders, as always, had their pride).

Cynthia would have to ask her father that, after she'd had a good, long rest.

~oOo~

Donal had made his weary way to Rockraven. His mother knew him well and had a plate of cheese, wine, and bread brought for him. The rest of the ceremony—whatever it must end up being— to officially become "the Rockraven" so his freemate marriage to Cynthia MacDougal would bring peace and alliance to both kingdoms, would happen after he'd rested.

He was glad Namia had waited on the ceremonial aspects, as he was exhausted. Dealing with Charger was one thing; dealing with bandits, another. He'd run into two more bandits— fortunately not together, as these were much more devious than the two he'd brained. No, these he'd had to outrun.

He hoped he'd not led them straight to Rockraven.

Granted, the small-holders—the Piccardy family, the Almarins, and their dependents—were fine hunters, and should be able to keep the raff off long enough for the alliance-marriage to take place.

Discussing none of this with his mother, he ate, nodded, and went to rest.

The morning would come soon enough. Then he'd find out just what his mother intended…and whether or not it was something he could live with.

~oOo~

It was now time for the wedding. Cynthia was dressed in the traditional MacDougal plaid and leather breeches, as she had refused to wear a skirt. (It was unfortunate, she'd always thought, that women were not allowed to wear kilts.) She'd told her father that Donal must take her as she was, or no deal.

A COLD, BLEAK DAY IN THE HELLERS

They'd assembled upon the boundary line between the two minor kingdoms, where a hunting lodge had been festively decorated in honor of the occasion. Her father looked nervous, especially as he was dressed mostly in dark colors...those had never suited him.

Her father had dimmed his fire today, so she could shine.

Dori walked beside her, as they made their way into the hunting lodge. There was a long hallway, she dimly remembered from a trip she'd made there with her father in her early teens...after that, there was a room with a hearth, which probably had a blazing fire.

Dori said nothing, which was possibly just as well. Cynthia felt unsettled enough as it was.

When they'd made it into the room, she saw a well-featured man in his prime, dark of hair and eye, standing in front of a makeshift altar. (Fortunately, it wasn't a specific type of altar, as she was not a *cristoforo* and had no interest in becoming one either.) He wore the traditional blue and scarlet of the Rockraven as a sash that crossed from the top of his shoulder all the way to the bottom of the black kilt he wore. The shirt underneath the sash was a pristine white.

Beside him, his mother stood. Cynthia had only met Namia once, long ago, but she'd have known Namia was related to Donal—for surely, this was he—from the shape of her head and eyes. She, like her father, wore dark, plain colors.

As this was an alliance marriage, Dori would stand with the crowd, while her father would be her main witness. Donal didn't seem to have brought a paxman with him, but even if he had, his mother would have had to be his main witness anyway.

They didn't have to say much, Cynthia didn't think, except to agree to become freemates. (She was trying not to think of the traditional Highland bedding ceremonies, as she wasn't looking forward to that at all.) But she did not want to be the first to speak.

~oOo~

Donal stood in front of the altar and waited for his intended bride. His mother stood behind him, so he had no one else to look at except the vision in the traditional MacDougal plaid. How she'd found a shirt and overcloak in those colors so quickly was something he couldn't answer…then he shook himself into sense.

If he'd had to describe Cynthia MacDougal to his brethren at Nevarsin, he'd have told them she was tall, slender, and attractive. She had green eyes, he thought; that was rare in this part of the world (and rumored to be rare elsewhere on Darkover as well). Her hair was strawberry-blonde and cropped just below her ears for convenience.

His mother let out a hiss when she'd apparently noticed that Cynthia was wearing breeches. He, though, didn't mind at all.

What had his mother expected, anyway? Cynthia had spent the last ten years or so as a member of the Sisterhood of the Sword. They didn't wear skirts; that would just cause trouble in combat.

Besides, Cynthia looked quite dashing in them. (In the best of senses.)

Once she reached the altar, she turned toward him. He grasped her hands, and said this:

"I, Donal of Rockraven, hereby pledge to take Cynthia MacDougal as my freemate. I will love her, and cherish her, and listen to her and take her advice as she's had many interesting experiences that I quite frankly haven't—" his mother probably didn't like that, but oh well "—and I will do right by her, as well as my family, her family, and all of our various smallholders. This I pledge."

Cynthia looked like she was about to pass out, but after a beat managed to reply.

"I, Cynthia MacDougal, hereby pledge to take Donal of Rockraven as my freemate. I will honor him, and my family; I will do my best to learn to love him, as he seems a man of good will and no malice."

Donal heard his mother hiss at that, too, but had no time for it. He was instead watching Cynthia's father, who was nodding his head benignly.

Cynthia went on with, "I will do right by him, and our

families and smallholders. This I pledge."

Then Cynthia's father stepped up. "I, the MacDougal of the MacDougal clan, approve and endorse this marriage. Further, I pledge alliance, whenever it is needed, between the MacDougals and those of Rockraven."

Donal saw, out of the corner of his eye, his mother Namia step up.

"I, Namia of Rockraven, also approve and endorse this marriage of equals. I, too, pledge to hold to the alliance between our two respective families and kingdoms, whenever it is needed, and however it is required."

Here in the Highlands, Donal knew, the small gathering of others in this hunting lodge expected him and Cynthia to kiss. It didn't have to be an intense kiss, which was just as well; he'd astonished himself, in some ways, by pledging to love and cherish Cynthia. (It was acceptable to him the way she'd put it, though, as loving someone took time.)

He did not want to do anything Cynthia wasn't ready for.

He was a bit surprised when she stepped forward and pressed her lips softly against his. It was brief and feather-light; still, he smiled, as he could not help it.

"Now, let's eat!" the MacDougal roared.

The various people assembled pounded their walking sticks in approval, and they proceeded to the next room, where tables awaited them that groaned with food.

~o0o~

The dinner was just getting started when three men in torn leathers ran into the hall. Cynthia recognized one with the distinctive Piccardy features, while another was one of her father's Aldrik factotums. "Bandits!" the Piccardy yelled. "Riding up the pass! At least fifty! About twenty, twenty-five minutes out! And they have *cralmacs* with them!"

Cralmacs? Really?

The crowd started to murmur but held to discipline. They were Highlanders, and the threat, while imminent, was not yet at their doorstep.

Cynthia, without realizing it, had already jumped to her feet.

Dori, at her left, was beside her in an instant; so was her new husband, Donal. She looked to her father, who was after all the MacDougal, and he gave a sort of "carry on" wave.

She guessed she was happy he'd let her handle this, but what a way to start a new marriage!

She addressed the Piccardy after Donal gave a "you go first" gesture.

"Where?" she asked.

"About three miles out, give or take a few furlongs," the Aldrik put in. He was dark-haired, blue-eyed, and had six fingers, indicating some *chieri* blood somewhere. "But I felt the *cralmacs* try to communicate. They were forced into helping the bandits somehow, perhaps by some new way of using *laran*. They said if we could release them, they'd serve us. But they are tired of fighting blameless humans."

"That's...odd," Donal put in. "I've never heard of the *cralmacs* doing that. I thought they were, at best, beasts."

"No, they have minds...I've met a few before. They don't think the way we do, much, and they have a strange—"

Cynthia cut the man off. "I'm sorry, but we have bigger fish to fry right now."

He looked at her. Perhaps he'd never heard that Temoran proverb before. Oh, well.

She raised her voice. "Men and women of the Hellers, of the combined MacDougal and Rockraven families, we must take up our arms! Go, now, to the armory—" (Fortunately, this was nearby. One of the few concessions her father had allowed her was to make absolutely sure weapons were available as the best time to strike at them would assuredly be during this wedding.) "—and grab whatever you need."

Men started pouring out of the hunting lodge, as the third man stepped up to them.

"I'm Raul, visiting with my brother in Aldrik. I might be useful to you. I'm an animal healer."

"For the *cralmacs*?" Donal put in.

"Yes. They truly are, most of them, the most inoffensive of creatures."

Cynthia thought, *Well, it takes all kinds.* But outwardly, all she did was nod.

"What armament do we have?" Dori asked, ripping the peace strings off her sword. "How many?"

"Twenty-five men are here from both families," Cynthia said heavily. "Not counting my father. A few of the women are good with slung stones, too." She knew that wasn't much against fifty bandits.

Donal held up his wooden staff, which looked to be solid. "I've brained some bandits with this, recently. Perhaps some of the retainers can use a staff as well?"

"Good thought," Dori said, before Cynthia could. "I'll talk with the women—" who were still around, as Highland women were not meek and did not flee danger unless ordered to "—and see what I can do with them."

Cynthia nodded again, and Dori was gone.

"You can swing a sword, right?" she murmured to Donal.

"Yes, though I haven't done much of it lately," he said. "I put mine with yours, in the outer hall." He smiled, which lit up his face despite the gravity of the situation. "I'm going to assume it's yours, anyway, as it's the only sword with peace strings in the hall that's obviously seen a high degree of action."

She closed her eyes. They had some help. It wasn't just she, Dori, and Donal against the bandits, though her father sitting this one out was a surprise. Still…

"I have a thought," Donal said, as they went into the outer hall to grab their swords. "They'll expect us to come at them with horses or chervines, as they are mounted."

"And?"

"Why don't we lay an ambush? Trip the horses, and some bandits will no doubt be thrown. With luck, a few will be incapacitated right there. And if we keep to higher ground, we can drop things on them—"

"I've heard of a new Compact, something the large families like the Aldarans are trying to implement. That would not allow us to have weapons that leave the hand. Have you?"

"Yes, but…not everyone's agreed. And so far, everyone I've

talked to at Nevarsin believed the Compact would never apply to bandits."

Cynthia sighed and thought hard. Donal's plan was probably as good of a plan as any. And she said so, adding only, "If we get to close tactics—"

"I know what to do, and so do you. But I'll take your lead. This is what you've spent your life doing, and I'd be a damned fool to get in your way."

What an unusual man! Maybe they would get along, at that... provided they could get through this mess.

The men, and more than a few women led by Dori, came back inside the hall. "We're ready," Dori said.

"Good," Cynthia said. "Now, what I want you to do is—"

~oOo~

The fight had taken twenty minutes, if that. The men were disoriented, possibly by something the *cralmacs* were doing—or maybe the Aldriks had more *laran* than Donal had ever considered. None of their forces had harmed the *cralmacs*, while the *cralmacs* refused to harm them in turn.

Ten of the bandits had survived. Donal was questioning them, as Cynthia had sent the rest back to be triaged (including the *cralmacs*, who'd been sent straight to Raul as he'd asked).

"We heard about the wedding," one man said. He'd lost an eye in the fight and bore many rips and tears in his grimy leather clothing. "We knew we could take the lands if we hurried."

Donal shook his head. "We're never unarmed in the Hellers. And we're never unwarned, either." He added the last because it never hurt anyone to believe their betters had eyes in the back of their heads. Or the equivalent skill in using *laran*, for that matter.

"We were wrong," another man, whose arm had been cut off at the elbow and had already been roughly cauterized (as they were not inhuman monsters). "We would serve you, if you allow."

"Truly?" He put as much sarcasm into that as he could. "That's a Hell of a way to find retainers, isn't it? By fighting them?"

A third whistled lasciviously. "I saw your bride. She's—"

"Not for you," Donal said shortly.

"We'd heard there were more women here," a fourth one put in, which was just as well. Donal had been about to brain the third one. "Our valley was lost due to *clingfire*, and all the women and children were dead. They targeted the family homes, first!"

Donal let his voice become gentle. "I'm sorry for your loss. But—"

The fourth one went on with, "I know I shouldn't have joined these men. On the trail, though, as one man, if I hadn't joined them, I'd have died."

Donal looked at him with fresh eyes, as the others were led off. (He wasn't the only questioner; just the last.) "Why?" he finally asked.

"I'm your brother-in-law. Marius."

"Which sister?"

"Sherri, er, Sherilla," the man stammered. He was short, dark, plain, and like the others, looked like he'd been through Hell.

Yet Donal was inclined to believe him.

"Sherilla is dead?" Donal asked. "How long ago?"

"Four years? Five?" Marius tried to count. "I lost everyone, and everything...raiding seemed like as good a way to die as any."

Donal asked the Aldrik, one of the witnesses, to go get his wife. He hoped Cynthia would know what other questions to ask, as Marius's bereavement seemed genuine.

That's why Sherilla stopped writing, he couldn't help but think.

Cynthia brought Dori along, as apparently, Dori had some talent with *laran*. ("I don't use it, much," she'd growled earlier. But I can tell if someone's lying.")

"What goes on?" Cynthia asked.

"This man—Marius, he said his name is—may be my brother-in-law. I want to know if what he says is true." He left it at that, as he did not want to influence things further.

Cynthia asked questions, gently but directly. "Why were you here? I'd noticed you weren't fighting...you'd stayed with the *cralmacs*, right?"

Marius nodded. "Yes. I don't know much about them. But they've been kind to me. When I've cried at night, after the others were asleep, they've brought me water. Or held my hand. Or just looked at me with compassion. They obviously are not animals."

"Raul told us that," Dori said. Her pale blue eyes grew urgent, hot. "Are you indeed Donal's brother-in-law, Marius?"

Marius said yes, and Dori nodded in confirmation.

"Then my sister is dead," Donal said heavily.

Cynthia went on with more questions, then sent Marius with Dori to find a place to rest. "He's not a bandit. He's family."

Dori and Donal, together, said, "Witnessed," before Dori took Marius's hand and led the broken man away.

"I'm sorry for your loss," Cynthia said, hesitantly. She put a hand on his arm. Her leathers—which she'd donned before the fight began—were soiled, but not as heavily as his own. "Tell me about your sister?"

And so he did, as they went off to start their lives together.

FIELD WORK

by Margaret L. Carter and Leslie Roy Carter

Born into a Navy family in Washington, D.C., Leslie Roy Carter lived all over the United States, as well as in Argentia, Newfoundland, while growing up. After receiving a B.S. in Physics from the College of William and Mary, he was commissioned as an Ensign in the U.S. Navy. While serving as a naval officer, he earned an M.S.E.E. from the Naval Postgraduate School. His career as a surface line officer took him to many ports, such as Pearl Harbor, Long Beach, San Diego, and Charleston, culminating in command of the frigate U.S.S. Reid. After his retirement from the Navy, he worked as a defense contractor for ten years. In addition to writing, as holder of a private pilot's license, he devotes much of his time to volunteer service with the Civil Air Patrol. He and his wife, Margaret, have collaborated on a four-book fantasy novel series, beginning with *Wild Sorceress*, and several stories in the Darkover anthologies.

Reading *Dracula* at the age of twelve ignited Margaret L. Carter's interest in a wide range of speculative fiction and inspired her to become a writer. Vampires, however, have always remained close to her heart. She holds a Ph.D. in English from the University of California (Irvine), and her dissertation, later published as a book, included a chapter on *Dracula*. In the course of numerous cross-country moves as a Navy wife, she taught college English classes and worked for over twenty years as a legislative editor for the Maryland General Assembly. She has authored books and articles on vampirism in literature, as well as editing an anthology of scholarship on *Dracula*. In fiction, she has written horror, fantasy, and paranormal romance novels and novellas. Her most recent publications include a dark paranormal Lovecraftian romance novel, *Against the Dark Devourer,* and a light paranormal Christmas romance novella, *Chocolate Chip Charm.* Her short stories have appeared in various fantasy and horror anthologies, including several Darkover and Sword and Sorceress volumes. Margaret and Les live in Maryland and have four children, several grandchildren and great-grandchildren, a St. Bernard, and two cats. Please visit her website, Carter's Crypt: *http://www.margaretlcarter.com*

Terran botanist Alex Dubois escorted his Darkovan friend and colleague, Calum MacAran, into one of the biological specimen storage rooms in the science building of the Thendara base complex. There he opened a climate-controlled drawer to show off his latest find. The dried sprig of violet-blue, delicately bell-shaped flowers didn't look like much resting in a compartment with a batch of other plant samples.

At first sight of it, though, the visitor said with a broad smile, "Of course, I recognize this. It is rare, and it grows only on and near the land of my family, as far as we know. Where did you get it?"

Alex picked up the specimen carefully between finger and thumb. A dusty ghost of fragrance wafted to his nose. "One of our local sources found it in an herb shop. He had never seen it before, so he thought we'd be interested. The shop owner said that it came from the Kilghard Hills. That's why I thought of you." During the three years Calum had worked part-time for the Terrans, Alex had grown friendly with him.

Calum was the younger son of a minor noble family, slender, russet-haired, and a few standard years younger than Alex's own late twenties. "We call it *amaryseth*, commonly known as the sapphire bell. It is related to *kireseth*."

Alex returned the sprig to its compartment and closed the drawer. "*Kireseth*—the ghost wind flower? Does this one produce hallucinogenic pollen, too?"

"No, *amaryseth* is not dangerous like that. A tisane brewed by steeping its leaves is sometimes used to awaken suppressed *laran*."

With only a noncommittal smile and nod, Alex said, "Part of our work here at Thendara is to gather your world's folklore and to sift pearls of fact from legend."

Calum smiled back, patient as usual with the topic they'd covered many times before. "You mean how *laran* functions. I am acutely aware of your scientific interest in our 'magic.' You may be applying your rules to our behavior with science-based theories that do not fit well."

Alex held up a finger as if lecturing. "The lore about the flower also called the golden bell speaks very clearly of psychoactive plants—common enough throughout the universe—but they rarely affect anything except the mind of the partaker."

The Terran led the way out of the specimen storage room into the corridor and shut the door behind them. As usual, Calum blinked in the white light that, as he'd occasionally remarked to Alex, glared uncomfortably in contrast to the illumination of Darkover's red sun. He laughed. "I know what you think of us. Superstitious natives with their legends about magic."

"I wouldn't call you that."

Calum worked with the Terran embassy and scientific staff as an animal husbandry expert and an interpreter and had perfect command of Earth's standard language, but he remained thoroughly Darkovan. Alex would never be so rude as to dismiss him as "superstitious."

"Getting back to the *amaryseth*," Alex said. "Have you seen this effect firsthand?"

Calum nodded. "Only once, when I was dosed with it myself in my late teens to stimulate any latent gift I might have. My *laran* was so slow in developing that my parents and the visiting *leronis* who tested me worried that I might not possess any measurable amount. It turned out, after one dose of that substance, I do have the family gift for rapport with animals. It is weak and erratic, enough to work upon domestic creatures like hounds and chervines. Wild beasts, perhaps not."

"I've noticed how you seem to have what we call the touch of a 'horse whisperer,' but real magic? Hardly."

"No matter what the common folk call it, laran is scientifically based—even if it is not a discipline your scientists would recognize—not magic in a supernatural sense. And the

MacAran gift of animal rapport consists of more than a talent for beast-taming."

"Are you saying you can read their minds?"

"Not literally, as if they had thoughts expressed in words. I can sense their emotions and to some extent control their actions." He sighed. "Sometimes, with the domesticated creatures I mentioned. With other kinds of animals, it comes and goes at random. My parents and siblings have a stronger, more reliable version of the Gift. Not like one of our legendary ancestors who bonded with ferocious birds of prey, but well beyond my level."

With a wry half-smile, Calum added, "I suspect my weak *laran* explains why, after I finished my stint in the Guard, my father gave me permission to stay on for over half of each year in Thendara to help with my cousin's fur-trading business and assist you with your research animal stock. He was probably glad to find a useful occupation for the embarrassing younger son." His shoulders twitched as if to shuffle off the unpleasant thought. "Not that I do not enjoy my work here. Interpreting for you *Terranan* gives me an insight into how your people think and respond to our culture. It is, as you would say, a double road for me."

A what? Oh, maybe a two-way street?

"It's none of my business, of course," Alex said, "but doesn't your family appreciate your, uh, interpersonal skill set? Between dealing with your uncle's customers and interpreting for us, you have the makings of a diplomat."

With a self-deprecating laugh, Calum said, "I doubt Father devotes thought to what I do here, much less places high value on it. In his view, *laran* is far more important."

While Alex wouldn't deny the mere existence of psi powers—Earth's psychologists had confirmed them—he couldn't swallow the extreme claims made for Darkovan mind-magic. Still, he also couldn't help being curious about the alleged properties of the rare plant. "Do you think *amaryseth* might have the same effect on Terrans as it does on your people? After all, we share a common ancestry. It would be interesting to test that hypothesis if we had a generous supply instead of one withered sample."

Calum halted in the middle of the corridor and turned to face him. "That is possible. If you are truly interested, I could guide you to the spot where they grow on my family's land. I always go home at this season and stay through harvest. I will be leaving in less than a tenday to make it there by Midsummer. Why not come along?"

As much as the idea of identifying a new species in its native habitat appealed to him, Alex had qualms that an aristocratic family might not welcome an off-worlder's intrusion. "I wouldn't want to impose on your folks."

"Your presence would not present a problem. We have plenty of room for guests. My parents take a dim view of Terranan, but they will welcome a friend of mine. You can spend the festival with us, and afterward, my father's guardsmen will escort you back here with samples. As it happens, they bloom at this time of year."

"Thanks for the invitation. I'll ask my supervisor what she thinks of it," Alex said. He hadn't done any recent trekking across the landscape, but he could get back into the routines of field work quickly enough. The prospect of personally gathering the flowers was too intriguing to pass up.

~o0o~

Alex's department head, Dr. Midori Narita, leaped on the idea as soon as he told her about the invitation.

"Of course, you must accept MacAran's invitation. Given how most of the Comyn feel about us and how seldom they let us travel freely outside the designated areas, this is an unparalleled opportunity. It's been over twenty years since first contact, and we still don't know nearly enough about this planet. You're ideally suited for this investigation." She ticked off reasons on her fingers. "Because of your botanical expertise. Because you're well versed in roughing it on the land. Because you know how to ride. Because you've had self-defense training from having served in the backup team for Base Security."

"A lot of good self-defense training will do me when I'll be out there without modern weapons."

"Nonsense, Security will be tracking you through your computer note-taker. And you will, of course, have a subcutaneous emergency location transmitter installed, per station policy."

"Yeah, I know, the standard dog leash. That will help you find my remains in the stomach of one of those banshee birds. The mountains where I'll be going are said to be crawling with them."

Ignoring his half-serious doom and gloom remark, Midori continued, "Most important, you speak *casta* better than anybody else in this department. MacAran won't have to constantly translate between you and his family."

All good points, granted, and he couldn't deny how exciting the prospect of cataloging a rare plant was. "I just hope it doesn't turn out to be a wild goose chase—seriously, a flower that stimulates magic powers?"

"You're the one who's always raving about the thrill of discovering new botanical species unique to this world," she reminded him.

Alex replied with a rueful chuckle, "You've got me there."

~oOo~

Three days later, Alex and Calum set out from Thendara mounted on a pair of chervines and leading a third as a pack-beast. Again Calum had reassured Alex that hospitality for a guest, even an unexpected visitor, would be freely offered. After several days of relatively easy travel—once Alex became reaccustomed to riding and stopped aching from the hips down—they turned off the Great Northern Road toward the MacAran lands. Their path gradually sloped upward. The well-traveled route with roadside inns gave way to a narrow track, hardly more than a trail winding through an old-growth forest. Here it became obvious that chervines suited the rugged terrain better than horses would have.

Conifers towered overhead, blocking sunlight to create a cool, dim atmosphere. As a result, little vegetation grew on the ground, carpeted with a layer of dried needles. Alex made mental notes of the mosses, ferns, and a few other species, memorizing the details to record on his tablet during rest periods. Whenever convenient, he asked Calum to stop long enough for snapping photos and collecting samples, which he tucked into his specimen pouch. Birds and squirrel-like rodents flitted and scampered through the branches. The sharp fragrance of the trees, similar but not identical to the scent of Terran pines, pervaded the air. Grateful for his thermal jacket, he stole frequent glances at Calum, who left his fur-lined cape in a pack until twilight closed in.

When Alex complained as they were building a campfire on their first night without the comfort of an inn, Calum said, "You're actually cold? It's almost Midsummer."

"Summer night here is more like late fall where I grew up." Alex huddled closer to the fire and fed it wood while Calum rubbed down their mounts.

"They really respond to you," Alex observed.

Calum shrugged. "In my bloodline, this level of animal empathy is nothing special, just the minimum expected." He delved into his saddlebag and doled out a meal consisting of bread, cheese, dried fruit, and strips of smoked meat. Alex offered his freeze-dried, complete individual meals. He poured water into a bag of powder and shook it up well.

The Darkovan took a spoonful and grimaced. "You eat this *willingly*? It tastes like stable sweepings."

"True, but one packet will sustain human life under environmental conditions from minus fifty to plus fifty degrees Centigrade. It's engineered to provide every nutritional need a human requires."

Calum filled a plate of his own food and passed it to Alex, who nibbled a piece of the smoked meat.

"A little dry—it will suck the water out of your mouth in an instant," Alex said.

"If we were going to be on the trail for more than a few nights, we might snare a couple of rabbit-horns for stew, but otherwise, it would hardly be worth the trouble."

"So there is game in this forest? Now, if we had a blaster..."

Calum frowned. "You know that the Compact forbids the use

of ranged weapons."

"Yeah, which is why I said *if*. After all this time on your world, I still don't fully understand that taboo. I know weapons that don't require combatants to come within arm's reach of the enemy are prohibited, but why is the rule enforced so strictly?"

"The Compact was forged after the *laran* wars of the Ages of Chaos. All these lands were devastated by the energies of fire, thunder, lightning, and earthquakes. The prohibition is meant to guard against forces of mass destruction at ranges beyond the view of actual battlefields, death from afar, with no chance of defense. Our *laran* weapons were much more powerful than your hand blasters."

To Alex, this history sounded only slightly more plausible than Terran legends of sunken continents. True, his own planet had waged nuclear wars, but those obeyed the laws of physics, not mythical magic. Out of courtesy, he didn't pursue the topic any further.

While Calum checked their mounts one last time, Alex laid out his sleeping bag. Calum unfolded his blanket roll and sat staring, as Alex stripped down to his underwear and crawled between the metallic sheets.

"Let me guess—that sleeping bag is engineered to provide an enclosed temperature environment of whatever you set to be comfortable between..."

"Ambient temperatures of minus fifty to plus fifty degrees Centigrade. Good night, Guardsman MacAran."

~o0o~

Mid-afternoon of the next day, the last before they were due to arrive at the MacAran estate, Calum halted his chervine. "Would you like to take a brief detour and view the sapphire bells in the wild right now? We're close to where they grow most profusely."

Alex eagerly agreed, and they turned off the main track onto a trail barely wide enough in places for the chervines to pass between the trees. At last, they emerged into a meadow carpeted with tiny, violet-blue flowers. Alex inhaled a deep breath of their fragrance. It bore a faint resemblance to Terran honeysuckle.

"I'm surprised the local herbivores haven't nibbled them down to the roots," he said, already mulling over possible methods to prepare live plants for transportation back to Thendara.

"Fortunately, animals like the leaves but not the flowers. They don't graze on these plants until after they've bloomed and gone to seed."

"And you guarantee their pollen doesn't have psychoactive effects like *kireseth* blossoms?"

Calum shook his head. "As I told you back in Thendara, that requires a decoction."

"You're sure your family won't mind if I harvest a few plants later, roots and all?"

"I will ensure that you do not take too many."

Alex snapped both panoramic and close-up photos. He then gathered several handfuls of blossoms, wrapped them in a cloth packet to separate them from the other samples, and tucked them into his pouch. Once he'd finished, they rode back to the main road.

Late in the day, the muffled clop-clop of hooves on the turf a short distance ahead broke the silence of the forest, although they could not yet see who approached. The curve of the narrow, winding trail obscured the view. Calum reined his chervine to a stop at the verge of the trail to make room for the approaching riders, so Alex did the same.

When two scruffy-bearded men on chervines rounded the bend, Calum raised a hand in greeting. His voice held a note of caution as he said in *casta*, "Rolf, what brings you out here?"

The older of the two, his chestnut hair and beard peppered with gray, answered in the same language, but haltingly, as if not used to speaking it. "Why, to welcome you home, *vai dom*."

To Alex's eye, the man's grin looked more sly than welcoming. *They know each other? Calum doesn't look exactly delighted to see him.*

Alex's unease was validated when both of the riders drew their short swords. At the same instant, two more armed men appeared out of the trees, one on either side of the two riders.

"Home with a slight detour, that is." The one called Rolf dismounted, brandishing his sword. "Come along peacefully, and you'll be all right."

"Lord MacAran does not look favorably on his kin being threatened. Put up your weapons, and I will pretend you didn't say what you just did."

The dismounted men grabbed the halters of Calum's and Alex's chervines. The animals struggled to break loose, rearing as they backed away. Calum flipped over his chervine's back and vaulted to land on his feet, drawing his sword and yelling to Alex to flee. Alex jerked his foot out of the stirrup and kicked the man wrestling with his mount, knocking him off balance. The man fell forward but held onto the halter, jerking Alex's chervine downward. The doe stumbled to her knees. Alex flew off and crashed into the bushes. He landed so hard, he was momentarily stunned.

Calum engaged the leader, Rolf, driving him back up the trail, and was about to disarm him when the mounted ruffian lunged forward and struck Calum with a club, knocking him to his knees.

Alex jumped to his feet and hurled himself toward the man hanging on desperately to his chervine. Seeing Alex coming, the man released the animal and recovered his dropped weapon., Alex's chervine bolted back down the trail. The ruffian holding Calum's chervine let it go and moved to the side of his friend, who was still occupied with Alex.

That man rushed Alex, swinging wildly at him. Alex ducked inside to assist the man's forward momentum with a toss over his back. Turning to face the second bandit, he stopped dead and froze. Rolf had Calum's neck jerked back, his blade pressed against his bared throat. In rough *casta*, he ordered, "Stand down, *Terranan*, or your Comyn friend dies."

Alex raised his arms with open hands, the universal sign of surrender. He winced while the two men he had just bested grabbed an arm each and pulled them behind his back. Forcing him to his knees, they secured his arms together with rope. When finished, they jerked him to his feet and led him to where Calum kneeled before the bandit leader.

Rolf smirked at Calum. "Don't worry, *vai dom*, I don't plan to kill you. You're worth more alive." He gave orders to the pair flanking Alex, and they went to retrieve the chervines and equipment. While the third man watched Alex and Calum, Rolf searched through their belongings, ignoring Calum's aside from a brief scan and minutely examining Alex's. Rolf jabbed a finger at the belt pouch Alex wore. "What's in there?"

"Just plant specimens. I'm here to study them."

"That is the truth," Calum put in. "My word of honor."

Rolf snorted, then returned his attention to rummaging through the rest of the items. He called out to his henchmen, and they hurried over to see what their leader was so excited about. Rolf pointed at Alex's tablet computer.

Alex turned his head to face Calum. "Those guys' body language sure looks like they're trying to decide if they have a problem with my continued existence. Am I wrong?"

Calum, who had been listening to the outlaws while rubbing his head where the club had struck it, croaked at them in *cahuenga*. "You do not want to harm my friend. If you murdered a *Terranan*, they would hunt you down and slay you without mercy."

Rolf waved Alex's computer recorder at his captives. "This thing is a magical talking device. They send messages like a Tower. With it, they will find us and kill us."

"Then we smash it with a rock," another ruffian said, demonstrating.

Alex groaned, "All my notes—my pictures—no!"

"Better to lose your records than give these men a reason to eliminate you," Calum said.

The bandits were ruthless in hammering Alex's recorder into splinters. Calum turned to Alex. "If you had not brought it, you would not have been in danger of getting killed on the spot."

"It was keeping us out of danger—one tie to rescue," Alex said in Terran Common. "As soon as Base Security loses communication with personnel in the field, protocol is to search if, and only if, they have lost contact with the person as well. We do lose communication occasionally; the second tie is a subcutaneous emergency locator beacon embedded in my chest. That ELT will still be broadcasting my position. If we don't get away from these guys soon, and word of our capture gets out, my people will know of my kidnapping, and any goodwill between us will be compromised."

He cast a worried glance at their captors, deep in intense conversation.

"What's all this about, anyway?" Alex asked.

"My best guess is kidnapping for ransom." Calum called out to Rolf, "If you keep him alive, the Terrans will pay a ransom for him. Let my father negotiate for both of us."

"Good point. Then I guess we're stuck with him," Rolf grumbled in *casta*. Switching to *cahuenga*, too fast for Alex to follow, he barked orders at his men.

They shoved the two captives toward the chervines and gestured for them to mount. Minutes later, Calum and Alex were back in their saddles, bound hand and foot.

"You do not have to do this," Calum said to their captors. "I know the weather for the past couple of seasons has been hard on the whole region, but if your situation is this desperate, why did you not appeal to my father?"

"Would he have listened to us?" A sneer twisted Rolf's mouth.

"Did you even attempt to reach out to him?"

"That's what we're doing right now, with you along to get his attention."

Calum sighed. "If you are expecting a lavish reward for returning me, you will be sorely disappointed. What makes you think my family has heaps of gold to spare?"

"They're sure to have more than we do. Now shut up."

They rode along for several hours, with the two men's feet loosely restrained by ropes passed under the chervines' bellies and their hands bound in front of them. At least, their arms were no longer tied behind their backs, nor were the bonds tight enough to cut off circulation. As Alex quickly discovered, though, he had no hope of wiggling free from the expertly tied knots. Not that either of them could have escaped anyway, with two kidnappers riding in front of them and two behind.

"To look on the bright side," Calum said in a low tone, "they are taking us in the right direction, toward my family's estate." He nodded toward the bandit leader. "He liked your idea."

"My idea? You've made me a major obstacle to our people's continued cordial relationship. Terrans don't bargain with extortionists."

"He does not know that, Alex. This happens all the time. Refusal to negotiate is a concept foreign to our culture."

Alex shook his head. "As soon as the parties to this interaction make contact with each other, our lives are time-limited. How is Rolf going to get in touch with your father?"

"By rider, most like."

"And how many days will it take to settle the deal? My superiors won't wait that long before they begin a search. We need to get away from these men as quickly as we can."

Calum shouted something to Rolf. Rolf replied in *cahuenga*. Aside from the honorific *vai dom*, Alex caught only a word here and there.

"What was that?" he asked Calum.

"He confirmed my guess. He will send an intermediate to negotiate. He also said we will not be harmed if we behave. We are too valuable."

"Valuable? Good to know, maybe they'll lower their vigilance. Well, I don't have plans to misbehave anytime soon."

The tedious trek dragged on, relieved only by a break during which the captives were allowed to retreat into the trees like leashed dogs, with two men holding the other ends of the ropes and keeping watch, their mistrust evident. The one Alex had flipped over his shoulder kept his hand on the hilt of his sword.

When they had taken care of necessities, they were led to the campsite chosen for the night and tethered to large trees.

"What are they saying?" Alex asked in Terran Common.

"They're discussing how large a ransom payment they expect to get for me," Calum replied in the same language. "Considering the recent poor harvests, they will be gravely disappointed. It is probably what drove them to this wild scheme in the first place. Yet they cling to the mistaken belief that all Comyn are rich."

"Not?" Alex offered a wry smile despite their uncomfortable position.

Calum shook his head. "Our wealth is in land, not money. My parents can barely keep the manor in repair. Unfortunately, my earlier appeal to Rolf failed to counter his illusions."

Alex glanced at the bandits. "What about me?"

"They consider you a bonus. In their minds, the *Terranan* possess infinite wealth. They are discussing what your superiors will pay for your return."

Alex laughed out loud at that idea. "The budget wouldn't even cover an aircar to shorten this trip. As I said, they won't pay money for me, not if it means negotiating with outlaws, so I hope your father does as you suggested. I shudder to think about the tongue-lashing I'll get from my boss for landing in this predicament in the first place."

"It is hardly your fault."

"At the least, she'll probably say I shouldn't have slacked off from regular self-defense drill."

Calum sighed. "Four against two. Our chances were not good to begin with. Father will certainly give me the same lecture for letting myself get captured."

"If I'd been allowed to carry a blaster—"

"We have already discussed that. You know how fundamental the Compact is to our culture and why."

"Yeah, I hear you. Wouldn't this be a great time for you to strike them with lightning?"

Calum said with a dry chuckle, "Even if it were allowed, that power does not fall under animal empathy."

"Then it would be a good time to summon a pack of wolves."

"We have large carnivores in this region, but I cannot sense any nearby. Besides, I lack sufficient confidence in my skill to control wild beasts. It would be unfortunate for them to eat us instead of chasing off the kidnappers."

"Not my first choice either. But, well, as I understand it, you have *laran* and these guys don't. Is there some way you can use it against them?" Alex asked the question more to keep his companion's spirits up than in hope of getting a useful answer.

"Maybe we do not require lightning bolts or fierce man-eating animals to aid our escape. Maybe we can use something more subtle." Calum nodded in the direction of their captors, who were casting suspicious glances at the two men whispering in an alien language. "We must wait until they settle down."

A couple of hours dragged by, while the campfire burned down to a dim glow. Alex's arms cramped despite his attempts to flex his muscles. Eventually, the outlaws crawled into their bedrolls. One man on guard crouched next to the fire, which backlit his silhouette. He spent more time gazing into the flames than watching the captives.

"Amateur," Calum murmured. "I suspect they lack practice with life as outlaws."

Farther away from the firepit, the chill kept Alex from falling asleep for a time. He occupied his mind with reviewing the unfamiliar plants he'd observed during the trip, in hopes he could reproduce his notes. Before long, he drifted into a half-doze. He came awake with a start when Calum whispered his name. Their snoring captors were faintly illuminated by the banked fire.

"You have a plan?" he whispered in Terran Common.

"I might be able to use animal empathy to free us. First, I need to find out whether my Gift is capable of summoning a hawk. Without a diversion, we will not be able to escape even if we untie ourselves."

"Unless we deal with these ropes, a diversion wouldn't be much help, either."

Calum closed his eyes and frowned in concentration. Minutes of silence crept by as his fists clenched, and he trembled as if straining to lift a heavy weight.

Alex stared up into the branches, the largest of Darkover's four moons visible between them. Seconds later, a large bird flew overhead, silhouetted against the moon. Calum had actually summoned a hawk! The bird swooped low enough for Alex to hear the whisper of its wings. It glided over the campsite above the sleeping bandits. One of them mumbled in his sleep and turned over.

The bird dove toward the man on watch, who jumped to his feet, waving his arms. The hawk pulled out of its dive, soared upward, and perched on a high limb.

Calum opened his eyes and stared at it. "Come back—" he whispered.

Instead, the bird emitted a single screech and flew away into the night.

Calum muttered a curse under his breath and slumped against the tree. "I should have known I could not control a creature that wild."

The guard glared at them. "What's with that talking?"

Alex rotated his shoulders. "Kind of hard to sleep like this."

"Well, try harder." The ruffian resumed his former position.

Alex murmured, "You almost did it, closer than I expected. Give it another try."

The Darkovan's shoulders drooped. "What is the point? That attempt took all the mental strength I have."

"Sounds like you're buying into your family's opinion of your limits."

"I fear they are right."

If there's the slightest chance this could work, he just needs a little shove. "If you're already giving up, maybe so. What happened to the wondrous powers of *laran* your ancestors wielded?" Alex forced himself to adopt a scornful tone to spur his companion to a more intense effort. "Nothing but fairy tales after all? Just as I thought."

Calum replied in a furious whisper, "You have that little trust in my word?"

"So far, I haven't seen a single thing to make me believe. If your mind-magic is real, show me. Get us out of this mess. As they say back home, put up or shut up."

"By Zandru, if we were not friends—" Calum broke off, the anger fading from his voice. "I see what you are doing. All right, I will try again." He gazed into the distance. "Maybe if I make contact with creatures a little less ferocious…"

Calum closed his eyes and frowned in concentration. The branches overhead rustled, and a faint chorus of chittering wafted on the night air. Both men looked up. Dozens of tree rats thronged the limbs and scurried down the trunks. Alex jerked in shock when one of the rodents landed beside him and bit into the rope fastening him to the tree. A second animal was doing the same to Calum.

"Do not startle them," the Darkovan said in a barely audible voice. "It is difficult enough to keep this many under control. Not easy to make rope fibers taste like nuts."

Alex stifled a nervous laugh. He had to struggle even harder to stay immobile when clusters of animals swarmed over him and started gnawing the bonds around his wrists. Meanwhile, another group ran to the picket line where the outlaw party's chervines were tethered and ate through the line strung between two trees. By the way the riding-beasts shuddered and rolled their eyes, yet didn't make a sound, Alex knew Calum must be controlling them at the same time. The line dropped to the ground, and the pack rushed to clear each chervine's lead off the line. Fortunately, the man on guard didn't notice the rodents' quiet activity.

Alex let out a sigh of relief when the tree rats finally retreated.

"Now for the diversion," Calum said. "If this works, I fear that our chervines will panic along with the others."

"You can't control them and create the, uh, diversion at the same time?" After the marvel he'd witnessed, Alex wouldn't put any animal-related feats past his companion.

Shaking his head, Calum rubbed his wrists where the rope had chafed them. "What just happened stretched my limits further than I thought myself capable. I am not certain I can manage the next step."

"Hold on, what about the *amaryseth* flowers? If they bring out latent *laran*, could they boost your power?"

"*Amaryseth* is not normally used in that way, but they must be steeped in hot water, which we lack."

After ruminating on the problem for a moment, Alex said, "What if you just chewed and swallowed the blossoms by themselves?"

Calum straightened up. "As far as I know, that has not been tried, certainly not by anybody I know of. The *leronis* who tested me never mentioned that method as an alternative."

"If you think it might be too dangerous—"

"More so than being kidnapped for ransom? I shall take my chances."

Digging into his pouch, Alex retrieved the most recently gathered packet of samples. With one eye on the half-dozing guard, he scooted nearer to Calum and set the package on the ground. Calum inched close enough to pick it up. Both men retreated to their respective trees.

Calum unwrapped the small bundle, stripped the flowers from their stems, and stuffed them into his mouth. Grimacing, he chewed and swallowed.

"That bad?" Alex asked.

"Bitter." A shudder convulsed the Darkovan. He doubled over, clutching his temples.

Alarmed, Alex started to crawl toward him. Calum waved him to a halt. "I can handle it." His voice slurred a bit. "That hawk—it is still nearby. I feel it." His eyes widened, and he panted as if he'd been running.

"Are you all right?"

"Just a headache. Let us finish this."

Rotating his cramped arms and flexing his fingers, Alex stood upright. Still dubious of his companion's welfare, he studied Calum in the dim light from the fire. "If you're sure you're okay, leave the chervines to me. I'll hang onto them and do my best to soothe them while you do the rest." Over the past few days of helping to tend the animals, he'd won their trust as well as rebuilding his former confidence as a rider.

"So be it." After drawing a labored breath, Calum withdrew into a trance-like state.

With a cautious look at the three sleeping brigands, Alex crept around the perimeter of the clearing toward the picketed chervines. The guard on watch, catching sight of him, ran in his direction.

A dark, winged shape swooped from the trees and flew into the man's face. *The hawk! Calum called it back!* The outlaw dropped to his knees with his arms wrapped around his head while the huge bird's wings battered him.

With any hope of stealth ruined, Alex sprinted toward the chervines. The pack animal snuffled him, apparently in hope of a treat, when he grasped its reins. With his free hand, he got a grip on the reins of the other two chervines.

Noises of flapping and chirping drew Alex's attention back to the treetops. A flock of sparrow-sized birds gathered in the branches, their number increasing by the second.

The outlaws, awakened by their comrade's screams, threw off their blankets. Rolf was the first to notice the captives had gotten free. Before he could act, though, at least ten of the small birds descended on him. At the same instant, his followers were likewise mobbed by flapping wings and pecking beaks. Other groups of birds flew in the faces of the bandits' unsecured mounts, which stampeded from the camp.

Struggling to keep their chervines from following, Alex yelled to Calum to mount up, breaking him out of his trance. Rolf fought his way toward Alex, swinging wildly around his head with Calum's prized sword and shouting for his men to stop the captives. Calum grabbed a chunk of firewood and, ducking a wild punch, landed a powerful blow to Rolf's head. The bandit leader crumpled in a heap.

Calum retrieved his weapon and stared for a second at the trio of outlaws. As the flock attacked their victims in a renewed frenzy, he stumbled to the chervines Alex was restraining. Alex had to help Calum into the saddle before he could mount himself.

They fled from the campsite with the pack beast on a leading rein behind them. Calum slumped over his chervine's withers, his arms wrapped around the animal's neck.

After about thirty minutes, they slowed. Calum swayed in the saddle, on the verge of toppling over. Guiding the chervines off the trail, Alex helped Calum dismount and recline against a tree.

"The animals," Calum said between gasps for breath. "The forest is full of them. I can *feel* them all. Cannot...shut them…out."

After Alex gave him a drink of water, Calum's breathing began to calm. Alex glanced backward up the trail. "What happens when the outlaws catch up with us?"

"They will not." Calum managed a feeble smile. His voice still sounded weak, but at least he wasn't panting now. "I mentally commanded their chervines to run at top speed in the opposite direction."

"What are you going to do about Rolf and his merry men?"

The Darkovan cast him a quizzical look, but Alex decided not to try explaining the ancient Earth legend of Robin Hood. After a moment's silent thought, Calum said, "No doubt Father will send out armed search parties to track them down. That should not be too difficult, since we know who they are, and they are likely to make contact with their families at some point. I recognized two of the others besides Rolf. What punishment they shall receive, I cannot say. If the past two years' poor harvests drove them to outlawry, we should try to do something about that situation."

"Would your people accept help from us? If I can talk our liaison office into deciding we should assist, maybe we can arrange some kind of trade of favors."

Calum frowned. "My parents may not look favorably upon such a plan. But even they will have to admit sooner or later that the times are changing. We shall see."

"Here's where your potential diplomatic skills might come in handy. Would you agree to bridge the gap between your clan and us outworlders if possible?"

"That idea has merit, if this effect of the *amaryseth* is not permanent. At this moment, my brain is so inundated with animal emotions I can hardly think. I have always wished for stronger *laran*, but this—!" He shook his head as if bees buzzed in it. "As far as I know, this is a totally new phenomenon. My family will want a *leronis* to study it."

"Could we help with that, too? Our botanists and your *leroni* teaming up to analyze the plant's chemistry?"

Calum rubbed his forehead. "Technicians from the Towers deigning to share research with *Terranan*? Well, since your ships

first came here from the stars, stranger things have happened."
With another half-smile, he asked, "Thinking of trying the
plant's powers on yourself?"

Alex held up his hands in mock horror. "Whoa, witnessing
mind magic is one thing, but inviting it into my own brain? One
step at a time, please."

TO REACH FOR THE STARS

by Lillian Csernica

Lillian Csernica's short stories have appeared in *Weird Tales, Fantastic Stories, Citadels of Darkover,* and *The Year's Best Indie Speculative Fiction Volume One.* Her Kyoto Steampunk short stories can be found in the Clockwork Alchemy anthologies *Twelve Hours Later, Thirty Days Later, Some Time Later,* and *Last Stop on the #13.* Lillian's historical romance, *Ship of Dreams,* is set in the Caribbean of 1725 during the Golden Age of piracy. The novel is available through Digital Fiction Publishing. Lillian has also published a nonfiction ebook, *The Writer's Spellbook: Creating Magic Systems for Fantasy.* A genuine California native born in San Diego, Lillian currently resides in the Santa Cruz mountains with her husband, two sons, and three cats. Visit her at *lillian888.wordpress.com.*

Two days out of Thendara, riding north by northeast for Serrais, Maya felt uneasy. Between Thendara and Serrais lay the Kilghard Hills. Maya had been raised in those hills, trained to read the terrain in case of landslides, sinkholes, or forest fires. She knew how to listen for certain sounds and silences. With the Midsummer Festival just two weeks away, the warm days, cool nights, and good visibility should have made this a routine mission. Even so, as the shadows of late afternoon grew longer, the prickling between her shoulders would not go away.

The problem was the Terrans. Someone had convinced Lord Serrais to send two Terrans along to further safeguard what lay among the supplies in the wagon.

Maya rode at the head of the escort, watching for any strange trail signs or movement in the undergrowth up ahead. Her eyes were on the terrain, but her mind kept turning to her sister Renunciates. Hanna, slim and strong with a crooked smile and a short mane of black curls, rode to the left of the wagon. Yareli, stocky and weathered with two short silver braids, rode on the right. Annika rode just behind the wagon with Dalia riding behind her, alert for any trouble on their back trail. Annika kept herself tidy, her single golden braid wound into a neat bun, her tunic and leggings clean. Dalia could stand still in an empty room and come out looking like she'd rolled down a muddy hill. She wore a black cotton scarf wrapped over her mouth and nose to keep out trail dust. Maya wished the scarf could muffle Dalia's endless supply of off-color jokes.

The wagon carried two drivers, local men from Thendara. Two more local men rode alongside, each armed with knives and swords.

The other Terran, a man named Thorpe, rode alongside the wagon. Thorpe stood head and shoulders taller than any other man Maya had ever seen, built burly and solid like a soldier. His hair had been shaven so close to his head Maya couldn't tell what color it might be. His pale eyes reminded her of hoarfrost.

"You look worried."

Keegan rode up alongside Maya. Lean and wiry with plenty of silver in his black hair and beard, Keegan was the captain of the transport team. Keegan was a spaceport worker from the Terran Empire. Maya had met him a number of times in some connection with raw materials or handicrafts being bought and sold in the Terran Zone. Keegan knew everybody in the import and export business. He claimed he stayed on Darkover because the lower gravity made his banged-up joints ache less.

"Terrans make me nervous."

Keegan grinned. "They make me nervous too. I'm guessing there's more than fancy cloth and dainty food for the Festival."

Maya shrugged. "Not much worth stealing from Ridenow."

"Depends on what you need and how bad you need it." A cold note in Keegan's cheerful voice made Maya glance at him.

"You think so?"

"I hear a lot of gossip in the Zone. Most of it is the liquor talking when folks are off duty."

Maya noticed all the careful qualifiers in that last sentence.

"So, nothing to worry about then?" she asked.

Keegan stared straight ahead, his expression stony. "Aw hell, there's always something to worry about." He dropped back into his position alongside the wagon.

Maya's heart started to pound. That sounded like a warning. What did Keegan know?

~o0o~

Just after sundown Maya called a halt for the night. A clearing close to the trail provided enough space for the tents and a modest fire pit.

"Dalia. Annika. Take first watch."

They dismounted and handed the reins of their horses to Hanna, who also took charge of Maya's and Yareli's mares. Dalia walked to the west side of the camp and Annika to the east. Every quarter hour they would turn left and move to the next cardinal point on the compass. Maya helped Yareli carry her cooking gear from her horse over to the middle of the campground.

Keegan dismounted, stretched, and tied his horse's reins to a wooden ring on the side of the wagon. then ambled over to Yareli.

"Ma'am, if you don't mind me asking, what's for supper?"

"Stew."

"How about I send somebody to gather wood and somebody else to find some meat for that stew?"

"That would be most kind, Mr. Keegan."

"They know enough to stay close, yes?" Maya asked.

Keegan grinned. "I told them to be home before dark. I can pitch in too. We've got a shovel just made for digging a fire pit."

Maya looked at Yareli. whose expression was a mixture of amusement and wariness.

"Are you trying to be nice to a little old lady, Mr. Keegan?"

"No, ma'am. I believe fair is fair. If you're doing the cooking, it's only right I chop wood or fetch water or similar."

Yareli studied him a moment longer, then nodded. "Fair is indeed fair, Mr. Keegan. That would mean supper is ready all the sooner."

Maya began laying out the Renunciates' bedrolls. Keegan had a word with the two men who'd ridden alongside the wagon, then brought a Terran shovel out of the back of the wagon. An oak handle with a steel scoop. Keegan plunged it into the dirt and set his foot on the top of the scoop. He worked his way around a circle three yards across. The task allowed Keegan to keep an eye on the entire camp. Maya looked around.

"Keegan, where's Thorpe?"

Keegan straightened up. "Carson! Where the hell is Thorpe?"

The wagon driver stopped rubbing down his horse just long enough to shrug and shake his head.

"He was standing by the wagon," Hanna said. "Did he wander off into the woods and get lost?"

Dalia snorted. "Hard to lose something that big."

"Dalia!" Maya snapped.

"Thorpe hasn't said a word all day. He probably went off to have a little privacy. Bouncing up and down in the saddle all day can't be easy on a man's—"

"*Dalia!*"

"—trousers. He's just off somewhere making a few adjustments."

~o0o~

Maya sat staring into the fire. Every now and then she'd poke at it, then add more wood.

The two wagon guards had returned bringing armloads of dry evergreen and enough small birds to make the stew more than just broth and root vegetables. Thorpe came trailing in behind them with a water skin slung across each shoulder and a sloshing bucket dangling from one fist. Everything had worked out just fine. Only it wasn't fine. The water skins must have been folded up empty inside Thorpe's saddlebags. There, or inside the wagon. Did Thorpe know what the Renunciates had been hired to protect? Who was he? Keegan would know, but Maya was reluctant to ask him any questions. If he answered her, he might ask a few himself. Fair was fair.

"You look like you're guarding a prisoner." Keegan sat down next to her, holding two mugs of tea. He held one out to her.

"Thanks." Maya took the mug and sipped at the steaming brew. "My grandmother had a saying. 'Remember, fire will never be your friend. If you're careful, you can make it your ally."

"Sounds like a wise woman."

"Keegan," Maya murmured. "Are we going to make it to Serrais?"

Keegan drank a long swallow of tea. "I sure hope so." He also kept his voice down. "If we don't, we don't get paid, do we?"

"I'd rather be poor than dead."

"That's the problem, isn't it?" Keegan's smile turned grim. "Some people would rather be dead than poor."

Four times Maya found a reason to walk along one edge of the campground. The terrain itself held enough interest. Limestone meant she might find caves. The thought of caves brought a sharp pain to her heart. On many an afternoon, she'd gone exploring the local caves with her little sister Bria. Maya shook off that memory before it led to others more painful. Just as Dalia and Annika had moved around each quarter of the compass, so did Maya. She was careful to cross from north by northwest down to south by southeast, then north by northeast down to south by southwest. From the leather wallet at her belt, she took a roll of plain brown cord strung with small brass bells. The breeze in the treetops, conversations round the fire, and the snapping and crackling of the fire itself provided enough noise cover while Maya anchored one end of the cord to a fallen tree limb or clump of sturdy greenery, the paid out the cord until she'd paced off that quarter of the compass.

Maya took the second watch with Hanna. The night deepened, the evening turned cold, and one by one people sought their bedrolls. Maya stood guard to the west, watching over her sisters and listening for the slightest tinkle.

~o0o~

They appeared out of the darkness like a heavy mist.

Maya turned to her left, ready to walk to the eastern point of the compass. Annika took two strides north. Sudden gray shapes surrounded her and dragged her backward into the trees. Annika screamed.

Maya leaped over the sleeping forms and ran at the sounds of bodies thrashing through the undergrowth. Shouts and curses poured out of her mouth. Annika came stumbling out of the trees, her braid hanging askew, blood on her tunic. Hands reached for her. Maya shoved Annika behind her and lunged, her long knife in hand. She slashed and stabbed at the tall gray shadows. They fell, cursing her in *cahuenga*.

"Maya!"

Maya spun around. Two bandits had Yareli backed up against a tree. Hanna came running from over beside the horses. She had a dagger in hand and took aim. The blade sank into the back of one bandit. He collapsed against the other bandit, knocking him sideways. Before the second bandit could rise, Yareli buried her long knife in his back. Hanna bent to snatch back her dagger.

Shouts and screams erupted behind the wagon. It creaked and rattled, rocking in its axles. Something heavy struck it again.

"*Banshee-humping son of a Ya-man's dog!*"

The roar came from behind the wagon. Only Dalia could curse like that. Maya ran toward the wagon. Just then two bodies came whirling out from behind it, clawing and kicking and cursing. The firelight gleamed on Dalia's blonde hair. Her enemy wore a hooded gray cloak.

Dalia hit the ground, pinned beneath the bandit. They struggled, thrashing around in the dirt. Maya caught a fistful of the man's hood and pulled it off. Under the hood, he wore not just the dust mask. More black cloth covered the man's head, tied at the back of his neck. Dalia got one hand free and tore away the dust mask, taking the black cloth with it. Red hair gleamed in the light of the torches. Maya stumbled back.

"A Comyn? Here?"

"Ridenow?" Dalia stared up at him, mouth agape. "*Trevyn Ridenow?*"

"Hello, Dalia." The Comyn backhanded Dalia, slamming her down against the dirt. Blood ran from her split lip. "Did you really think I wouldn't find you?"

"You know him?" Maya snapped.

"He's why." Dalia shook her head. Her eyes focused on Maya. "Why I joined—Guild."

Fury exploded inside Maya. "Get off her! *Now!*"

"Stand down, Amazon." Ridenow clamped one hand around Dalia's throat. "Or she will suffer as only a Comyn can make her suffer."

Maya froze. That was no small threat.

"He's a Ridenow! He's got no *laran!*" Dalia struck upward. The heel of her hand hit Ridenow under the jaw and snapped his head back.

Maya hit him with the hilt of her long knife. Ridenow sprawled in the dirt, holding his head and moaning.

"Stupid Dry Town slut!" Ridenow fought free of the cloak. "You will suffer for striking your betters!"

"Better than what?" Now Dalia sneered. "Looks like the Ridenow Family still don't amount to much if you've turned bandit!"

"Bitch!" Ridenow lunged at her.

Annika screamed. Maya spun around to see Thorpe twisting the golden length of Annika's braid around her throat. He raised his fist, making Annika strain on tiptoe. Annika kept gasping, left hand dragging at her braid, right hand straining to reach the dagger stuck in her thigh.

"Be still, Amazons. Or your little sister dies."

Trevyn Ridenow staggered up onto his feet. He slapped dirt and twigs off his cloak, then stood upright and sneered. "Useless. Nobody wants you as women, and you just can't fight like a man. Pathetic."

"Shut up," Thorpe said. "Go get what you're here for. You've wasted enough of my time."

Ridenow opened his mouth, shut it, then gathered his cloak around him and huffed off to the wagon.

The two remaining bandits stepped forward, standing to either side of Thorpe.

"Drop your weapons," Thorpe said. "Right now, or I'll make you watch while she slowly strangles."

A look of total peace settled over Annika's features.

"Avarra's vengeance be upon you, Terran. No man uses me. Never again!"

Annika tore the dagger from her thigh and plunged it into her own throat.

"*Annika!*"

Dalia let out a howl and charged. The bandits stepped in front of Thorpe. Dalia lashed out with a fist that hit one bandit in the face and spun him around. She threw herself on the man's back.

"Hanna! Yareli!" Maya yelled. "Go! Get back to the Guild House!"

The two women ran for the horses.

The bandit stumbled backward under Dalia's weight and crashed into Thorpe. Thorpe's hand twisted in Annika's braid kept him anchored to her body and threw off his balance. He went down on one knee. The bandit grabbed Dalia by the hair and dragged her forward over his shoulder, flinging her into the dirt. Dalia rolled, coming up with both hands empty. The bandit fell over. Dalia's long knife stuck up from his chest.

"Brother!" The last bandit ran at Dalia.

Thorpe dropped Annika's body and ran after Hanna and Yareli.

Maya sprinted toward the bandit and leaped, hitting him hard enough to knock him off his feet. They rolled together. Maya held on tight, rage giving her strength enough to pin the man's arms to his sides. They fetched up against one of the tree trunks lying half-buried in the grass. Maya slammed the man's head against the tree trunk. He stopped moving. Maya scrambled up, running for Thorpe.

"Ridenow!" Thorpe bellowed. "Stop them! Stop the Amazons!"

Thorpe reached into his jacket. The firelight glinted off Terran metal.

Maya gasped. An off-world weapon. "Hanna! *Get down!*"

A bolt of hot white light shot out and hit a tree on the far side of the horses. The tree exploded, raining broken branches and other flaming debris down on the forest floor. The horses panicked, kicking and rearing. Maya saw Yareli silhouetted against the flames. Hanna tackled Yareli and rolled her away from the fire. Thorpe sighted along his pistol.

Crack!

Thorpe jerked forward and fell on his face. Behind him stood Keegan holding a broken tree branch in his right hand. His left arm dangled at a bad angle. Blood ran from a wound at his temple.

"Thank you," Maya said. "Now whose side are you on?"

"My own." Keegan tossed aside the branch. He bent to take the weapon out of Thorpe's hand and toss it at Maya's feet. "Be careful." Keegan swayed. "Point it. Pull the trigger. Ridenow is still—" His eyes rolled back. Keegan fainted.

Maya stared down at the pistol. weighing her choices, hearing the hunger of the forest fire roaring behind her. Embers drifted down around her. She forced herself to pick up the weapon and tuck it into her belt pouch.

"Hanna! Yareli! Are you still close by?"

"Here!" Hanna waved from the horse enclosure. She sat astride her own horse. Yareli had managed to mount up as well. They struggled to calm the other horses long enough to free their reins. The horses bolted into the night.

"Take Keegan with you," Maya said. "I think his left arm is broken."

"He's Terran!" Hanna fought to keep her horse under control. "It's a hard enough ride for the two of us!"

Maya stripped a cloak from a bandit, spread it out, and rolled Keegan onto it, then dragged Keegan over to the horses. "Keegan is important. He knows something."

"Are you sure?" Hanna asked.

"We save him, we save ourselves. Do it!"

"Maya! I've got your mare!" Yareli yelled above the hiss and crackle of the fire.

Maya looked around. Dalia had disappeared. Was she chasing Ridenow, or working with him?

"Ridenow betrayed us," Maya said. "I'll catch up as soon as I can."

"But Maya—

The upper half of the tree blazed like a Midsummer bonfire. Snapping and crunching from above heralded disaster.

"Go!" Maya screamed. "The tree is falling!"

Maya ran for the cave she'd spotted while she was stringing the bells. She lay there, trying to quiet her breathing. The smoke hadn't spread this far into the cave. If she kept low, she might buy herself a little more time. Ambush. Bandits. And Annika. Annika was dead. Maya couldn't even bring Annika's body back for a decent burial. Tears flooded Maya's eyes and ran back into her hair. She rolled onto her side and hugged her knees to her chest, tucking her head down to muffle her sobs. Never before had she lost a sister on a mission.

Leather scraped on stone. Maya kept still, letting her breath out slowly.

"Maya?" Dalia's voice, the thinnest whisper. "Maya?"

Maya closed her eyes and drew a deep, silent breath. She caught the scents of sweat, horse, and the sap of the trees they'd ridden through on the trail up into the Kilghard Hills. Why would a Comyn be trying to find Dalia? It couldn't be a coincidence that Ridenow turned up here among bandits. Maya curled her fingers around the hilt of her boot knife. A pebble skittered off a stone and bounced off the back of Maya's thigh. She rolled backward, plowing into a pair of legs. Dalia fell forward and landed with a grunt of pain.

"Seven hells, Maya!" Dalia started to shove herself upward.

Maya planted her knee between Dalia's shoulder blades. "Are you a traitor? Are you?"

"What? Me?"

"You knew a Comyn was involved."

"Not until I pulled off his mask!"

Maya thought about the shock on Dalia's face, in the tone of her voice. How hard the Comyn hit her, enough to stun her and draw blood.

"Maya, please! I figured out why Ridenow is here. He came to meet Thorpe halfway between Thendara and Serrais."

"Prove it."

"My best proof is putting bruises on my ribs right now. I can't show it to you until I at least turn over."

"The jewels?"

"Yes and no. They're part of it, but not the most important part."

"Keep talking."

"Take my weapons. Tie my hands. Just get off me and let me breathe!"

"Fair enough." Maya pulled Dalia's long knife out of its scabbard and laid it aside, then did the same with Dalia's boot knife. She freed the scarf from around Dalia's neck. "Both hands behind your back."

Dalia obeyed. Maya wound the scarf around Dalia's wrists and tied it off with double knots. "Up on your knees. Then turn around and sit with your back to the wall."

Dalia obeyed. "Why are you sitting here in the dark?"

"Making more fire didn't seem like a good idea right now."

"If you want to see what I found, we need light."

Maya patted herself down and pulled enough twigs and leaves from her hair and clothing to make a small pile of tinder. She did the same to Dalia and found three sticks the length of her forearm stuck through Dalia's belt. "What are these for?"

"Poking the bushes and checking for deadfalls."

Maya was oddly gratified to know Dalia had been paying attention during Maya's talk on safety in the forest. Maya chose two of the sticks and snapped them in thirds. She set them into a cone shape over the tinder, moving slowly and carefully so she didn't knock it all over. From her belt pouch, she took flint and the piece of rock Grandma had given her on the day she taught Maya how to make fire. Maya whispered a prayer to Avarra, then struck the flint against the rock. One feeble spark fell, then winked out. Maya struck again. More sparks fell. And again. The tinder caught and glowed, then tiny flames began to lick along the sticks. Maya snapped the third stick into pieces and carefully fed the growing fire.

Dalia sat there breathing and wincing. The last few tears trickled down her cheeks, cutting trails through the dirt. "Trevyn Ridenow is from a branch of the Family who had interests in the mines and the cattle in the Dry Towns. His father would come to Shainsa on business and bring the little tyrant with him. 'I'm a Comyn. I'm a Comyn. You live on *my* land.' Every chance we got, the Dry Towns kids tried to beat the Comyn out of him."

A snort of laughter escaped Maya. "Must have been a lot of beatings."

"Not enough. Trevyn always said he'd be the one to make the Ridenows bigger than the Hasturs."

"Did anybody take him seriously?"

"Somebody must have. Here he is in a deal with Terrans to smuggle starstones."

Maya's jaw dropped. "He's not just out to steal the jewels?" She frowned. "But... Comyn are connected to their starstones, aren't they?"

"Comyn who have enough *laran* to use a starstone."

"So he's not carrying a real starstone?"

"Once you see what's bruising my ribs, you'll understand."

Maya freed the laces at the neck of Dalia's jerkin. She reached inside and pulled out a pouch made of fine fabric. The braided drawstring cords had been cut. Maya moved back out of reach, set the knife beside her knee, and untied the cords. Three gems tumbled out onto her palm, one as big as the tip of her thumb, the other two half that size, all clear light blue and cut in the shape of a teardrop.

"How did you get hold of these?"

"The better question is when. When the bandits hit us, I spotted Trevyn digging in the back of the wagon, going after the jewels."

"So where is the real starstone?"

"Down in the bottom of the pouch."

Maya found enough bits of leaves and twigs to keep the little fire burning. She turned the pouch upside down and shook it out onto her palm. Out tumbled a small bundle of silk. Inside lay a gem that matched the size of the smaller teardrops, its color a milky blue.

"How do I know this is a starstone?"

"The pouch was in Ridenow's left hip pocket."

"How—" Maya paused. "You weren't really stunned by that slap, were you?"

Dalia grinned.

"Where would a Ridenow get a starstone?"

"Trevyn is obsessed with being the one who brings glory to the Ridenow name. He's more than capable of stealing a starstone from one of his younger and more powerful cousins."

"Why was Ridenow looking for you?"

Dalia's cocky air faded. "Trevyn Ridenow hates me. After I ran away from home, he swore he'd find me."

"What, for beating him up when you were both children?"

"When I was ten and Ridenow was twelve, I caught him putting his hands on my eight-year-old cousin."

"You turned him in?"

"I knocked him out. Hit him hard enough to lay him out flat."

"You knocked out a Comyn? And in the Dry Towns?" Maya nodded. "I can see why you ran away. How far did you get?"

"I made it all the way to the spaceport."

"All by yourself?"

"All by myself." Dalia smiled. "I got a job working at a restaurant that made the kind of food Terrans eat." Her expression twisted, a grin tempered by the taste of something sour. "I had a roof over my head, a bedroll by the hearth, and two meals every day."

"Impressive. How did Ridenow find you?"

"He must have seen me in Thendara. His uncle is Lord Serrais. Trevyn likely whined his way into coming along when the Council was meeting."

"Bad luck."

"That's Ridenow. The ones who aren't crazy are just plain stupid."

"Ridenow might be crazy, but Thorpe is dangerous."

"He's not dead?"

"Not dead enough. If somebody paid him to organize the transport and the ambush, he's most likely a mercenary from the Terran Empire. He could have fighting and survival skills we've never even heard of."

"Fine. Shoot him."

"What?"

"You've got his pistol. Shoot him."

Maya took out the pistol. Just two black metal rectangles with a trigger in the corner where they met. All edges had been rounded and polished smooth. It gleamed with oily menace. Such a slender shape, not as heavy as she might have expected. So plain, when it contained such terrifying power. Maya picked up one of the smaller blue gems.

"Comyn use starstones to boost their *laran*. Is *laran* energy?"

"Maybe."

"I wonder...." Maya set the starstone side by side with the blue gem. "Is Ridenow ambitious enough to try bringing laser weapons back to Darkover?"

"And break the Compact?" Dalia shook her head. "The Terrans who came into the restaurant would joke about Comyn and their 'magic rocks.' Sometimes they'd whisper about starstones being worth a fortune."

Maya stared at the starstone, thinking about ice and cold winter nights and the stories her grandmother told about ancient times. *Laran* was a curse, she said. Stupid people who wanted more than they'd already been given used *laran* and starstones to interfere with how babies were made. Grandma said history called that time the "Ages of Chaos." Terran weapons shot energy. Could starstones make that energy even stronger? Maya poured the three blue gems and the starstone back into the pouch and tied off the silken cords. She dropped that pouch down inside the collar of her shirt.

"Sit forward."

Dalia didn't move. "What are you thinking?"

"We have to get back to the Guild House. Hanna and Yareli will give their report, but we have the proof."

Dalia hitched herself away from the wall and leaned forward. Maya freed the double knots and began unwinding the scarf from around Dalia's wrists. She rolled the pistol up in the scarf and tucked it into her belt pouch.

"So now do you trust me?" Dalia asked.

"I trust you to know if you betray me, you face Ridenow and his Terran friend all by yourself."

~oOo~

Maya crept to the mouth of the cave. The air smelled wrong. It stung the back of her throat like the dyes the weavers used. The fire's strength had lessened, even the sound of it devouring the forest. There was no time to be sure. She gave Dalia a nod.

"Ridenow!" Dalia yelled. "Ridenow! Can you hear me?"

"Get out here, you little bitch!"

"Shut up, Trevyn! I just wanted to know if the Terran had killed you yet!"

"Amazon." Thorpe's deep voice rolled out through the night. "What else do you want?"

"Hey! Thorpe!" Dalia yelled. "Trevyn's got *two* stones! Make him show you the other one!"

"Comyn carry one stone," Ridenow yelled. "The one that belongs to that Comyn!"

"Then what were you carrying in your left hip pocket?"

The sudden silence made Dalia grin.

"I want to make a deal, Thorpe," she said. "Just between you and me."

"What have you got to offer?"

"I can tell you how Ridenow thinks he can cheat you."

Ridenow's shouting and cursing drowned out Thorpe's reply.

"*Quiet.*" Thorpe's command echoed off the cliffs. "Amazon! Tell me exactly what you're asking for."

"I want to get off this planet. I want to see the galaxy, all the amazing things the Council won't let the people of Darkover even know about."

The certainty in Dalia's voice shocked Maya. Had all those years working in the Terran Zone given Dalia a taste of life on other worlds? Did she really want to leave Darkover?

"What do I get out of this deal?" Thorpe asked.

"I've got the starstone. The real one."

"She's lying!" Ridenow yelled. "I've got my stone right here!"

"Whatever he's got in that pouch around his neck," Dalia

said," it's not a starstone."

"Can you prove that?" Thorpe asked.

"Make him prove I'm wrong! I've known the little prick since he was ten years old. Trevyn Ridenow doesn't have enough *laran* to blow his own nose, never mind use a starstone."

Maya expected more shouting, but Ridenow said nothing. She strained to hear the sound of voices. Any words were lost in the wind rushing through the trees.

"Come out, Amazon," Thorpe said. "Where's your friend Maya?"

Maya gripped the pistol in her right hand and held one end of the scarf inside her left fist. Dalia wound the scarf around Maya's wrists twice, keeping it loose, then tucked the end down in between. Maya walked ahead of Dalia. They left the cover of the undergrowth and stepped out onto the cleared ground near the trail.

"Here she is."

Dalia rested her palm against Maya's back. Maya jerked forward and dropped to her knees.

Ridenow strode toward Dalia. "Give me my stone!"

"Wake up, Trevyn," Dalia said. "You've served your purpose. Nobody cares what you want."

"You're going to learn who your masters are!" You—"

"Ridenow," Thorpe said. "What did I tell you?"

"Only Comyn can touch starstones! That a whore like this laid her filthy hands on it—"

Thorpe caught Ridenow by the back of his cloak. "Shut up and keep still."

Ridenow freed the clasp and let the cloak fall away. "How dare you lay hands on a Comyn? Without me, you had no hope of getting a starstone! You—"

Thorpe drove his fist into Ridenow's stomach. Ridenow fell onto all fours, retching.

Maya dropped the scarf. brought her hands around in front of her, and leveled the pistol at the Thorpe. He stared at Maya for five heartbeats. Those cold empty eyes were unblinking. His mouth split open in a grin like the edge of a scythe. Thorpe stuck his right hand in his pocket, then held up a metal cylinder the length of Maya's little finger and the thickness of a broomstick.

"You can't do much without the power cell."

May held that cold stare and tightened her fingers around the slender butt of the pistol. The ridges on the flat sides dug into her palm. She gave Thorpe a cold smile of her own.

"If you're so sure, keep on coming."

"That's funny, you talking about being sure. Do you even know who's standing behind you? Do you know Little Miss Dalia is the one who made the deal between me and Ridenow?"

Dalia burst out laughing. "Never happened."

"Little Miss Dalia said she wants to get off this backwater planet. She wants to see the galaxy. That takes a lot of money."

"You're lying, Terran."

"Am I? Maybe you'll believe this. I told Miss Dalia if she didn't follow my instructions to the very last detail, I would go tell your Guild Mother how Miss Dalia likes to visit the Terran Zone, whoring herself out to anybody who wants to bed a Free Amazon."

"You killed Annika. That's all that matters right now."

"Don't be stupid, Amazon." Thorpe took two casual strides closer. "Do you know anything about laser weapons? They burn." His grin widened. "You know about fire, don't you, Maya? Your little sister died because you were—"

"*Shut up!*"

"—too slow! She burned, Maya. Her skin blistered. Her blood boiled. Her bones—"

Maya screamed. The smoke, the embers, and the stink of burning flesh from the bodies of the dead bandits filled her head with horror. A Midsummer party. The young people all gathered down by the creek. Maya sat holding hands with Sam, just talking, skipping pebbles, and watching the sunlight dance on the water. She smelled smoke, just a little, and thought it was one of the cook fires. By the time she saw the smoke billowing through the trees and ran to ring the fire bell, it was too late. Bria had wandered off to sit in the shade, playing with her doll. She lost her way in the smoke. Falling branches trapped her. The fire found her before Maya could.

Fire killed Bria. Fire gleamed in Thorpe's cold, dead eyes. He made white fire, so much worse than burning trees. Thorpe wanted more than he'd already been given. He wanted starstones. He wanted power. Maya could give it to him. She pulled the trigger.

Another bolt of hot white light shot out, blazing straight through Thorpe's chest. Twenty feet behind him a boulder burst into chunks that smoked. Thorpe fell flat on his back. Despite the heat and smoke and glowing embers, Maya stood there shivering.

Ridenow straightened up and wiped his hand across his mouth. "This is perfect!" He let out whoop of laughter. "I'll turn you in for using an off-world weapon. You'll be executed, the Renunciates shamed, and my Family will be the heroes of Darkover!"

"Shut up, Trevyn." Dalia snatched up the fallen cloak, flung it over Ridenow's head, and spun him around until he ran head-first into a tree.

~o0o~

Maya's bones ached with every jolt in the saddle. The uneven ground made riding pure torture. Her only consolation was knowing Ridenow was hurting even more. Dalia had tied him up, gagged him, and slung him across the saddle of their third horse. The gag was a necessary alternative to letting Dalia kill him. His steady stream of cursing, whining, threats, and pathetic attempts to negotiate left Maya with a headache on top of her cracked ribs.

The sun lightened the horizon as they began their descent onto the trail that would take them back to Thendara. Maya drank in the soft light and the cold sweet air. She still didn't know what had stopped the fire. Right then she didn't care. They still had a long way to go before she and Dalia could rest inside the safety of the Guild House. Maya had plenty of evidence, but the evidence could lead to a variety of conclusions. Would his Comyn blood lend Ridenow's story of betrayal by the Renunciates a credibility Maya could not outwit? Maya brooded on that while Ridenow grunted and raged behind his gag.

The sun cleared the horizon and its light flooded the plain below. Dalia raised her head and squinted into the fresh brightness.

"Riders." She cocked her head, eyes shut. "Six... No, ten. Good horses, light arms on half of them. Soldiers' weight on the other six."

Maya reined in. Her horse didn't like that. The mare knew they were headed home and yearned for her familiar stable just as Maya longed for her bed. "How soon?"

"Soon. We can't get up the trail fast enough to outrun them, not with Ridenow slowing us down."

"Then we wait."

"With a captive Comyn in plain sight?"

"Aside from that red hair, he looks nothing like a Comyn. If Ridenow wants to play bandit, he should learn what happens to bandits who get caught."

Dalia grinned. She guided her horse alongside Ridenow and jerked his gray hood down to hang low over his forehead.

Maya watched, heart pounding, head aching. Then she saw Hanna waving and the glitter of sunbeams in Yareli's silver hair.

~oOo~

A week later Maya sat beside Dalia in the front row of a large room in Terran Headquarters. Beside Maya sat Rhona, their Guild Mother. Beside Dalia sat Hanna and Yareli. Up on the stage stood one of the Terran officials. Maya had lost track of all the complicated ranks and titles. She was still tired. Once the Comyn Guard had taken possession of the starstone and the Terran Spaceforce agents had seized Thorpe's pistol, the rest turned into a blur of questions and meetings and more questions. Loud clapping on all sides brought Maya back to the present. Rhona walked up the short flight of stairs and crossed the stage to the lectern where the Terran official stepped aside with a bow.

"Today we give thanks for the safe return of our sisters," Rhona said. "There is one who can be with us only in spirit. Let it be known that Annika of Thendara House died by her own hand."

Gasps and murmurs swept through the crowd.

"This was an act of supreme courage. By taking her own life, Annika prevented the leader of these despicable criminals from holding her hostage in order to make our sisters surrender. Annika's sacrifice gave power back to our sisters. With the blessing of Avarra, the Renunciates stopped a terrible crime that might well have caused great suffering to all peoples in all corners of the Terran Empire. Our beloved sister Annika chose her own life, and her own death. Let us share a moment of silent gratitude."

At the end of the ceremony, Maya rose to follow Rhona and her sisters into another large room decorated with flowers and garlands. For the next hour, Maya smiled and nodded and accepted the best wishes of strangers she doubted she'd ever lay eyes on again. At last, Dalia led her to another building in the vast Headquarters compound. An infirmary. In a private room, Keegan lay in a bed. Wires ran from various machines to the bed and under the blankets that covered him.

"Good to see you." Keegan looked thinner. The bruise at his temple had faded to blues and greens.

"How are you feeling?" Maya asked.

"Damn lucky. Thorpe was wanted in five systems."

"Can you tell me what happened to the fire?"

"I'm told Armida Tower got word about a forest fire and relayed that to Thendara Tower. Terran HQ spotted it too and sent out its airborne rescue team."

"Flying fire fighters?" Maya tried to imagine it. To actually fly above the fire...

Keegan smiled. "They have chemical sprays that smother the fire. Three of them covered the area in time to contain it before it spread to inhabited areas."

"Aside from us," Dalia said.

"That's right." Keegan looked Maya in the eye. "I'd be dead right now if it hadn't been for you telling your sisters to take me with them. I want you to know I'm very grateful."

"You saved us first. Thanks to you, I got the pistol away from Thorpe."

"What happened to him?"

Maya took a slow, shuddering breath. "I shot him."

Keegan nodded. "Good for you."

"No." Maya shook her head. "No."

Keegan pointed to a thick brown envelope lying on the table beside his bed. "There's no way to explain just how big a difference you've made by stopping Thorpe." He shrugged. "I figured maybe this might help."

Dalia opened the envelope. "Papers?"

"There was a bounty on Thorpe. The terms were 'dead or alive.' The Spaceforce officials are convinced the Renunciates were responsible for making sure Thorpe never left Darkover. So you get the bounty."

Maya and Dalia spoke at once. "Annika deserves some of it."

"Yes, she does. Your Guild Mother has agreed to see to that. Rhona will make sure the right people see these documents and give you what you've earned." Keegan lay back with a sigh.

"We should go," Dalia said. "You need to rest."

Maya followed her to the door.

"Maya," Keegan said.

"Go on," Maya told Dalia. "I'll be out in a minute."

Dalia left, closing the door behind her. Maya looked at Keegan, and Keegan looked back at her.

"If you ever want a job," he said. "You come talk to me."

"Fighting fires?"

"Every world in the Empire has some kind of fire. We need good fire fighters."

Maya smiled. "I'll keep that in mind."

FIRE SEED

by Diana L. Paxson

Diana L. Paxson has been writing since the 1970s. She is the author of thirty novels, seven non-fiction books, and, with this publication, a hundred short stories. She lives in a multi-generational, multi-gendered household in Berkeley. She is currently working on a non-fiction book about the Norse goddess Freyja and learning how to reissue some of her out-of-print novels and stories.

Fire weather...

I emptied the wastewater from breakfast into the pot where our housemate Ramona was growing herbs and straightened, sniffing the air. I could smell nothing worse than garbage lying in the lane between us and the inn. In the week since Midsummer there had been neither snow nor rain, and folk had passed from blessing the fine weather to complaining about the temperature, but the sky was still a translucent shade somewhere between amethyst and blue.

The kitchen door opened and my freemate, Cassilde, came through. She licked a finger to test the wind. "The wind is from the east. We won't be called to the fire lines unless it blows from the north with news of a fire in the Thendara Hills."

When the devil winds kindled the mountains, everyone heeded the call to fight the flames—Comyn and peasant, man and woman, the law-abiding Renunciates of Thendara House and our little community in what some called the Forbidden Guildhouse on the other side of town. If fires sparked in the hills beyond the Valeron, the call would come.

In this weather, it was all too likely. I felt sweat bead my forehead and wiped it away with my sleeve.

Cassi turned to go back inside and then stopped, pointing.

A thin figure was striding up the lane. A youth, I thought, at that age when limbs lengthen unexpectedly and one struggles to master a new body while trying to comprehend a changing soul. A scarf of the sort farmers wore in the country around Neskaya framed a head crowned with a fluff of ash-brown hair, like one of the birds that wade among the reeds beside the Valeron.

Closer, I realized it must be a girl. She was wearing a pair of loosely gathered Renunciate breeches that I remembered mending when I still lived at Thendara House, and despite her height, her cheeks bore no trace of down.

"Mestra Kiera?" Her eyes went from my freemate's motherly form and blonde curls to my own lanky frame and ginger hair.

Blue eyes...bright as a matrix shard, bright as the eyes that had enchanted me that year when I was getting some long-deferred training at the tower at Neskaya and living in the Renunciate Guildhouse in the town.

"Evanda's mercy!" I breathed. "You must be Mhari's child!!" I looked up, and up. "Leona! How you've grown..." She colored up, shifting from one foot to the other as I fought down memories.

"Mestra Kiera, my mother sends greetings and calls on your promise to foster me!"

"Well, for Evanda's sake, don't keep her standing on the doorstep!" Cassi rescued me. "Come inside, both of you! I think that Ramona can find something to fill a growing girl," she went on, shepherding us both inside.

Our little kitchen had none of the settled comfort of Thendara House, but in the past three years, we had made the two-story cabin behind the inn into a home. Embroidered curtains hung in the windows and drying herbs hung from hooks on the walls.

"How did you get here?" Cassi asked as we all sat down

"Signed on to drive donkeys with a pack train carrying raw cralmac hides. We got in at sundown." The blue gaze shifted to Ramona, who was flipping barley cakes in the iron pan.

I tensed. From the front, Ramona's figure was womanly enough, but from the back, her strong shoulders still identified her as the man she once had been. Would that be a problem?

"I see that you went first to Thendara House," I said, pointing at Leona's breeches.

"That's where my mother said you lived." The blue eyes narrowed. "They fed me and gave me a bath and new clothes—I journeyed here dressed as a boy—and then sent me here."

A wise choice, I thought, counting the years. Mhari's child was poised at that moment just before a girl blossoms into womanhood. It was an age when the relationship between a girl and her birth mother is often strained, hence the custom of sending girls who had grown up in a Renunciate Guildhouse to another town to spend their Housebound half-year.

"I am surprised they told you how to find us—" said Cassi as Ramona set the cakes, still sizzling, in front of our guest and drizzled them with blackfruit jam.

"Some of them did not wish to. They said you did not have a proper place for me, but they have three other young ones and I could share the girls' room with them there. But I told them my mother and you had promised to foster each other's children and so I should come first to you. And then Mother Doria said an oath must be honored, and that I have to make up my own mind where I want to be."

I do not think that this one needed telling..., I thought, considering that frown. *She is the kind who will always choose her own way.*

"Oaths?" Cassi raised an eyebrow and it was my turn to blush.

"It was before I met you, *breda*—" I said repressively, relaxing as she laughed.

"So you went to Thendara House and they told you that Kiera was here," Ramona tucked a greying curl back beneath her kerchief. "What else did they tell you?"

Once more the girl flushed, but her level gaze did not falter. "Mother Doria said that you and your freemate had chosen your own path, but she was obligated to let me meet you, and if—if it did not work out, I would be very welcome there."

"Huh!" Ramona snorted. "Kind of her!"

The blue gaze turned from me to Ramona and back again. It was not that of a water bird, I thought then, but some bird of prey.

"What did she mean?"

"She meant, my dear, that we are the next thing to outlaws here," a new voice answered, low and sweet as a well-played viol.

We all turned. Ariana had paused half-way down the stairs, her light skirts settling into graceful folds. In this heat, instead of wool, over the skirt she wore only a tunic of thin linen in silver grey ornamented with an interlace of purple flowers, and a lavender silk scarf instead of a shawl. Her black hair was coiled and held at the nape of her neck with a butterfly clasp. Somehow, in that outfit, her grey eyes had an amethystine glow.

As always, at the sight of her I felt at once a lift to the heart and a momentary dissatisfaction with my own serviceable garb. Leona was gazing as if Evanda Herself had suddenly appeared, a common response from those seeing Ariana for the first time. Aware of her audience, she posed with even more feminine grace. Then she laughed and took the last few steps down into the room.

"Ramona was a man, but the Goddess changed her soul. As a boy I was born, but the blood of the Fair Folk is in my veins—" she waved a six-fingered hand, "and She changed my body, too." She paused, watching as Leona's eyes blazed—with shock? Horror? Hope? That last seemed unlikely, but I could not tell. "The good women of Thendara House call us abomination for all their talk of freedom," Ariana went on, her Hellers accent growing stronger. "We have been allies, of sorts, but that be another tale."

"What about you?" Leona fixed me and Cassi with another of her blue stares.

Cassi's gesture embraced the room. "We are here because we love them...," she said quietly, and smiled. For a moment all of us were silent, thinking about what we had gained, and lost, for that love.

"So—" Ariana said brightly at last, "now that you be here, you'll be needing something to do—you look nigh on fifteen— old enough to take the oath of a Renunciate, or a freemate, or to marry a man—" she shuddered, "if that be your way."

Cassi and I traded glances. We had taken oath to each other. The commitment we had made to Ramona and Ariana was harder to classify.

"Have you thought about what you want to do?"

"Oh...yes...but..."

"She doesn't have to plan the rest of her life right now! The poor child has just left home!" I took a breath and turned back to the girl. "For as long as you have need, you are welcome to stay with us here!"

"Well enough," Ramona said then, "but in the meantime, as Ariana says, we must find you some occupation. What can you do?"

"A little of everything, I suppose. I am good at chopping wood and fixing things when they go wrong. I can milk a chervine or dig a garden, shoe a horse and mend its gear. At Neskaya, when they saw how big I was getting, they gave me the outdoor jobs."

That was no surprise. Leona had been a Midsummer Festival child, and I recalled Mhari saying that the man who sired her had been tall.

I looked at her with approval—guiding expeditions was my trade, and I had no apprentice. Even if I had wished to give birth, I had always feared that any child of my body might be claimed by my Comyn kin, like the half-brother my oath-mother had borne to Edric Ridenow. But Mhari had given her daughter my own mother's name. Who better to follow me than this girl who might have been my own?

"Ariana is a dressmaker now, but when she first came to us, she worked at the inn," said Cassi, "I think they have enough maids, but they might take you on to help in the stable. Are willing to work with men?"

"I did on the journey here..." Leona said softly. "They thought I was a boy."

"And your work for the house can be to keep the wood box full!" Ramona exclaimed.

~o0o~

I had just brought in a basket of marlberries for dinner when I heard voices outside. One could not call the lack of rain unseasonable—if Thendara was ever temperate, this would be the right time of year for it, but the ground was getting hard and dry. Better to use them up now than to let them wither on the vine.

"Are they treating you right at the stable?" Ariana's voice came clearly through the window.

I stuck my head out and saw her coming with Leona up the path.

Leona shrugged. "In the stable, they make jokes sometimes, but they mostly leave me alone." Suddenly she grinned. "I heard a story about how you and Cassi and Mama Kiera defended yourselves from a mob. I think they are afraid of what you will do to them if they don't leave me alone. But I don't want to need a defender! I heard that at Thendara House they teach women who have to work with men how to act so they won't think of them as female."

Adriana paused, her features for a moment twisting in remembered pain. "Raised in a Guildhouse, I'd guess ye have not had many dealings with men. The very way the body moves says who ye are. A woman's center is in her hips. Look now—" She advanced a few paces with studied grace. "But this is how I walked when I was a boy." Another few steps, and suddenly I was seeing the lithe youth who had been Adrian. Then she stopped, shuddering like a dog shaking off rain, and was the Adriana I knew once more. "Walk as if ye could carry the world on your shoulders and ask for more."

Leona nodded, started forward, and became the boy I thought I had seen coming up the road.

"Yes, that's it. And swing your arms a little. Sprawl a bit when you sit down. Men are always wanting to claim more room."

They were of a height, but now Leona looked taller. She took another few steps, shoulders back and head high, then turned, favoring her teacher with a heart-stopping grin.

Oh dear, I thought, watching them.

~o0o~

"Can't you sleep either?" The bed creaked as Cassi turned.

I started to reach out to her, but it was too warm for any contact of skin on skin. For the past week, Thendara had been baked by a wind that felt as if it was blowing all the way from the Dry Towns. We'd pushed the covers to the foot of the bed and lay naked on the sheet, but though with darkness the temperature had gone down, there was not a breath of breeze.

"Would you believe that the Terrans are *enjoying* this weather?" she said then. "A group of them came chattering through the market, comparing it to some vacation spot on Vainwal. I am not going back to the Square tomorrow. No one will be buying gloves until it cools down. If I stay here I can use the time to make more."

"At least you *have* work!" I replied. "No one is going anywhere. I might as well join Leona at the stable, mucking out stalls."

"Where you can keep an eye on her?"

"She may be almost fifteen, but she seems very young! I was afraid she might fall for one of the boys, but Adriana is the one she watches. I know it's normal for a girl her age to worship an older woman, and the goddess knows Ariana's story is romantic, but I'm afraid she'll be hurt, and—"

"You sound like her mother—" said Cassi.

"I feel as if I am!" I exclaimed. "I braced Mhari with my own body while she was giving birth, and if I have the Ridenow Gift of empathy at all it was surely active then, for I felt every pain. I held Leona before the midwife put her into her own mother's arms." I swallowed, remembering the heart-jolt as that tiny hand gripped my finger. "And now she's almost grown!"

But not yet a woman—on the threshold of puberty, Leona had a kind of ungendered beauty that reminded me of Ariana in those desperate weeks before her body transformed to match her soul.

"She has left one mother already," my freemate replied. "She may look like a fledgling, but she is ready to try her wings. Here she feels safe. Try to bind her, and the gods know where she may fly."

~oOo~

"If you won't wear something pretty, at least let me loan you a tunic! Do you want the women at Thendara House to think we keep you in rags?" I held out the yellow linen tunic I wore to meet prospective clients, matching Leona's mutinous glare with a glower of my own. I was wearing creamy Xerasian silk, part of the reward sent to my oath-mother Caitrin n'ha Laurian for a service performed long ago, and a firestone pendant that had been my Comyn father's gift to me. The stone was a rarity, created when great heat transformed the rather undistinguished crystals that formed in faults and veins hidden in other stone into something that looked like captive flames.

"Why do I have to go at all? I don't know any of these people. I'm not an Amazon…"

"Yet—" said Cassi. "Is that what's bothering you? It's a chance for them to get to know you, and you'll learn something about our heritage."

The arrival of the invitation had affected all of us in differing ways. We had known that a celebration of the day the Guildhouse fought off an attack by an outraged husband was being planned, but whether their current cordiality would extend to an invitation was not clear. Ramona was a chef at a Terran tourist hotel and could not get the time off even if she had wanted to go, but the invitation *had* been addressed to our household.

I knew they would want to see Leona and perhaps persuade her to make her oath there, and I wanted the girl to meet my oath-mother and her partner, Stelle, who were the closest to grandmothers the poor child had.

"Are you ready?" Adriana called from below. It was a pity that her gender transformation had included painful monthlies, but perhaps she would enjoy having the house to herself for a peaceful afternoon. "I brought hats from the shop to shade you from the sun!"

The seamstress who employed Adriana also had a Trade City clientele. In the past weeks, straw hats had been selling well. It still seemed strange that we should need protection from our red sun's gentle rays, but even a bit of portable shade would be welcome. Thendara House already thought we were odd. Our appearance in such alien gear might be a useful distraction.

Certainly, they should have no other reason to look down their noses. We were obviously making a success of our odd household, healthy, well-dressed, and well-fed—and we had a new generation, this daughter of my heart whom the Goddess had sent when I had abandoned any thought of ever having a child.

~oOo~

"For more than two centuries, Thendara House has been a refuge. We have been attacked by words and by weapons, but we survived. Today, we celebrate the two-hundredth anniversary of one of our greatest battles."

Mother Doria laid a gnarled hand on one of the battered copper plates bolted to the door. Though she was flushed from the heat, I was relieved to see that she looked well, for she had been a friend to us. But I hoped her speech would be short, for the rest of us were packed into her office and the corridor on the other side.

"A woman called Rima n'ha Janelle came to us, wife of a merchant who had abused and insulted her in a multitude of ways. Her husband, unwilling to release his possession even though he had rejected her, brought an army of mercenaries and tried to burn us down. This door bears witness to that day!" She ran her hand down a gash where fire had blackened the timbers beneath the metal. "We won then, as we won a few years ago when a mob came here because they believed that one of our women had brought the Yellow Plague. Kiera n'ha Leona led our defense that day!"

My cheeks heated from more than the weather as the girl beside me turned, eyes wide.

"But that is a tale for another celebration!" exclaimed my oath-mother's freemate, Stelle. "Raelle is whispering in my ear that today's feast is ready, so in the name of the Goddess, Mother, release us before the ghost of the merchant takes his revenge by suffocating us in here!"

The confusion as the crowd at the door tried to unknot resolved itself into laughter, and we streamed across the yard into the cool shadows of the Armory, where long tables had been laden with platters of roasted meat and sliced cheeses, bread and hard crackers and sauces to dip them, bowls of fruit, and little cakes. To prepare all this, the cooks must have stayed up all night.

By the time we had filled our plates, darkness was falling. The temperature was, if not cool, almost temperate, and feasters had dragged chairs and benches into the open space beside the gardens where a trellis supporting a Terran grapevine netted the glowing purple of the evening sky. A soothing murmur of conversation filled the air.

Cora, who had been the youngest of the Guildhouse children when I was living here, had pressed Leona into service with the other two younglings who were refilling goblets from ceramic jugs. One was just emerging from childhood, another a little older, and the third, a dark-haired girl already developing a bosom, seemed just about Leona's age. I looked up as a trill of laughter floated through the air. Leona had been hesitant about the party, but she looked as if she were having a good time. Was it really right for me to keep her with our odd crew when she could be here, enjoying all the amenities of a long-established community and the companionship of other girls?

Mother Doria held out her cup and Leona came to her side.

"Will you have wine, Mother, or tea?" she asked, with the little tip of the head that suggested respect without servility.

"Wine, my dear, with thanks for your good manners. But of course, you were brought up at Neskaya. They trained you well." She watched, smiling, as Leona poured. "You have seen a bit more of Thendara House today. How does it compare, now that you know something of our history?"

"You were the first Renunciate Guildhouse, is it not so? At home, they taught that it was easier to establish the houses in places like Neskaya and Arilinn because of the battles you won."

Others were gathering to listen. My oath-mother, Caitrin gave me a thumbs-up from the other side of the crowd.

Mother Doria's smile broadened and she waved at the other girls. "Do you hear that, my darlings? I would you had listened to your lessons so well." Her gaze returned to Leona. "Perhaps we need you here to help us teach them. You are past fourteen, are you not? Just the same age as Lina." She nodded toward the dark-haired girl. "When you are fifteen, you can take your oaths together and share your half-year training here. It always goes better when there are two of an age."

"No."

Leona's reply was a single syllable, but from it, a murmur of confused speculation expanded like ripples from a stone tossed into a pond.

"What do you mean?" Mother Doria's reply was equally soft, but it spread silence.

"I will not take the oath.."

"But she must—" said someone. "Look at her! She is an Amazon already in all but name!"

Mother Doria's gaze turned to me, her smile warping into a glare. "What does this mean? I could have told her you were dead. I sent her to you to keep an oath. Her mother trusted you! *I* trusted you to raise her in our ways!"

"What did you expect, putting her in that household of perverts!" Now the comments, and the accusations, were coming from every side.

"We have not even discussed it!" my freemate exclaimed. "The decision, whatever it may be, is hers." We all looked at Leona, who stood trembling, eyes white-rimmed as a stag-pony with a banshee in view.

"Have you not started your courses?" Mother Doria tried to gentle her tone. "Sometimes a girl is past eighteen before they come. You are so well-grown, you look older than you are."

"I get them," she said in a low voice. "I hate them."

"Don't we all—" said someone, and the tension eased a little as everyone laughed.

"They are a nuisance," said Stelle, who was a midwife and our community's expert on female physiology. "But I have herbs that will ease you."

"I don't feel like a woman."

"Of course, you don't want to be one of those useless frills who can't lace their boots without a man to tell her what to do," Mother Doria replied. "But you grew up in a Guildhouse, surrounded by women. How can you not understand that a woman can also be strong and free?"

"Even an *emmasca* was born female and can claim sisterhood!" said someone else.

"You are a woman even if your bloods never come, as you are still a woman when they cease to flow!" Accusations set the air ablaze.

"It is a Forbidden Guildhouse indeed!"

"Of course, she's confused, living with those imitation women who are really still male!"

Suddenly, I was very glad that neither Adriana nor Ramona were with us here.

"They are more womanly than some of you!" Leona cried. "They have suffered to become what they feel themselves to be. Adriana is laid on her bed with cramps or she would be here today."

"Well, even those brought up in a Guildhouse have to learn how to be free women—that's what the half-year housebound is for," said Caitrin.

"You don't understand! All you women here—you are so fixed on being *women* that you forget what it is to be a part of humankind. But that doesn't matter to me. I am in the wrong body and I reject it. I refuse to be a woman at all!"

"You saw the door in my office!" Mother Doria exclaimed. "You know our history! Will you betray all that we have struggled to achieve for the sake of—of male privilege?"

"Maybe she's not really a girl!' came the cry. "Who knows what those perverts in the Forbidden Guildhouse might do!"

"Let's make sure!" Someone made a grab for Leona's shoulder, but she eeled away and jumped on one of the tables.

I sucked in a breath, stunned by how quickly a spark could become a devouring flame.

"I saw this child when they laid her on her mother's belly,

bloody and squalling! She was a girl child! There was no ambiguity there!" I strained to make my voice heard

Leona's rose above it. "I've watched when some poor soul came to the door of the Guildhouse at Neskaya seeking refuge and stood shivering while they stripped her bare, but you don't need to do that to me! I *don't* want to be your sister, Zandru take you all! I don't *want* to be female at all! There must still be one *leronis* left in Thendara who can make me what I want to be!"

Dishes slid and smashed as she leapt from the table and headed for the gate, her yellow tunic flickering past the bushes like a moving flame.

"Avarra save us, *is* there anyone left who has both the nerve and the skill?" Cassilde asked. Using a matrix to destroy a woman's female organs had always been a last resort, as likely to result in death as transformation. *Emmasca* women were welcomed by the Renunciates, but the procedure had been proscribed in the time of Lorill Hastur. The last such to live at Thendara House had been Camilla n'ha Kyria, who disappeared on an expedition to the Wall around the World a generation ago.

"If there is, she'll be down in that cesspit near the Terran Trade Center..." Stelle said grimly. "The one where we rescued...Adrian."

"I remember.' I swallowed sickly. He had been willing to risk his life to become Adriana, and now Leona was taking the same deadly path. Even if she didn't find a rogue matrix mechanic, there were others who wouldn't care if she were girl, boy, or cralmac if they could trap her. Would we be in time?

"Cassi, come with me. Caitrin, will you go to our house and bring Adriana? She got to know the area when she was hiding there. We'll meet at the market square."

Caitrin grabbed my arm. "We can't search the back streets of Thendara in party clothes. Stelle, you can fit out Cassi. Kiera, I'll loan you some of my field gear—and a blade."

~oOo~

The recent warm weather had done nothing to improve the city's smells. The extremity of heat might have abated, but refuse that would have been decently chilled or at worst grown dank in ordinary times had been stewed into a unique aroma. I pulled my scarf across my face as we approached the Market Square. At the end of the street, the Terran Headquarters building presented a blank face to the world. When I visited the place to renew my license as a guide, I had seen the Terrans cleaning their floors with blasts of steam. I wondered if their machines had the power to cleanse the whole square, and how bad it would have to get before they used them.

"What we really need is a good storm," said Cassi, hurrying along at my side.

I nodded. I could hardly see the stars, but that might have been because the Terrans always left the lights on in the square. I wet a finger and held it high. Was the wind bringing smoke from Venza, or was the valley of the Valeron funneling up clouds from the distant sea? It seemed to me that I felt a slight chill from the west. That might be a good sign, so long as the clouds did not bring lightning instead of rain.

"How did they get here before us?" Cassi pointed at the two figures just entering the other side of the square. "They must have run all the way!"

That was probably true, but Caitrin kept in good condition and Adriana was young. She had put on breeches for this expedition, and with them, some of the mannerisms of the young man she had been. It was like seeing with double vision to watch her there.

I had thought that Caitrin might take charge, but the first to speak was Adriana

"Let Caitrin and Cassilde go among the houses. I think Stelle has nursed folk in every hovel in the district, with Caitrin guarding her, an' Cassilde is the kind that a troubled soul will confide in. To them, maybe folk will say what they have seen."

I nodded. "And you?"

Adriana sighed. "I...know the places a child might be seeking a refuge. An' they be the places there'd be the most trouble. You should come with me."

~o0o~

As the hours of darkness passed my feet grew as sore as my

heart. We were sworn at by beggars sleeping in doorways. We stopped one rape and interrupted another couple whose female partner cursed us for ruining her trade. We poked into every trash heap, sent rats skittering down their holes, and found nothing. None of the ragged folk of the illegal tent villages had seen anyone of Leona's description, boy or girl.

I could not judge how much time had passed when our wandering search led us back to the Market Square. The sky was a solid darkness, but from time to time a little thunder grumbled in the west. A vagrant breath lifted the damp hair that stuck to my brow.

"Is your belly still paining you?" I asked.

Ariana shook her head. "Sometimes I think I invoke the cramping just to prove to myself that I am female! As soon as I pulled on my breeches, the pains went away."

I was relieved. As always when I spent any time with Ariana, her trace of the Ardais Gift roused my Ridenow empathy. Sitting here in the open Square, I realized that my fatigue came not so much from wandering as from leaving myself open to all that pain.

I looked around me with a sigh, limbs weighted by fatigue but muscles twitching with frustration as if lightning ran beneath my skin. *Let that be the only lightning,* I thought grimly. *Let my fears kindle the only fires we see!*

"At least, Leona was not wearing a skirt," I said aloud. "That may make her look less like a victim."

Ariana sighed. "Even now do you not understand? 'Tis not a girl we are looking for but a desperate boy."

But I am seeking a girl... I thought grimly. *Leona is my* daughter, *my proof to Thendara House that I am a true Renunciate.*

"Is it dawn already?"

I roused to see Ariana pointing. The sky beyond the angular silhouette of the Regent's palace held a red glow.

"That's north, not east..." I said slowly. The direction of the Thendara Hills.

My nostrils flared as I took a deep breath, and the acrid scent set alarm bells ringing in the oldest levels of my brain. But no—it was with the ears in my head that I heard that ringing—a high clangor from the watch tower on the city's northern side. In another moment, the deep-toned tolling of the bell in the center of the marketplace began to shake the air.

The Fire Bell... My gut clenched at the sound.

"We've got to get home—" I grabbed Adriana's arm and pulled myself upright. "Change clothes, get our gear, and be ready when the wagon comes to take us to the fire..."

"But what about Leona?"

"She—*he*—will have to take her chances. When that bell rings, everyone who can swing an axe or lift a shovel is bound to answer the call."

~o0o~

The fire-break wound like a brown serpent along the rim of the lower foothills, edging the slopes where the nut trees grew. Grunting, I dug my shovel into the earth to widen it, twisting to lever up a clod and turn it over so that the tangle of dry grass and dead moss it bore could not fuel a surface fire. Then I straightened, working my shoulders back and forth to release the strain, and adjusted the broad straw hat I wore.

For two days, I had labored with the crew to which I'd been assigned. Would this band of bare earth be enough to keep the fire from surging down through the forests to the farmlands? The western sky blazed with banners of crimson and gold as if it, too, were burning, but at least it was not the dreadful blood-colored pall that had covered the sky at dawn. A lurid light glowed on the fields beyond the city and gleamed from the river Valeron.

A lightning strike had started the fire on the Thendara Hills, a wilderness of heath and wildwood whose rocky peaks were visited only by miners seeking gemstones and herders whose goats had wandered away. Driven by a wind from the north, it had turned those heights into a seared and smoking wasteland, spiked by the charred skeletons of resin trees. Ash was already powdering the dark soil of the firebreak. When I looked behind me, I saw the top of the ridge outlined in flame.

Even through my mask, the air came harsh to the lungs. The

wind gusted fitfully. Would it carry the flames to a new source of fuel or drive them this way to starve on the bare ground we had cleared with such toil today?

I shook my cramped fingers. They were sore, but the gloves Cassi crafted were treasured by those who battled forest fires. The ones she had made for me were backed with hardened hide that laughed at sparks, sewn from blister-defying kid-skin tailored to the shape of my hand.

Responsibility for the defense of the hills to the north of Thendara lay with the commander of the City Guard. When he learned that Cassilde was with us, he set her up by the healers with a basket of scrap leather to do repairs and if possible make more, proclaiming that her skilled fingers were too valuable to risk wielding a rake or a hoe. She and I were the only oathed Renunciates in our household and thus required by law to be here, but Ramona had volunteered to run a feeding station and Adriana, who had fought fires in the Hellers when she was a boy, was wielding an axe somewhere down the line.

From the woods below I heard a donkey complain, and one boy swearing while others laughed. Evanda be praised, the water carriers were here! Long ears wagged above the bushes as the donkeys picked their way along the hillside, led by boys judged too young or weak to work on the line. Wooden barrels were tied to the pack saddles. I licked my lips at the sound of water sloshing within them, for I had emptied my own water bottle long ago.

One by one, the donkey drivers tugged their beasts up the hill to offer water to a worker on the line. The last boy started toward me, but for every step forward, the animal bucked sideways, so they progressed at an angle up the hill. When they reached me, I was still laughing.

"'Tis not funny," he growled, his attention still on the donkey, whose hindquarters were swiveling ominously. "You Zandru-begotten beast, stay still and let me give the woman her drink, or I'll tell Ramona to carve you into collops for the stew!" He got the spigot on the barrel open and looked up at me.

For a moment he, I, and the donkey were all still. My own

eyes widened as I met an appalled blue gaze.

"Leona! You're safe! Why did you—"

"Call me Leon!" came the hoarse reply.

The slim shoulders slid through my reaching hands. The donkey reared, then driven and driver were sliding back down the hill, water from the barrel splashing uselessly across the stones.

Like my tears.

~o0o~

That night, the wind changed. The firebreak we had finished the day before had held the flames, but now the wind was gusting eastward, threatening Hali. As we gulped down a hasty breakfast, the camp seethed with rumor—the Regent had asked the Terrans for assistance—no, the Telepath Council was doing a working or they were summoning a *leronis* from the Armida Tower. The only thing certain was that on the heights above us the fire still advanced in a wavering line a hundred varsts long.

Smoke had reddened everyone's eyes. Only Cassi knew that mine were sore from weeping. But at least the dangers Leona faced now were the ones we shared. Clearly, the other donkey drivers accepted her. Until she spoke, even I had been fooled by the illusion that she was a boy.

But was it an illusion? Ariana's transformation had been a miracle, but I had fought for Ramona's right to claim her inner identity even though her body had not changed. Why could I not look at Leona and do the same?

Because she is your future. Because she is the only child you will ever have, an inner voice replied.

As the wagon that was taking us to the new day's labors lurched and rattled up the road I found myself wondering when it had become so important to claim Leona as my daughter. Even if I had had any interest in the process by which one gets with child, I had been scarred by the anguish my oath-mother suffered when she had to give up my half-brother, Donal. With no guarantee of a girl-child to raise as a Renunciate, I would not risk that pain. And then the Goddess had sent me Leona, bright, healthy, and glowing with the beauty of my own first love.

Today's task was to protect a hamlet that stood in a hollow in the hills where two ancient roadways crossed. Haggard cliffs rose around it, broken here and there by old landslides, and split by the rocky canyon carved by the stream. At another time, I would have found it beautiful, for the rocks were banded in many colors, studded with outcrops and inclusions that sparkled in the sun.

The extreme heat of the previous week had passed, but it had leached all moisture from the tall grasses beside the road. People were already scything them down and raking grass and fallen leaves to be carried away. As I hurried to join them, a donkey brayed. I felt my heart clench. Was Leona with them? Would I rather know that her flight from me had carried her to safety or have her faithful to her duty here?

To the south, the Valeron River gleamed beneath a sky whose usual lilac had acquired a brownish overlay. Northward, the stain was darker, but pewter clouds were billowing in the western sky. Could they save us? Fire fed on wind, and the wind would reach us before any rain.

At midday, the donkey boys brought food and stayed to bring up water from the stream to wet the shingle roofs and carry cut brush away. The air was hot, but the day was growing darker. No longer trailing yesterday's bright banners, the descending sun had become a crimson disc in a sullen sky. When I left my crew to join those who were loading the donkeys, no one objected. When our eyes were not on our work, we nervously searched the cliff tops for the first flare.

But despite that intensity of anticipation, we were taken by surprise when the fire finally came.

Darkness was falling. I had worked my way to the bend in the road where Leona was tying a last bundle of brush to the donkey. The wind had come up, and flames were surging down the hill. It gusted again, sending a shower of flaming foliage across the fading sky. I staggered in a blast of hot wind, sight for a moment blanked as a nearby resin tree exploded into flame. A frantic look showed fire already arching across the road behind me, ahead, a recent rock fall revealed a gap in the cliff where nothing grew.

I dropped my rake and ran.

Leona reeled away as the donkey reared, and I grabbed her, half-guiding, half-dragging her toward that opening in the rocky wall. As we dodged behind the first boulder, I threw my body over hers and shoved her down. Heat seared my nostrils as the flames blasted over us, and I ground my face into the cool stones. For a moment, we could not breathe.

Then it was past, and we lay gasping, listening to the soft hiss and crackle of burning vegetation, punctuated by the groan and crash of falling timbers and the crack as rocks exploded, superheated by the flames.

Leona coughed, and I rolled aside so she could breathe. The air was still hot enough for perspiration to dry before it could bead on skin.

"I feel like an ingot in Zandru's forge..." Her words came hoarsely, and then, "Thank you."

"There is no debt between a mother and her child," I answered, flicking a floating ember away. My heartbeat was beginning to slow. We were not safe yet, but survival was a better wager than it would have been a few moments ago.

"Is that how you think of me?"

"If you will allow it—and if you will tell me why you ran away!" It was now full dark, but we could see each other in the firelight reflected from the rocks above.

The answer came slowly. "You have to understand. When I left Neskaya, I thought it was just being in a small Guildhouse in a small town that stifled my soul. I thought that the House in Thendara, with the spaceport and all those Terrans so near, would feel more—open—but even a few hours there was enough to show me that Thendara House was worse than Neskaya. It held even more women, all of them mirroring each other so that was all that they could see! When they told me you were a Forbidden Guildhouse, breaking all the rules, I thought that with you I could be myself at last."

"What did we do wrong?"

"Nothing, except to be what you are...women who have suffered much to know what being a woman means. I *do* understand what Ariana and Ramona have gone through to match their bodies with their souls. Better than you do, I think. I'd guess you have always been comfortable with who you are."

Not always... But it had been my identity as a comynara that I'd rejected, rejoicing when I found that as an Amazon I could be both female and free.

I got to my feet and peered out between the two great stones through which we had dashed. On every side, the land was burning, crown and ground and no doubt the surface below. Even in stout boots, no one could cross it now. I wondered how long it would take to burn out and cool, and whether anyone would come to look for us.

"And you are not?" I asked softly, sitting down again. Was she like those women who had come to Thendara House bruised and bleeding, hating the female bodies that had kept them helpless?

"I was not raped, if that's what you mean!" That came with a scornful shake of the cropped hair. "I grew up hearing about women who had been hurt by men. If I hated myself, it was because while knowing all that, I still felt like a man inside."

There was more smoke in the upper air. I crouched back down, watching embers swirl up to join the sparks that shone in the sky. Like them, the daughter I had wanted so much was slipping away from me.

"I don't want to change because I am greedy for a man's power," she added after a little while. "I was raised by strong women. Mother Ysabet at Neskaya can stare down the Captain of the City Guard."

"Then why?"

"When I work alongside men I feel *comfortable*... I can love you. I am honored to claim you as kin, but a part of your household I can never be."

Was it a trick of the light or a change in expression that made the clean curves of cheek and brow and jawline suddenly so clear? My Gift had always been unpredictable, but stress awakened it, and I knew that everything he was saying was *true*. My breath caught. I was looking at *Leon*. Beneath the image of the daughter I had so desired, he had always been there.

"Can you..." he swallowed. "Do you think you could be mother to a *son?*"

I sat up and hugged him. He might be fourteen, but a part of him was still an unacknowledged child.

"You will have to meet my brother. I used to mother him when I was still a girl. I think I can remember how to love a little boy, though I don't suppose you will be little for very long—" Working in the stables had been good for him. There was muscle in the shoulders on that thin frame, and surely he had grown an inch since he first appeared at our door.

"But you must promise me this—" Memories of the past days shook me and I gripped his hand. "Wear a man's clothes and a man's name, but swear you will not seek out a *leronis* to make you *emmasca.* That operation was dangerous even when done by an expert, and I would not let the kind of hedge-witch who might agree to do it now neuter my dog!"

"I understand," he sighed. "But until I do *something,* my body will be in a constant battle with my soul. How much does it cost to go to Vainwal? I've heard they can turn you into *anything* there—"

"—into things that would make some of my sisters in Thendara House faint," I agreed. "But maybe my brother will help us. The Ridenows have business interests on Vainwal and he often travels there. We'll find the money somehow."

Throughout that night we talked, while the wind slowed and the embers faded and the world wheeled on toward dawn. In his short life, Leon had been a good observer. His view of the Neskaya Guildhouse put my experience in Thendara in perspective, and his perspective on his mother made me realize that my life would have been very different if I had stayed with her there.

But then, I suppose, he would never have been born, and I was beginning to suspect that without Leon n'ha Mhari—or whatever he chose to call himself—the world would be a less interesting place overall.

When at last the sun rose, we looked out on a blackened landscape, seared and charred down to its bones, but the clouds rolling in from the west were not brown but silver grey, pregnant with rain.

"Those would have been welcome yesterday," said Leon. "But better today than not at all."

Perhaps, I thought as I watched him picking his way through the ashes, *but would we have had this night in Zandru's forge to burn all the misunderstandings away?*

"Did you know that there are seeds that only fire can awaken?" I answered. "Come next spring, this whole field will be in bloom."

A stone turned under Leon's foot. He reached out to the cliff face to keep from falling, swore, and jerked his hand back again.

"It's still hot!" He leaped back as part of the cliff face shivered and fragments began to fall. "Is the stone still burning? Look there!"

Within an outcrop of the rock, a dozen fiery points of light were glowing. I told myself they must be catching the light of the rising sun.

But the cliff faced west.

"Give me your knife—" Heart pounding, I showed him how to hold my hat against the cliff, and began, very carefully, to pick at the stone. One by one, the crystals fell into its crown, coruscating like tiny suns.

"Firestones..." Leon whispered.

"Fire seeds," I echoed, "transformed, like you, by the flames."

NOR IRON BARS A CAGE

by Rosemary and India Edghill

India Edghill is an award-winning author of historical novels and science fiction and fantasy short stories. She's a multi-time "Cauldron" winner for her stories in *Marion Zimmer Bradley's Fantasy Magazine*. She owns far too many books on far too many subjects and is owned by three Cavalier King Charles Spaniels.

Rosemary Edghill (who also writes as eluki bes shahar) is a *New York Times* bestselling, multiple-award-winning author. She has won the "Cauldron" awarded by *Marion Zimmer Bradley's Fantasy Magazine* on several occasions and also collaborated on four novels with Ms. Bradley. One of her short stories was nominated for the Rhysling Award, which is given for SFnal poetry, and she has been a Philip K. Dick award panelist and survived.

"No," Oraine said, her voice shaking even as she strove to hold it steady. "No, I will not marry him! Are you mad, brother? *Marry a Dry Towner?*"

The shutters over the windows of Oraine's bedchamber rattled fiercely, as if more in tune with Oraine's temper than with her brother's. The winter wind found every crack and crevice in Firehythe's walls—and there were many, for there was no money for repair.

Piotr neither shouted nor threatened. He merely nodded, as if her answer was only what he had expected. "Yes, and it will be a good match, dear sister. Who else do you think I can find for you?"

"But I'm a Ridenow!" she cried plaintively. Surely he could not be serious! Comyn married Comyn and always had. Her heart lurched with fear—not for herself, because Piotr could hardly mean it—but for him. Madness stalked their line as all knew. Had it come for him out of season?

But Piotr only looked calm and grave, as he had for as long as she could remember. "And we're the poorest branch of a poor family. You have no dowry—must I waive your bride-price as well? Shall I find a farmer for you? One in the far Hellers, to spare your shame?"

His tone was so matter-of-fact that Oraine found herself trying to imagine being a farmer's wife in the distant mountains. Marrying some *cahuenga* metayer who counted himself rich if he had a chervine to draw his plow; accustomed to dropping to his knees as his Comyn overlord rode past.

It sounded even more impossible than marrying a lord in one of the Dry Towns. "No, of course not! But—"

"But what? I'm sorry, Oraine, but there are too many girls in this family—and you've neither the beauty nor the *laran* to make you an appealing wife." The blunt truthful words struck as painfully as a blow. Piotr seemed to sense that; he hesitated, then added, "If there were more money, but—"

But there isn't.

And Piotr was right. Tanaquel Ridenow—their mother—had died in childbed, birthing yet another daughter, who, mercifully, had not survived her, and her husband Corus had wasted what little wealth remained in drinking, hunting, and running up ruinous debts. It had almost been a blessing when he had joined Tanaquel in death, leaving Piotr—of Tanaquel's eight children, the only male child—to become lord in his place: master of farms that produced more stones than crops, overlord of forests that were repositories of blight, possessor of dilapidated manor houses and a crumbling keep...and vassal to Lord Ridenow at Serrais, who was meticulous only in his demands for Firehythe's tithes and taxes. By sheer perseverance, Piotr had managed to find adequate husbands for Oraine's two older sisters. Their lovely younger sister had somehow managed to entice an Alton lord to take her as his latest wife, for even a husband who'd already buried two wives and sired half-a-dozen children was preferable to none. The three youngest girls might look to

Allucquere to find them fosterage among the Alton clan, but any potential husbands they might attract must be willing to accept a slim dowry—or none.

As for Oraine—

I am not beautiful, nor am I the eldest, nor have I any particular laran. *I have no dower at all, save myself.* The mere fact that she was a Ridenow wasn't enough to overcome those obstacles—except, apparently, in the eyes of a Dry Town barbarian. *Does he think taking a comynara to wife will gain him status in the Domains? If so, he's a fool.* Then, as she strove to summon up yet another refusal, a small voice whispered in her mind, *But if he* is *a fool, perhaps I can rule him....* The thought horrified her enough to make her next words far too loud and harsh.

"I *won't,* Piotr! I will not do it!"

Her brother's abashed, almost apologetic, expression changed. Familiarity—rather than *laran*—told Oraine his anger was a cloak for a desperation perilously close to despair.

Not that the knowing made any difference.

"You will do as you are told! If you don't, I—I'll send you out to find your own way! Perhaps you'd rather be carried off by the cat-men? Lord Vardo of Daillon has paid well to have you, and I have promised you to him. And you can stay locked in your room until we leave for the wedding!"

With that, Piotr stormed off in such a fury he forgot to lock her door after he slammed it. Not that it mattered, for as he'd so rightly said, what choices did Oraine have? Without *laran,* no Tower would take her in. Without *laran,* dowry, or Allucquere's beauty, no man would want her—let alone fall so desperately, so madly, in love with her that he would carry her off from her brother's keep. Besides, where would she meet such a paragon? The last time there had been guests at Firehythe—other than the occasional snowbound traveler—had been during the funeral rites for Lord Coran.

Her only other choice was to escape Firehythe—somehow!— and join the Free Amazons.

Not that I know where to seek them out, nor have any idea

what to say should I encounter one. So far as Oraine knew, she had never seen one of the mysterious Renunciates, and all she knew about them came from the songs sung at Festival times—they dressed and lived as men, earned their bread as mercenary soldiers, and were oathbound to slay themselves should their true sex be discovered.

She thought long and hard, and decided she wasn't Free Amazon material. Not only did she have no desire to abandon living as a woman, and even less to become a soldier—but even the Amazons would, she supposed, demand a dowry to take her.

'Nothing is given for nothing.' Her old nurse's oft-repeated catchphrase might as well have been the family motto.

That left her exactly two choices. She might throw herself from the highest tower of Firehythe—assuming she could reach it, as the way to it was through one of the condemned wings—and assuming she could gain its parapet before its stairway collapsed beneath her.

Or...

She could do as her brother commanded, and marry a man who would take her into the Drylands, there to live chained and locked behind high walls until the day she died.

Instead of unchained, and bound by custom?

Oraine sighed and stared out the narrow bedroom window. The day was dim, and clouds mantled the vast mountain forest that surrounded Firehythe. Imagination showed her what eyes could not: to the north, the Kilgard Hills and the two rivers—Carthon and Kadarin—that gave the Ridenow Domain what wealth it possessed. Beyond them—could she but see so far—lay the great icy peaks of the Wall Around the World.

To the east, Thendara and Lake Hali. To the west, the Sea of Dalereuth. And between the rivers and the sea, farther to the west, the desert which was to become her home.

Perhaps it will not be so bad, she thought, gazing over the mountain forest. *Perhaps— Perhaps he will be—* "Kind" was probably too much to hope for, but perhaps the man would ignore her, once he had what he wanted from her.

And all too soon, I will know, for the future rushes upon me, and I have no way to see into it.

All she had was hope that obedience would be rewarded.

~oOo~

Appallingly, Oraine discovered her grim future was even closer than she'd feared. The same day she had been informed of her fate, she and her sisters and all the keep serving-women were set to work stitching and weaving, for Piotr said she was to be married before the first snows fell, and it was already late spring. Tenday to moonturn, the time flew by, with Oraine barely cognizant of what outcome her aching fingers stitched to serve. The house carpenters built chests to hold the bride-gifts, the herb-women made cordials, decoctions, medicines, and jams, the looms produced ell upon ell of fabric, fleece upon precious fleece was washed and tanned and combed...Piotr would bestow upon her as much as he could in the way of bride clothes and household goods, rewarding her docile acceptance in the only way possible to him. Oraine knew it was proof of his love for her, but what the head knew could not soften what the heart feared.

At her wedding, she would be riding into an exile as absolute as death.

~oOo~

Midsummer festival was scarcely over when the cortège to bear her away gathered in the courtyard, and on the morning of her departure, the cruelest blow of all fell.

Her rooms had been stripped of their hangings and furniture already, and the eiderdowns removed from her bed the moment she rose from it. *Could they not have waited until I had ridden out?* Oraine thought bitterly. She knew why it was, of course. Most of the keep's servants would be accompanying the wedding party, and those remaining behind should not find themselves burdened unduly by tasks that could not wait—such as beating and airing bedding before the winter damps set in. Even the chair she sat in and the mirror she gazed into would shortly vanish— the mirror to be crated in straw, as it was one of her bridal gifts.

The room was still filled with the chests that bore her clothing, and Marja had opened several of them looking for shawls and gloves and ribbons that had been too-hastily packed away. Now she stood behind Oraine, brushing and braiding her hair.

"I shall miss you, *domna,*" the serving-woman said with a sigh. She set the brush aside and began to braid Oraine's hair with ribbons.

"Miss me?" Oraine's voice was flat with shock, as if she already knew the answer.

"When you are gone." There was a hint of anxiety in the servant's voice now, and her hands stilled in their careful weaving.

She thought I knew already, Oriane thought. *How could I expect her to follow me into slavery*—she *has no one to pay her kinsman for her!*

For an instant she drowned in terror—alone!—*alone!*—in an alien land at the mercy of a barbarian! No one to talk to, no one who remembered the glitter of the mountains' icy crowns and the soft song of the wind through the pines.

But she was a Ridenow, born and bred, and so she reached for the butterfly clasp that stood waiting. It was a pretty thing, of carved bone inlaid with copper wire, and one of the few jewels she owned.

"And I shall miss you, Marja. Take this to remember me by," she said, holding it out.

"Oh, *domna,* I cannot! It is too fine for me," Marja protested.

"You will not be there on my wedding day," Oriane said. "I must give you your gift now."

At last, Marja took the clasp, and Oriane rose to her feet to clasp it into her tirewoman's hair.

If I am to be a slave, I must become accustomed to serving.

~oOo~

Each day the party traveled took Oraine farther from everything familiar to her. Though the party was large—for the trade route between Shainsa and Thendara was bandit-infested—she was one of only three women in it. The other two were drover's wives, at least as old as Oraine's nurse, who were here to lend the expedition—and her presence in it—a certain propriety—and who were so aged-roughened that they probably would not be tempting prizes for Oraine's affianced husband. She tried not to shudder every time she thought of what awaited her. Everyone knew the men of the Dry Towns were barbarians, and no child raised in a poor hill-keep could be ignorant of the mechanics of mating.

They were three days upon the road before Piotr was finally willing to tell her where they were bound. The name meant nothing to her, for she had never been more than a day's ride from Firehythe in all her life, but relief at her continued docility made Piotr garrulous, and so Oraine soon learned that Su Horma marked the beginning of the Drylands and the end of Comyn influence: less than a village, uninhabited for most of the year. There was a well there, though at this season it might well be dry.

Her bridegroom awaited her there.

~oOo~

The pine forests had given way to thickets of softwood, and then they too vanished, leaving the land clad only in harsh pale grasses and wild bramble hedgerows. Each day was warmer than the last; at a time when heart and memory told her that the air should bite with the promise of snow and autumn mist rise up through the forest mast, it felt as if she was somehow riding into summer. Oraine discarded her cloak, and then as many underskirts as she could, and rode now without even a shawl over her shoulders. This far from the Carthon River there was no water to spare for washing, and the drovers' wives knew about camp cooking and beast doctoring, not hairdressing and caring for wardrobes. Oraine could do much of a tiring-maid's work, but some tasks required four hands—or more. By the third day of traveling, she had surrendered to the inevitable and wore her hair braided into a single long plait that she managed to pin into an untidy coil at the base of her neck. In the strangeness of everything else, the thought that she was going unadorned to her wedding—becoming more plain and dowdy by the day, where custom would have her adorned and caparisoned—was just one more unfunny joke.

~oOo~

Piotr came to her tent one morning to suggest a ride as the caravan prepared itself to move forward. Tired of keeping to the caravan's plodding pace, Oraine eagerly accepted the offer.

But it had been a trick, however well-meaning.

"See? Lord Vardo has come to meet us."

Piotr had not told her how near they were to Su Horma the night before, so that she might have one more untroubled night's rest. Now she discovered the rendezvous was barely half an hour distant. At the bottom of a low rise, Oraine could see a caravan twice the size of theirs. Shock held her mute and still as Piotr took the reins from her hands. Even if she had known their destination, what could she have done? Fled to her tent and refused to come out?

A man—it must be Lord Vardo—came on foot, to meet them. He was tall and brawny, with the straw-colored hair of a Dry Towner. He wore flowing trousers tucked into wide-topped boots, and crossed baldrics bore his two swords and a pair of jeweled daggers. Both biceps and forearms were laden with rings, most of them copper.

Piotr reined in, raising one hand in greeting, and—swiftly, fluidly, as if this were any ordinary meeting—dismounted from his horse and turned to help Oraine down.

The moment was now. The event was real beyond denying. She was about to be sold like a sheep at market. She only realized that unconsciously she had been clinging to the hope of some miraculous deliverance when that hope finally and conclusively died. Sky and earth reeled about her, her heartbeat thundered in her ears, and she fell, rather than alighted, from her horse into her brother's arms.

~oOo~

"As we agreed, Lord Vardo, here is my sister Oraine," Piotr said. "Her dowry-gifts follow. They will be here within the hour."

There was a moment of silence. Lord Vardo inspected her clinically; Oraine stared at him and did her best not to give way to the giddy darkness closing in on her. As they stood there, two of Vardo's men joined him. They were dressed in much the same way he was, save that instead of rings on their arms they wore studded leather bands. Were they Lord Vardo's paxmen? Oraine heartily wished she knew more about the Dry Towners than a few stanzas from some doubtless-inaccurate ballads.

"You said we were to be married under law and in the style of the Comyn," Lord Vardo said at last. "Where is your priest?" He spoke *casta* with the harsh sibilant accent of the Drylands, but at least it was comprehensible.

"We have no priests such as yours in the Domains," Piotr answered. "I am the head of my line. I will marry her to you." He turned back to his horse to remove a flat wooden box from its saddlebag, holding it level as he opened it for Lord Vardo's inspection. Inside it were two sets of silver bracelets inlaid with copper. One of Oraine's earliest memories was of turning the pretty silver things round and round on her mother's wrists as she sat on her lap.

These were Tanaquel Ridenow's marriage bracelets.

A thousand conflicted feelings swirled through Oraine. Awareness of this last proof of love—for surely Piotr had once meant to close these bracelets about the wrists of his own bride? Terror at the fact that marriage *di catenas* would bind her to this Dry Towner for all time, even within the Domains.

Revulsion at the fact that the rings of the bracelets' pretty clasp—once meant to hold a matrix lock—would soon hold the locks and chains that turned her into a piece of property.

She breathed carefully, willing herself to calm, and thought she had succeeded as her brother spoke the words and summoned the Four to bear witness, but the touch of her now-husband's hands as he clasped the bracelets about her wrists caused her to shy away so violently that Piotr seized her by the shoulders.

There was a rasp of metal on metal as Vardo's two men-at-arms drew their swords. Suddenly nothing had ever seemed so ridiculous; hysterical laughter struggled to escape as Oraine realized those gleaming blades were drawn to protect *her*. From her own *brother*.

Oh, Blessed Cassilda, let me remain calm—

She bit her lower lip hard; if she began to laugh now, she

would never, never stop—

Lord Vardo held up his hand. "Peace," he said. "This woman is to become my wife, and her brother to become my brother. His *kihar* is mine."

In the stark silence that followed, Oraine could hear the wooden bells on the harness of the sumpter mules growing slowly louder as the Ridenow cortege approached. The moment of hysteria passed, leaving only despair.

"Adelandeyo, sister," Piotr said softly, taking his hands from her shoulders.

"Rot in Zandru's deepest hell, brother." Oraine's voice was low and even, and—mercifully!—steady. The step she took toward the man who now owned her seemed the hardest thing she had ever done. She hoped Lord Vardo saw only ladylike modesty in her downcast gaze, not the fear and misery chilling her bones.

After that first—that final—step, the rest of the day jumbled randomly in her mind, though later she reconstructed its events with painstaking care. A person—so heavily swathed and veiled as to be little more than an ambulatory bundle of fabric—came forward to silently escort her to a wagon. The vehicle was nearly the size of a trail hut, and every inch of its wooden surface was carved. The person—her jailer?—helped her up the four steps and saw her seated on a low padded bench. The interior was not dark, for the walls were not solid as she had first thought, but layers of overlapping screens through which the harsh sunlight of Su Horma made a pattern of stars on the walls and floor. A carpet covered the floor, a second bench faced the first, and a low table displayed its freight of glowing ripe fruits and unfamiliar delicacies. Perhaps her companion spoke to her, but Oraine did not hear. She stared at nothing, running her fingers—over and over—along the bracelets that bound her wrists.

She was property now.

~oOo~

Eventually, in a cacophony of shouts and whistles, Lord Vardo's entourage began to move. The prison-wagon lurched alarmingly—and creaked alarmingly—at first, but eventually, its motion became a kind of gentle swaying that Oraine did not find too difficult to tolerate. She had eaten nothing today, and it was now hours since she'd arisen heedlessly from her bed in her own camp, but Oraine cherished her discomfort as the one thing she could now claim for her own. She dreaded the moment they would stop for the night. *Was I wrong to accept this as the best of my choices—?* She tried not to think that, or think of the other alternatives open to her, all of which had been bad (and most of which had ended in death). But tonight, Lord Vardo would come to her tent and demand his marital rights, and she had only two choices. Accept him passively—or fight him. And if she fought him...

Even among the Comyn, he would be thought well within his rights to beat me as well as force me.

She'd made her choice, and now it was too late to choose otherwise.

~o0o~

When the wagon finally and mercifully stopped moving it was full dark. Oraine and her companion sat in silence until there was a knock on the outer door.

"Come, comynara," her veiled captor said, standing. It was the first time she (she?) had spoken since she had come to take Oraine to the wagon, and the voice issuing from behind the veils was deep for a woman. But perhaps this was an *emmasca*? The notion made more sense than the idea a Dry Towner would allow even a female servant out from behind his walls. Oraine could not even begin to imagine how she might frame the question, however—much less convince herself she had any right to ask—and so she followed the other silently and without question. When they stepped down from the wagon, Oraine realized that camp had been made around it. A few steps away stood the tent she was obviously expected to enter.

No chance to flee. And where would I flee TO?

The interior of the tent was even more luxurious than the wagon, and for all its strangeness, unexpectedly welcoming. The furniture consisted of a low wooden platform bearing a pile of furs—clearly meant for a bed—a table with two jugs, a cup, and a bowl of fruit, and a low chair, its wood prettily inlaid with a complex pattern in colored stones and shell. A small brazier warmed the air—the desert night was surprisingly chilly—and another carpet covered the ground, shielding her feet from the damp. Lord Vardo had at least tried to make her comfortable.

"Will the comynara dine?" Her veiled companion poured the cup full and brought it to her. Oraine sniffed at it cautiously, but it was only water, and suddenly she realized how thirsty she was. She drained it dry before she remembered the question she had been asked.

"I don't think so," she said. In order to be doing something, she walked over to the low table and refilled the cup. The water tasted sharp and cool, and she breathed deeply. She had to do something other than panic.

She turned around to face her companion. The other had removed her veil, and the face Oraine saw was utterly androgynous; hair and even eyebrows shaved away. It regarded Oraine with calm interest, but without curiosity.

"I am a stranger here," Oraine said. "I do not know what is expected of me."

Now the other looked surprised. "You are under Lord Vardo's protection. Nothing is expected of you." A pause, then: "Tomorrow we travel onward."

"How many days until we get...where we are going?" She could not bring herself to call her destination "home". Not yet.

"Only three, comynara," her companion said. "This one will leave you until it is time for sleep—if the comynara permits?"

Suddenly Oraine wanted nothing more than to be alone. She nodded abruptly and was relieved to see her gesture was understood.

Then she seated herself in the chair to wait.

For her husband.

~o0o~

When Lord Vardo stood in the doorway of her tent, she had to remind herself firmly that she was wed, that this was what she had chosen. *Be calm,* Oraine ordered herself. *This is no more than what all women face. You are his wife. He will not hurt you.*

The thought wasn't in the least persuasive. *Blessed Cassilda, help me endure this.*

Time seemed to slow; Oraine stared at him, hoping Lord Vardo couldn't hear the pounding of her heart. Hoping she didn't look fearful, but calm and self-possessed. *What is proper for me to say to him? Or must I remain silent? Or should I—*

"I am sorry," he said, his voice flat and his words oddly formal. "I know what you must expect, but we of the Dry Towns are not animals. I will come to your bed when you wear my chains. When we are truly married, and not before."

Then, as Oraine tried vainly to think of something—anything!—to say, Lord Vardo let the tent-flap close, leaving her alone with her chaotic thoughts.

Dare she believe him? If she let herself fall asleep, would she wake to find he'd come back in the deep night and seized her when she was helpless? *Don't be a fool,* she told herself. Lord Vardo didn't need to ambush her; marriage had made her his lawful property. *So he doesn't think us truly married—not yet.* Oraine wished she knew what sort of ceremony the Dry Towns used to celebrate a wedding. *I know so very little about the land I'm exiled to.*

Oraine sat upon furs piled upon the bright carpet—her bed for the night. *At least I will sleep alone.* She hugged her knees and tried to think calmly. Rationally. *All right, what do I know about the Dry Towns? About Daillon?*

The three Dry Towns—Daillon, Shainsa, and Ardcarran—were built near wellheads that ran deep into the earth to catch the precious liquid and draw it upward to the Dry Towns. *I wish I'd paid more attention when people spoke of the Drylands.*

The men of the Dry Towns were barbarians, harsh and cruel. Uncivilized. The women wore chains and had less standing than a cow or a horse. *Everyone knows that. Yet Lord Vardo claims he will not touch me until he believes us truly married.*

At the very least, his statement implied a certain self-control.

~oOo~

Each day seemed far too short as Oraine headed inexorably to her new home in Daillon. Lord Vardo did not approach her again. Each night she was immured in her tent with the taciturn companion, whose name she had not yet learned, for she-or-he ignored any question deemed unworthy of answer.

But even the longest journey comes to an end at last, and in the middle of a brilliant, beautiful day, the caravan arrived at its destination. Her destiny.

The Drylands city of Daillon.

~oOo~

Careful peering through the wagon's grillwork enabled Oraine to see at least glimpses of the city that she would enter and never leave. The sight wasn't reassuring.

Nothing like Daillon existed anywhere in the Domains. The enormous wall not only surrounded the city, it was higher than any of the buildings it guarded. In the sunlight, the wall glowed the red-brown of old blood. Oraine clenched her hands in her skirt and reminded herself that the color meant nothing. Given enough time, all sandstone weathered to that grim shade. But she sat back and didn't try to look out again.

The caravan stopped outside the city gate, and then Oraine heard the rumble of wheels over cobblestones as they traveled through the city streets. She listened to voices raised in— quarrels? Bargaining? It was hard to tell. All the voices were men's; no women's voices added their softer sounds to the babble.

At last, a hollow boom rang out behind her, and the wagon stopped. Every muscle tense, Oraine waited for what lay beyond what somehow had become the safety of her wagon.

The veiled servant opened the wagon door. "Come, comynara. You are home."

Home? I will never be home again. But there was no help; no escape. Oraine followed the servant out of the wagon and into a courtyard. Grim hardly began to describe her surroundings—and deserted as well. Bare stone walls rose on all sides, empty of all decoration. The only break in the featureless walls was a wooden door bound with wide strips of dark metal. The only people here were Oraine and her companion.

Oraine took a last glance around the desolate courtyard and

followed her guide through the doorway into her new world.

~oOo~

Beyond the door was a short hallway of dressed stone that was as featureless as the antechamber. At its end was a flight of stairs: six steps up, then a turn, then twenty steps, and another turn. At the top of the last step, Oraine beheld a corridor that could not have been more different than the one she had left.

High upon the wall were narrow windows, so high she could see nothing through them, but the light they admitted was more than sufficient to show her the wonders that surrounded her. The wall itself was of artfully carved and painted plaster—over stone, no doubt—and inlaid with colored stones as well. The floor was covered in a carpet rich enough to grace the keep of a Hastur. Spaced at regular intervals along the corridor stood urns nearly as tall as Oraine herself. Each urn bore a fruit tree—oranges, lemons, quince—and each was glazed with a polychrome design that blazed like jewels.

This was a display of wealth beyond Oraine's imagining or experience, and the only question in her mind now was: *With all this, what could he want with me?* The dowry-gifts that had seemed so lavish at Firehythe now seemed...

"Come, comynara, come," the eunuch said. "We must hurry."

Oraine swallowed hard. Such wealth must mean only one thing—this was the wing of the palace where Lord Vardo lived, and she was being taken to him.

But she was wrong. When the eunuch led her through the doors at the end of that splendid hall, Lord Vardo was nowhere to be seen. Instead, there was a room larger than any in Firehythe Keep, and one that made the hallway she had just left seem austere. The floor was made of colored tiles, their pattern as elaborate as a patterned carpet (just for comparison's sake, there were carpets laid out over them), and in the center of the room, water plashed and rang in the basin of an intricately-carved stone fountain whose bowl was lined with patterned tiles as fabulous as jewels.

The woman in front of the fountain was clearly awaiting Oraine. She was much Oraine's age. Her hair fell in thick amber braids to her hips, and her face was painted and tinted in such a way as to somehow make her look more real than her surroundings. She was dressed in all the shades of blue; a long tunic that shimmered in the muted light and fell below her knees, over it a wide sort of belt or sash that stretched from just below her breasts to just above the swelling of her hips, and over that a leather belt perhaps two handspans wide studded with an ornate design in copper and gold. Over all of this there was an ankle-length vest, so heavily embroidered and sewn with gems that it stood stiffly away from her body. To Oraine's shock, the woman wore trousers, not a skirt—beneath the hem of the long tunic she could see them gathered into a band just at the stranger's ankles. Her feet were shod in tiny gilded slippers, and the neck of the lady's tunic was intricately embroidered, and beneath it, Oraine could see the delicate pleats of some garment whose material was so fine and sheer that her skin showed through it plainly. A last surprise was the long, jeweled earrings that graced her ears, and on her wrists...

The sleeves of the tunic stopped just below her elbows, and on her wrists, she wore wide bracelets of pure copper. Copper chains as ethereal as cobwebs went from each bracelet through the loop on the studded leather belt.

"Greetings, and be welcome," she said cheerfully, smiling in a way that did not seem feigned in the least. Her voice was as beautiful as her clothes. "I am Jaora, and of course, I know you are Oraine."

Oraine stared at her, unable to think of any reply. *She is lovely. So why did Lord Vardo want* me? *Of course, he was able to buy me cheaply—*

"My husband's new wife." Jaora's sympathetic tone suggested that Oraine might need prompting to remember that fact.

Unable to summon words, let alone words of agreement, Oraine at last managed to nod. *Yes, I am Lord Vardo's new wife. I am his property, to do with as he pleases. I have no choice, whatever he does.*

Perhaps Jaora could read Oraine's thoughts—or more likely,

Oraine's expression—for her smile dimmed a bit, and when she spoke again there was a note of polite unhappiness in her voice. "Oh, I see. You are not pleased. Like all Comyn, you think us savages, here in the Dry Towns."

Oraine summoned up all the courtesy she could and bent her head in greeting. "No, *domna,* truly I do not."

Jaora's smile brightened again. "If you do not, you are a strange comynara indeed. At least, from all I have heard, for you are the first comynara I have ever met." In answer to Jaora's smile, Oraine found herself smiling too.

"And you are the first woman of the Dry Towns I have met." Oraine did not wish to admit, even to herself, the relief she felt to see that Jaora did not in the least resemble a beaten and terrified prisoner.

"But I shall not be the last—and you are most welcome here," Jaora said.

This still seemed odd, for Oraine was no *barragana* to be cosseted or ignored as Lord Vardo pleased, but a wife, Jaora's equal in status. Surely she must be angered by her husband taking another wife? Oraine tried to think of a tactful way to say this, but she was too tired and miserable. "Why?" she said at last.

Jaora was nearly startled into an outright laugh. "Oh, you will find that out soon enough! But I am being discourteous. You have had a tiring journey, and must be longing for a bath and a rest before we prepare you for your wedding. And for our lord's bed tonight."

Oraine tried not to flinch. *Tonight. Of course tonight. Lord Vardo must be eager to seal the marriage according to his own customs—and at least then it will be over with.* The delay of what was inevitable had rasped her nerves; no matter how bad the marriage bed was, at least she would know what to expect from him thereafter.

"Thank you, Lady Jaora. I would be most grateful for a bath."

The woman cocked her head quizzically. "'Lady?' That is not a word we use here in the Drylands," she said. "A female lord? That would be like dry water or hot ice! But come," she said, briskly and kindly, "you will bathe, and I will tell you all you need to know—for you must know as little of us and our ways as I of yours, were I suddenly whisked away to the streets of Thendara!"

She took a step toward Oraine, and Oraine found herself coming to meet her. Jaora took her hands, and the touch was cool and reassuring. The chains between her bracelets slid and whispered through the copper loop on the wide belt around her waist. "You truly don't mind that I am here?" Oraine blurted out. "That I have..." She could figure no good way to finish that sentence.

"What a strange place the Domains must be," Jaora said wonderingly. "To be kept there all alone, never seeing another woman, with no one to talk to. My dear one, I would not ask such a fate for myself nor wish it on any other. You are welcomed seven times over, and I am glad you have come."

"It's not like that—" Oraine protested, as Jaora slipped an arm through hers—the chains seemed to be very little impediment—and walked toward a doorway at the far side of the fountain. Oraine found herself stumbling through an explanation of her life at Firehythe—her sisters, the servants, and serving women, the people she saw every day.

"And now you have come here and left them behind," Jaora said sympathetically, "and that is sad, for in truth it is unlikely that they will be able to make the long journey to Daillon to visit you, even should their protectors agree. Come to that, it is not a journey I think *anyone* should have to make, especially alone as you were! Really, men have no sense whatsoever. I don't know what Nebran was thinking of when they were created."

"It is not that—Lord Vardo was—Piotr certainly couldn't— I mean, there was no choice. How else would I have traveled here?" She had never imagined in her wildest dreams that she would find herself defending the brother who had sold her and the man who had bought her.

"Well, if we leave it to men to find a way that is comfortable and efficient, we will be waiting forever," Jaora said. "Ah. Here we are."

The dampness in the air had made Oraine think they were

approaching the laundry—for if one wanted a hot bath at Firehythe, the laundry, with its enormous stone wash cauldrons, was the place to get it—but when they stepped through the doorway, she put that thought aside. Nobody in their right mind would boil laundry here.

The windowless room was completely tiled in the ornate patterns that Oraine was coming to accept as normal here. The air was fragrant with pleasant scents, and lamps stood in every niche, casting more than enough light for her to see her surroundings clearly.

Directly before her, there was a hip-height table of polished stone, as long and as wide as a bed. On the wall behind it were shelves that held a row of small baskets, each in a different color. To her right, Oraine could see two baths set into the floor—one the size of a washing cauldron and the other even larger. At the end of the room stood an additional tub, this one raised up on a dais, its sides so high Oraine could not see into it.

"You will find everything you need here," Jaora said, letting go of Oraine's arm.

"Oh please don't go!" Oraine said, feeling panicked. "I've never seen a place like this in my life! I mean, of course, I've *bathed*—" she added hastily, since by now she suspected Jaora thought the Comyn as barbaric as the Comyn thought the Dry Towners, "but...not like this. I mean, if it does not offend you—if it is permitted...." Oraine suddenly found herself fighting back tears.

"Why of course I will stay, Oraine, do not fear. Oh, my dear one, you must have had a terrible time in the Domains—I weep for all the women still abandoned there! But now you are home. Now let us get you undressed—and since you do not, as I was told, fear to have your body seen, we will have company who will see to us both."

Oraine had been in the middle of removing her shawl. She froze where she stood, turning back to Jaora to ask the meaning of her words, but Jaora had stepped away, clapping her hands sharply.

Summoned by the sound, six young women hurried through a

doorway Oraine had not marked before. They were all dressed very similarly—*Servants,* Oraine's mind supplied—and their bracelets were fettered with colorful ribbons instead of metal chains. When they saw Oraine they stopped, huddling together with wide eyes—and giggling excitedly.

"Aatxe and the Iratxoak come for you all!" Jaora said, sounding just like any woman trying to bring order to a collection of very young servant maids. "Hayette, come and attend the comynara! She must bathe and dress, to show our lord how carefully we care for what is his!"

Could property take care of itself? Oraine wondered giddily. Hayette approached her with some trepidation but negotiated the unfamiliar fastenings and layers with care, and soon Oraine was soaking in wonderfully warm water, surrounded by billows of scented steam. To her mild surprise, Jaora had disrobed to join her in the bath.

"It is not every day that Lord Vardo takes a new wife, after all," Jaora said. "And I would be as foolish as Durraman's donkey did I not take some of your pampering for myself."

Oraine smiled a little drowsily. Before they'd gotten into the bath, Jaora had sent one of the maids for wine and sweetmeats, and now Oraine held a fabulously-carved cup of some translucent pink stone and sipped cautiously at its exotic contents while one of the maids did something with her hair that felt absolutely wonderful (and which—so the girl assured Oraine—would make it as soft and shining as a spider-silk veil).

"There does seem to be enough to go around," Oraine agreed. It occurred to her that this was the first time she'd felt clean and warm and *safe* since she'd set out from Firehythe. "But is this—" About to ask if this was *all* these women did, she managed to bite back her words. She didn't want to be outright insulting to someone she was about to be locked up with, but if endless pampering was the life of a Drylands wife, she thought she might go mad from boredom.

Jaora flicked water at her from her position at the other end of the tub. "Did I not say this was a holiday for us all? Our days are full. There is food and drink to prepare, cloth to weave, and—oh!

You will see in time. You were not idle in the Cold Lands, and there is much to turn your hand to here if you choose."

"Thank heavens!" Oraine burst out involuntarily, and they both laughed.

~o0o~

When everyone deemed her sufficiently scrubbed and oiled and soaked—a massage had followed the luxurious bath—an enormous, but very sheer and lightweight, blanket was wrapped around her.

"Now it's time to garb you for your wedding. *Both* of us really should dress you, but don't expect to see Tallis here to help! That girl—oh, well, at least now I'll have someone sensible as company." Jaora took Oraine's hand and led her out of the bathing room and down another set of labyrinthine halls to what she told Oraine would be her apartments now.

Not just a room, but *rooms*. Oraine stared at what could only be described as brilliant, opulent comfort. She remembered the bedchamber at Firehythe that she had shared with all three of her younger sisters—the bed she had shared with Allucquere. *All this space, just for me?*

"I know they are not much to see as yet—we did not know what you would like, you see."

If the rooms were meant to be unadorned and barren, Oraine thought someone had failed miserably at the task. There were painted scenes on the walls, and the furniture, even the largest pieces, seemed airy and delicate. The only thing the rooms lacked were windows. The few windows in these walls were small, narrow, and so high up that it was not possible to see out of them. *I will never see the sky again—no, do not even think it!*

"But of course, you will alter them to suit yourself," Jaora finished. "Now come into your dressing room and see your wedding clothes."

A room just to dress in? Oraine began to think she was dreaming and would wake with her sister's cold feet pressed against her legs. The "dressing room" held more clothing than Oraine and all her sisters had owned in their entire lives. Some garments hung from ornate hooks, and she supposed more lay folded in the carved chests set at intervals about the room. Gilded shelves lined with velvet held hair ornaments and jewelry. A mirror almost as tall as she was leaned against one of the painted walls (for a moment Oraine wondered what had become of her own bride gifts).

And spread upon a wide padded bench lay what Oraine supposed must be her wedding outfit, every piece was dyed the flaming red of Sharra's fires: layer upon layer of fabulously-begemmed and embroidered cloth: shift, half a dozen underskirts, trousers, three layers of tunics, two vests... Even to Oraine's untutored gaze, the garments seemed archaic—or perhaps formal?—next to Jaora's own clothing. And every single piece made of spider-silk.

No, it can't be. All of this—all of it's— How rich IS *Lord Vardo?*

Oraine had never seen so much spider-silk in her life. Certainly, she'd never *worn* that fabulous material. All so expensive, so—she ran her hand over the skirt—so *supple,* so *delightful.* And all of the wedding clothes were not only created of spider-silk, they were lavishly embroidered with copper thread and embellished with turquoises, rubies, and pearls. So lovely—

She realized she was stroking the cloth as if it were a pet cat, and yanked her hand away from the shimmering fabric. *No! I am not to be seduced by meaningless gifts.*

But here, as she soon discovered, spider-silk was the stuff of not merely of clothes, but of *bedclothes:* sheets and pillows and the lining that turned a tumble of magnificent pelts into a soft warm blanket. But she was not given much time to admire the bed—or to dread what she would soon do there—for Jaora and Hayette were dressing her carefully, layer by layer, while another of the maids—Oraine thought her name might be Ysaba—was laying out paint-pots and brushes and tiny flasks upon a small table with a glass top.

"The wedding robes have been airing for a tenday," Jaora said cheerfully, "and we are blessed by the fact that my lord is on such terms with his elder brother that he would loan them, for I promise you that is not always the case! But of course, Mirram would have it so, and Jorik will deny her nothing—"

It was something of a relief to realize the robes were only a loan, not a gift; Oraine couldn't imagine anything she might do that could warrant such a fabulous gift. *Unless I am to walk all the way to Thendara in Council Season and assassinate King Stephan. With no weapon but my nonexistent beauty, I suppose...*

She realized that while she'd been cloud-gathering, Jaora had gone on talking, scattering names through her speech like flowers in a spring meadow, and expecting Oraine to know exactly who everyone was.

"But Jaora—who are these people?" Oraine asked. *And what do I need to do about them?*

"Why, Mirram is Lord Vardo's mother, and Jorik is, of course, the eldest brother. Who else?" Jaora glanced toward the patch of sun on the wall—in just the same way, Oraine realized, as she herself had glanced out of her window at the sundial in Firehythe's old garden.

~o0o~

"But I must be sure to tell you what to do when you are chained and become truly my sister-wife. It is nothing to concern you, for our lord wishes this wedding very much. Now, since you have no lord of your own here, there will be less—" Jaora hesitated, then settled on, "fuss. All you need do is stand and wait, really—my lord and the toad-priest do all the work. Oh, and unless you truly wish to be insulting, hand the goblet back to your husband once you have drunk the water."

What goblet? What water? Oraine wasn't sure whether she wanted more information or less. Jaora was kind and helpful, but she did not seem to know how little they in the Domains knew of the Drylands.

"What would happen if I don't drink the water, or don't give him the goblet?" she finally said. Not that Oraine wished to be rude to Lord Vardo, of course. Not when he held her life in his hands.

"If you don't drink the water, you will be a concubine, not a wife. And not handing back the goblet—well, that just means you don't like the marriage." Jaora laughed, and continued braiding Oraine's hair. "But why wouldn't you like this marriage?"

Oraine could think of a dozen reasons, but none that Jaora would think at all sensible.

~oOo~

Her hair was braided, her face painted until it felt like a mask, and a dozen different scents were dabbed on her skin until the mixture of perfumes gave her a clangorous headache. She'd lost count of the number of layers of spider-silk she was wearing, and the gems and embroidery and sequins and beading on the outer layers seemed to encase her in heavy armor.

"There! You are ready," Jaora said at last, and Oraine turned to face herself in the long mirror.

But Oraine was gone. What faced her in the chill cool glass wasn't a woman, but a doll. A glittering prize. An object.

Just as Jaora was telling her that there might be a wait before she was summoned, another female servant (not one of those who had attended the two of them in the bath; they were all here and it would have been exceedingly difficult to dislodge them from a place where so much of interest occurred) came with a message that the priest was ready to begin.

Jaora and all the others accompanied her to the doors just beyond the fountain, but a guardsman stood upon the other side, waiting, and Oraine followed him without any other escort.

~oOo~

Down the stairs, along a hallway with many turnings, through an empty room, and down another hallway, narrow and dark. She wasn't sure she saw any of the rooms that Lord Vardo and his household normally used, as she had no notion of the layout of his keep, but it still seemed to her that Jaora had the better half of the bargain, for the rooms Oraine saw as she walked were grim and utilitarian, without any trace of color or softness. There were guards posted before many of the doors, and every one of them looked past her as if she was not there at all.

The door before which she and her guide stopped was of age-stained wood bound heavily with bronze. The man drew his curved dagger and rapped upon the door with the pommel. There was a sound of bolts being drawn back, and the door opened.

The room was narrow, low-ceilinged, dim, and windowless. Though she was certain she was still on the ground floor of Lord Vardo's keep, the insistent sensation of being deep in the earth was hard to ignore; the chamber even smelled damp, which added to what Oraine prayed was an illusion. In the center of the room was a black stone table, hip height and not very large, holding a pitcher and a goblet. Lord Vardo stood on the far side of it, facing the door. Two other men stood behind him— Guards? Witnesses?—and on the side of the table to his right stood another man.

No. Or yes. Surely this was the...eunuch?—who had accompanied her from Su Horma. The same unlined face and dark fathomless eyes. He—Oraine did not know quite how to name the priest, even in her own mind—wore a long coat of dark green leather that might have come from some enormous scaled beast, but otherwise, his clothing was indistinguishable from that of the other three.

I wonder whose reputation Lord Vardo was protecting, to have me accompanied to Daillon by a eunuch priest? she wondered suddenly. *Was it mine? Or was it...his?*

All of them seemed to be waiting for her to do something, and Oraine had never felt more like turning and running in her entire life.

Not that she'd get far, of course.

'Normally your father would accompany you.' This is just as *Jaora told me it would be.* Oraine struggled to remember all that she'd been told. Walk into the room. Stand facing Lord Vardo.

I am comynara. I am a Ridenow. I can do this.

Oraine stepped forward and took her place at the table. She even managed not to flinch as the door slammed shut behind her.

~oOo~

Jaora had said all she had to do was stand there, but there turned out to be more to the ritual than that. The priest spoke, and Lord Vardo answered, but the echoes in the bleak stone chamber and the thick Drylands accent made it impossible for Oraine to understand the words. Fortunately, no one cared whether she understood or not. Even more fortunately, she didn't have to say anything.

Drink the water when he offers it to you. Offer him water in return. Offer water to Nebran once you are veiled and chained—
Chained. Chained forever.

Oraine forced her mind away from those panic-inducing thoughts. This second wedding merely confirmed her fate. She'd already been married *di catenas. Perhaps I should have chosen to become someone's* barragana *instead—yes, and Piotr would have locked me up for that as closely as Lord Vardo will!* There were three destinies for a Ridenow lady: marriage, Tower, or death. Oraine had chosen marriage, and if it wasn't the life she'd hoped for—well, how many marriages truly turned out like the ones in the romantic ballads?

Her mind had wandered, but she was sharply recalled to herself as Lord Vardo picked up the pitcher. It was squat and round, made of a metal she had never seen before; darker than iron, with an odd violet sheen. The cup beside it was of the same exotic metal.

Vardo poured the cup full and held it out to her. She took the cup—it was surprisingly heavy—and drank. The water was icy and sweet, and tasted of iron.

"Now you must hand it back to him, in token that you wish to become his wife."

Despite herself, Oraine hesitated. *I can keep the goblet; he can't think I want this marriage...can he?* She looked at his face and could read nothing from his expression. But—

But he has been courteous to me. Even—

"Kind" was the word that came to her mind. *He has been thoughtful and kind—if only in the way a Dry Towner sees kindness to a woman....*

The priest began to frown, and Lord Vardo's face to harden. Oraine drew on all her courage and tried to smile. And held the empty goblet out, into Vardo's outstretched hands.

If her hands shook when she poured the goblet full again, if their shaking spilled water all over the table when she offered the cup to him, no one seemed to notice. Then Lord Vardo stepped around the table to stand beside her, settling a drift of spider-silk over her hair, and threading a copper chain through the loop on her belt to lock it to the bracelets she already wore.

She filled the cup one last time, and it was done.

~oOo~

The wedding night Oraine had so dreaded was less appalling than the moment she'd heard the sharp click as Lord Vardo locked chains onto her wrists. In every moment after that, she was constantly aware of the weight of the bracelets, the drag of the metal against her wrists, the singing rasp of the chain as it was drawn through the loop on her belt, the tug on one wrist when she moved the other. The sensation of being bound, shackled, *chained* seemed to be the only thing that was real. Even though the bracelets were lined in soft leather, and the chain itself no heavier than one she might once have worn as a necklace, Oraine felt them heavy as...

She didn't know what. The sensation of the chains pulling at her wrists was as horrible as it was outlandish. She tried not to move her hands; kept them folded at her waist to avoid that ghastly sensation.

When the ritual was done the priest conducted her back to the fountain in the women's courtyard. Jaora awaited her there, believing—rightly!—that Oraine would not be able to find her rooms again. In her rooms, two of the maids—Hayette and Ysaba—waited in Oraine's rooms to undress her and help her into a plain linex robe. Jaora had told her that by Dry Towns custom, the husband came to the wife's room; one less obstacle for Oraine to negotiate. And Lord Vardo did not keep her waiting long. The tapping at her door undid all Oraine's careful self-soothing and sent her heartbeat racing in panic.

Carefully coached by Jaora, Oraine knew that she must open the door to him. She had meant to do it with the serenity that would remind him that no matter what was to come, she was a lady of the Comyn, as far above him as the stars in the sky.

But her chains swung against the door and caught upon the ornate latch so that she could not step back and greet him as she was supposed to. Before Oraine panicked, Vardo lifted the chain in his hand and then let it drop between them.

There was an awkward silence. At last, Oraine managed to remember her role in this final part of the wedding ceremony. "You are welcome in my chamber, husband," she said, sounding breathless and terrified.

"And you are welcome in my house, wife." Another silence, and then Vardo said, "I suppose we had better manage this as best we can. I do not care whether or not you are a virgin, but I warn you, I want no Domain-witch tricks in my bed."

Apparently, her husband was nearly as enthusiastic about the wedding night as she was. *Why in the name of—of* Nebran!*—did he marry me, then?* But he was right; this marriage bound both of them, and it must be consummated.

Whether either of them liked it or not.

~o0o~

It had not been too bad. Truly, it had not. Oraine shuddered, and buried her face in her hands, biting back both nausea and tears. *This, any night he chooses. This, any day he commands it. Any time he desires me. I cannot endure it.* Tears she must not shed burned their way through Oraine's trembling fingers.

"Yes, weep." A shrill, angry voice rang out. "Did you think Lord Vardo would favor such a one as *you?*"

Oraine swiftly pressed back her tears and looked up. In the doorway stood a slender girl whose astonishing beauty made Oraine stare. Coils of shining gold hair ornamented with jeweled pins and glittering embroidered ribbons crowned her head, and skin pale as snow on the high Hellers gleamed against the deep chocolate brown of the clothing she wore. Malachite powder covered her eyelids; kohl lined her eyes and coated her lashes. Against the dark makeup, her eyes glowed the pale green of a cat's. Her fragile wrists were weighted down with elaborate copper bracelets and chains so heavily set with turquoises and river-pearls that Oraine wondered how the girl could lift her hands at all.

"Well, if you think that, you are wrong." This was stated with the absolute certainty that only the young could achieve, and despite her distress, Oraine smiled.

The girl stamped her foot. "How dare you mock me? I—"

"You, Tallis, are a silly child, and some day, if you are very good and work very hard, you may make our lord take notice of you. Until that day, girl, practice your needlework and your dancing—and cease troubling us women." Jaora walked past Tallis as if the younger woman didn't exist, ignoring Tallis's outraged gasp and stamped foot. After a moment, Tallis flounced out in a jangle of chains.

"I didn't mock her," Oraine said plaintively when she and Jaora were alone.

"Ignore Tallis; she's merely jealous and too stupid to hide it." Jaora lifted her hands gracefully and shrugged. Her jeweled chains glinted in the lamplight. "To think our lord and master favors her above all his other women keeps her content."

Despite herself, Oraine couldn't help asking, "Does he?"

Jaora laughed. "Who can say? He does his duty by her as he does it by me, and as he has done it by you."

"His *duty?*" Oraine stared at Jaora, baffled.

"Of course, and our master will always do as his duty bids him. He will dutifully lie with you at least once a week until you are with child—Nebran grant the day is soon!—so you will not find *your* duty too arduous, *breda.*" The homely *casta* term—one Oraine had never expected to hear again—filled her eyes with tears.

"Is that what you think? Truly?"

Jaora smiled and shrugged again. "It is our lord who must do all the work, after all."

"Work?" Oraine was so astonished by this interpretation of what had just happened to her that she found herself saying: "But don't all men, well, wish to— Desire to—"

"Take all women?" Jaora shrugged. "In their dreams, perhaps. But upon real nights? Our husband must desire to sleep sometime, and our sister-wife Tallis exhausts him."

"She'd exhaust *me*," Oraine said.

Jaora regarded her with interest. "Ah, are you a lover of women, then?"

"No, of course not." *So I think, at least. When would I ever have had the chance to know?* Oraine paused, then added, "But she does seem to have a great deal of—" She considered the matter for a moment, discarding the first words that came to her mind to describe Tallis, settling on. "—a great deal of spirit."

Jaora laughed. "Oh, I knew I would enjoy having another wife here! Two is a difficult number, especially when one of them is Tallis! Now come with me; you will feel much refreshed after another bath and a cup of wine."

~oOo~

While a bath—a much quicker proposition than the one she had taken upon her arrival—and probably more like what the daily routine was—and a change of clothes—to an outfit much more similar to Jaora's, but in a russet-amber—made Oraine at least feel clean, it didn't make her feel refreshed. By dint of polite insistence, Oraine managed to be left alone in her rooms afterward, though perversely, she found herself unable to settle there. Opulent as they were, the rooms still reminded her of a cave. She glanced up at the tiny barred windows. Sunlight still cast its patterns high on the opposite wall; from its color and its angle, she realized it was barely midday. She had arrived in Daillon at dawn and it had taken less than seven hours to see her wedded and bedded and...

Buried alive.

It was a beautiful tomb, worthy of a Hastur, but today Oraine couldn't find even mordant humor in that image. For the rest of her life, she would be imprisoned within these walls, unable to leave. Unable to see—to *go*—anywhere else. She would never again sit before a window to gaze out at the world. She would never again see anything beyond these walls.

Never again see the sky.

I can't endure it. I can't! Not the trapped feeling; not the ornamented prison; not a lifetime of being hidden away like a precious gem or a condemned prisoner; not being...*bound.*

Oraine stared down at the chains binding her wrists and yanked at them pettishly. Of course, they didn't break. She hadn't really thought they would.

Abruptly, she jumped to her feet. She couldn't bear to sit still for another minute.

~oOo~

No one stopped her, but if she'd craved solitude, she was not to find it. She was barely a dozen steps from her rooms before a serving maid rushed up to ask if there was anything she needed. Oraine could not persuade the woman that she wanted only to be alone, and finally she simply turned and walked away, hoping that would be an end to it.

It wasn't.

The woman followed her as she walked the hallways and courtyards, and every time they encountered another of Lord Vardo's female servants, she abandoned her work to trail after Oraine as well. Soon they were six, then eight, then Oraine stopped counting. No matter how many times she stopped, turned back, and assured them that she needed nothing and wished to be alone, it had no effect; her makeshift retinue continued to troop along after her, whispering and giggling to one another. It was Avarra's own mercy that Jaora and Tallis had not come to see what was going on as well.

It was also clear that not one lick of work was going to go on here today.

At last, Oraine could tolerate it no longer. She halted beside a stairway leading upward—the third she'd encountered, though she'd been too wary to explore where the others had led—turned once again to face her apparently entranced audience, and waved her hands. "Shoo! Scat! *Go away!*"

She'd forgotten her chains.

As she gestured, the metal flung itself around her fingers as if she were playing cats-cradle. Surprised and irritated, Oraine yanked with all her strength, and one of the tangled chains snapped free of its bracelet. Half of the women watching gasped, and the other half squealed, then giggled even harder. Appalled, Oraine hastily coiled the trailing copper links into her hand.

If I could just get away from them— She saw only one escape. She turned and ran up the stairway behind her.

This time, to her relief, no one followed her. At the top, she faced a door inlaid with designs of ripe grapes and blackfruit.

Blessedly, it was not locked. Oraine opened it and stepped through before anyone decided to dash up the stairs after her.

~o0o~

The first thing she was aware of was heat. The second was light. The third was of a vast sweeping sense of openness—the vault of the soaring sky above, a widespread emptiness all around her.

She was on the roof.

She was *outside.*

Oraine took a cautious step forward, barely able to believe it. Outside! And no one had stopped her—surely coming here must be permitted, if the door was not locked. She spread her arms wide and spun around in a slow circle just for the joy of it.

Then she plucked the end of the chain out from under her feet, coiled its length around her wrist again, and began to explore.

It was early autumn. At Firehythe they would be making the first forest harvests and planning how best to preserve the bounty of the orchards. The men would spend most of their time hunting, to fill pantry and larder and smokehouse with enough meat to see them through the winter. The skins of their prey would be salted and left to wait, as there were a thousand more urgent tasks that must be done before winter came.

In a tenday or so, the first snows will fall back home...

But not here. Here it was as warm as high summer. She walked slowly to the edge of the rooftop. There was a low wall, hip height, of stone latticework. She braced her palms against it and looked out. Around her and below her, the city of Daillon spread, surrounded by its red wall. Beyond it lay the Drylands, and in the far distance—easily a tenday's ride or more—the sweep of snow-covered peaks that marked the shore of the Sea of Dalereuth. She gazed at the distant mountains rapturously, glorying in their distance, at the wide, open plain which lay between them and Daillon, at the feel of the wind that plucked at her clothes and disordered her hair.

She registered a movement out of the corner of her eye and turned toward it. On the rooftop to her left, a young woman carrying a large basket had just come up onto the roof. She knelt upon a carpet, setting the basket beside her and taking a pouch from her belt. Oraine watched as the young woman reached into the basket and drew forth a dove. She attached something to its leg and then flung it into the air. The bird fluttered around her, circling once, then flew away. She reached back into the basket and lifted out another bird.

The chains around her wrists flashed as she worked.

I wonder what she is doing. Surely she cannot be sending secret messages—it's the middle of the day. And who could she be sending them to...?

Suddenly the young woman seemed to sense Oraine's eyes upon her. She stared over at Oraine, gazing first at Oraine's face, and then at her hands. The girl's eyes went wide, and she sprang to her feet, snatched up the basket and its remaining doves, and scurried off out of sight.

Oh.

Oraine looked down at her wrists. Her hands were pressed flat against the top of the low wall, and there was obviously no chain between them. Slowly she started to unwind the coil of chain from her left wrist. *I'd better figure out some way to attach it again...if I can just see how it is broken...* She turned her back to the wall, staring down at chain and bracelet to see if she could mend what she had damaged, but the weight of the chain kept pulling it out of her fingers.

A sound startled her and she saw that Jaora had come up to the rooftop, clearly in search of her. *It lacked only this; I would have been well-served if it were Tallis instead...!*

Jaora came toward her, holding out her hands. "Those silly rainbirds told me you'd come up here alone. I don't know what they were thinking—*thinking! Those* girls!—to let you find yourself abandoned like this."

Oraine tried to summon the right words to erase the worry in Jaora's face and voice. "I told them to go," she finally said, and Jaora shook her head.

"You are too kind, *breda.* But we hold your safety and happiness as our own. Always come to me, if you will not speak with the others."

The only thing to do was to promise that she would. "But

truly, Jaora—*breda*—I am not troubled." For the moment, it was true. But—"Tell me, have I trespassed? The door wasn't locked."

"Permitted in the women's roof garden? Of course, you are! But alone, and at midday? This is what you like?"

"Sometimes," Oraine said. "The sky is so beautiful."

"It's more beautiful at night, when you can't see everyone else's laundry drying! However, if you wish to be up here during the day, I'm sure at least one of those foolish children will be happy to bear you company."

"But perhaps they would not wish to..."

"They will do as their elders bid them," Jaora said crisply, "and besides, you must surely know that everyone is curious as a sand-rat about you. Now come down with me, for you should rest now. Tonight will be time for your stories, and ours."

Oraine sighed. Jaora only meant to be kind, after all. Whether the others were as well-intentioned, Oraine didn't yet know. "As you wish, Jaora. But I don't see what interest I can have for them. Or for Lord— for our husband. I simply can't understand why he married me. After all, I'm not beautiful, nor richly dowered. I came with nothing, compared to all he has already!"

Jaora stared at her. "You call trading rights into the Domains nothing?"

"Trading rights?" Oraine said blankly.

"To sell his sulfur to Lord Ridenow, if nothing else. And of course, all the wood!" Jaora sounded almost awed by the mere thought. In a land with no trees, the Ridenow forests must seem wealth indeed.

So I do not come with nothing. A warming thought; she brought value to her husband's house. Just as it would in the Domains, that gave *her* worth, and status. "Of course, for all the timber," Oraine said, smiling.

Jaora smiled back. "There, you see? All is well. Now—" Jaora reached out and collected Oraine's broken chain into her own hands. "Let us repair this—"

Oraine's face burned with embarrassment. "I'm so sorry, I didn't mean to. It's just—"

"Just that you were never permitted to wear them before, so

chains are strange to you. But soon you will feel more at home, more like a real woman—remember that all of us will joyfully aid you."

"Including Tallis?" Oraine couldn't resist that jibe, but Jaora merely laughed, and then examined Oraine's chain. Without fuss, Jaora repaired the damaged links with a quick twist of her fingers to the soft metal. "There, that should hold, if you are careful, and tomorrow the jeweler will mend it properly. Now, tell me truly—would you prefer heavier chains, until you become accustomed to wearing them?"

Heavier? No! Oraine managed to keep her true thoughts silent, merely shaking her head. "I must begin as I mean to go on," she told Jaora.

"Very wise, but do not trouble yourself over trifles. Now come back down with me—you should rest before tonight, for I guarantee you will be up until tomorrow's dawn!"

Jaora's words were far from reassuring, but Oraine obeyed. What else could she do, after all?

~oOo~

But when Oraine was summoned that evening—she had slept most of the afternoon, to her own amazement—it was not to Lord Vardo's bed, but to the women's rooftop. A feast was laid out there, and what seemed like dozens of women and girls lounged upon soft carpets and cushions. All of them turned to stare at Oraine with interest as Jaora led her to a seat. Even Tallis was there, scowling; an expression that made her appear both childish and jealous. Oraine longed to tell Tallis that she needn't worry; that Tallis could have all of Lord Vardo's affection for all Oraine cared. But she suspected Tallis wouldn't believe her.

Sighing, Oraine sat where Jaora indicated. *This is my new home now. These are my new sisters. I must make the best of it.* For a moment she thought she would weep at the thought; she blinked hard and gazed up, hoping to stave off tears.

She gave a small gasp of pure joy. Above her arched the same ink-dark sky she had gazed into, back at Firehythe. Six blazing stars—that was Cassilda's Harp. At least she still had that! And over there, at the far horizon—

"I know Cassilda's Harp, of course, but what is that?" she asked Jaora, pointing (carefully, for she did not wish to break her chain again; the air of tolerant amusement with which even the smallest girls regarded her difficulties with the wrist-chains was oddly embarrassing) at the spill of brightness. It looked like a river of stars; could that be possible?

Jaora tilted her head, ignoring Tallis's mocking laugh. "Ah, that is Zandru's Sword. Surely you know the tale of how Zandru tried to steal Cassilda's harp, and she blunted his blade?"

Oraine stared at the unfamiliar stars. Yes, if she looked carefully, it almost seemed like a sword blade pointed at the six stars of harp Cassilda held. "No, that tale I have not heard." Inspiration made her add, "Will one of you please tell the story to me?"

After that, Oraine had only to rest against the extremely comfortable cushions, sip honeyed wine, and listen. Eventually, exhausted by the day's events—was it only this morning she had entered Lord Vardo's house?—Oriane fell asleep, the sounds of women's voices murmuring softly in her ears.

~oOo~

One tenday passed, then another. Oraine learned that at midday, she could find privacy under the open sky, for no one else seemed interested in gathering on the rooftop then. The only ones who ever joined her there were the girls who tended the doves. They regarded Oraine warily, as if fearing for their birds' safety.

"Do they think I'll eat them?" Oraine asked Jaora one evening, and Jaora laughed. "Who knows what a comynara may do?" Jaora said teasingly. "More likely they fear you'll spy upon their gossip."

For it turned out the meek and pretty birds launched from every rooftop at midday carried information between women. The rings about the birds' legs could hold messages or even small trinkets, and they were cosseted as pets.

In fact, half the women of Lord Vardo's household kept pets of one sort or another, even the servants. Birds were common—there was a kind Oraine had never before heard of, with feathers brilliant as a starflower and a song like a harp. She saw cats, very small dogs, and even fancifully-colored fish in some of the fountains. She learned that the fish were friendly as puppies, and would half-leap from the water to take crumbs from her fingers.

And to her great surprise, the jealous selfish Tallis also had pets, as Oraine discovered while tossing treats for the fish one afternoon. A creature with the long body of a weasel and the coloring of a tabby cat undulated up to her and put its small paws on her knee. The kitsel stared meaningfully at the treats, and bristled its wide whiskers; Oraine smiled and offered it a morsel.

An outraged shriek startled both Oraine and the animal just as it reached out for the food. Oraine, startled, dropped the rest of the food into the pond. The fish swarmed for crumbs as Oraine stared at Tallis, who came running up to her and snatched up the astonished animal. "Karis! Don't you dare touch him, you— you *Comyn* witch!" Tallis snapped. She hastened off again, clutching the creature to her bosom, and making soothing noises to it.

I suppose that adorable creature belongs to her. But really, does she think I'll poison it? Startled, Oraine realized that probably was exactly what the tiresome Tallis thought. *She supposes I must be as envious as she is herself.*

I wish I could convince her otherwise.

But long before she'd learned anything else about her new sisters and her new world, Oraine discovered a truth that cast everything she thought she'd known into doubt.

Her chains could come off.

The chains that were the visible sign of ownership locked upon every woman by the man who owned her...came off. While Lord Vardo (like every other Dry Towns man, Jaora assured her) ostentatiously wore the keys to his women's locks hooked to his belt, the chains themselves could be unhooked, and the bracelets unclasped.

"How else can they be polished, and you tend to your own work?" Jaora said, when Oraine had once again tangled her chains and came to Jaora for aid. After unhooking and untangling the copper links, Jaora showed Oraine how to do the same.

"Yes, yes, all new-wed brides wish to wear their chains and bracelets *always* —" here Jaora rolled her eyes, clearly indicating this was a foolish desire. "But it is time you acted like a wife, not a silly young bride. And *breda,* you *know* what water does to copper!"

"But I only wear them because of Lord Vardo!" Oraine blurted out, and Jaora laughed and patted her shoulder.

"Very proper, but neither our husband nor his mother is here to witness your piety! Save such words for them!"

So Oraine refrained from arguing with Jaora, who had lived with chains all her life. Jaora, who could recognize that Oraine had not but could not understand just how alien her own life was to the bride from the Cold Lands.

~oOo~

Winter gave way to spring, summer to fall. Jaora had rightly said Oraine would be as busy as she wished to be. Most of the tasks were familiar: weave cloth, tend her own section of the gardens that filled the rooftop, craft cordials and preserves and medicines. And one night each week, Lord Vardo came to her room. They had nothing to say to each other, so their duty was performed in silence. And each month, Oraine discovered that she had not yet quickened with child.

Still, she thought one month when once again she realized she was not pregnant. *It's early days yet.* She frowned and began counting backward. Time was hard to keep track of now, but surely—yes, surely she had been here for a year. Yes, that was early days—but not so early as all that. *In another year it will be time enough to worry.*

She could not help the troubling thought that none of Lord Vardo's wives had any children—and Jaora, his first wife, had been married to him for ten years. But it was not long afterward that Oraine discovered what childlessness truly meant—for all of them.

~oOo~

She had gone up to the rooftop at midday as she always did. But today, as she walked across the warm tiles to the parapet, she realized she was not alone. From behind one of the potted rose bushes came the sound of piteous weeping.

As Oraine hesitated, Tallis's vivacious kitsel scampered over to her. Oraine bent to stroke it. *I suppose she has beaten one of her maids yet again. Lord Vardo will speak to her about this behavior if it continues, and then Tallis will be unbearable. But what is Karis doing here? Has Tallis...?*

Oraine stepped around the roses and stopped, for the woman crying so bitterly was Tallis. She was sitting with her face buried in her hands; tears dripped between her fingers and stained her spider-silk bodice. She didn't notice Oraine's presence—or even acknowledge Karis when the kitsel wormed its way into her lap again.

Oraine hesitated, wondering if she should leave, but Tallis was clearly desolate. Such misery demanded consolation.

I can't just walk away. I can't. Sighing, Oraine sat down and put her arms around Tallis. "Tallis? Tallis, look at me, please, and tell me what's wrong."

Tallis glared at her miserably. Her heavy makeup had streaked and smeared; Oraine realized that Tallis was much younger than Oraine had thought her. *Why, she is barely* Allucquere*'s age!* Tallis's breath caught on a sob, and she tried to pull away. "Have you come to gloat, then? To mock me?"

"Of course not. I heard you crying—"

She held Tallis firmly, and the girl suddenly flung her arms around Oraine and sobbed wildly. Oraine stroked Tallis's back. "What happened? Let me help, please."

"No one can help! I've prayed and prayed to Nebran, and still nothing. It's been three years!"

"What did you pray for?" Oraine said. She knew Tallis wanted to be the favorite, but it was unlikely that Lord Vardo would ever treat his wives with anything other than scrupulous equality.

Tallis sat back and stared at her as if Oraine were the younger of them. "A child, of course. What else?"

"But you're so young— Tallis, how old are you?"

"I'm past sixteen, and still not pregnant! Oh, I am *cursed!*"

Oraine wanted to shake her, but that wouldn't do any good.

"You're not cursed. You have many years of childbearing ahead of you. You need only be patient." It might not be true, but this was no time for harsh reality.

"But—but suppose our lord—well—*can't—*" Another sob from Tallis. "Without a son, what will become of all of us?"

Enlightenment dawned, cold as a winter sunrise. It was not just for herself Tallis wept, but for her future—*their* future. Without a son, who would take care of Lord Vardo's women when he died? It really wasn't so very different from the Domains—if Piotr had not been there to assume the mantle of head of household when their father died—and to take responsibility for his half-dozen sisters—their fate would have been grim beyond the telling. They might have ended their days as servants in some Ridenow household—and at that, such drudgery would have been a far kinder fate than starvation in some hovel, or becoming a hill bandit's temporary toy.

No wonder Tallis wept. If Lord Vardo couldn't quicken his wives— *Well, he'll have to. There are ways to aid conception. And once a week may not be enough.* Oraine couldn't believe she was thinking like this, already plotting ways to ensure her unwanted husband took her to bed more often. But looking at Tallis's desolate expression, Oraine knew she had to consider their future.

The *women's* future.

She hugged Tallis. "Don't cry, and don't worry. You'll have children. I know it."

Tallis stared at her with wide eyes, her lashes sodden with tears. "You do? How?"

"I—I just know." Oraine decided the lie was justified. The girl needed comfort now, and hope. "And— And— There are cordials we use in the Domains. I have brought some with me. And I can make more if I can find the ingredients here."

Certainly, there were legendary decoctions of *kiriseth* that could quicken a statue or wake desire in a stone, but Oraine was no Keeper, to handle the forbidden flower. The cordials she had brought with her were simple ones to restore vitality in the sick, or a woman after childbearing, or to cure the ailments—so common outside of rich households!—that came of eating only one sort of food for a very long time.

But hope is the best medicine of all.

"But why would you help me?" Tallis sounded as sulky as one of Oraine's own younger sisters.

Oraine stroked the girl's hair. "Because, *bredilla,* we must make our own happiness here. And so we all must aid one another."

~oOo~

Jaora took Oraine's confidences and explanations to heart, for Tallis had only expressed the sorrow Jaora held close to her heart. Ten years and no child! Oraine could not imagine facing such a terrifying unknown with such tranquility.

But what was even more surprising was Jaora's solution to the matter.

"You must meet with our Lord's mother," she said decisively. "Indeed it is past time that you two met."

"But Jaora! I cannot possibly—" she gasped, and Jaora laughed.

"Will you say to me that a comynara of the Cold Lands lacks courage, when I have seen it demonstrated a thousand times? Come, sister, we have preparations to make."

~oOo~

For the first time in a year, Oraine set foot out of Lord Vardo's keep, to travel (in Jaora's company, and in a litter carried by armed guards, with more such guards walking on every side of it) to his mother's home.

The two of them were welcomed with ceremony of a sort Oraine would once not have known how to navigate; she and Jaora delivered their freight of small gifts and written messages, sipped *jaco* with Lord Vardo's mother while speaking of inconsequential things, and then—only after every formality had been satisfied—did Oraine broach the subject of their visit.

Lord Vardo's mother listened carefully to Oraine's rather embarrassed explanations. Of course, she had heard something similar before—from Jaora—but Oraine came with explanations and suggestions.

"For it isn't at all useful to be dutiful and fair if such dutiful fairness doesn't come at the right times," Oraine said. "You would not leave the breeding of an *oudrakhi* to such schedules, so why should you leave the matter of a son?"

When Oraine stopped speaking, Mirram merely nodded.

"As you say, Second Son's Third Wife, this is indeed a problem for my son. I thank you for informing me, and you may be sure I will tell him what he needs to know." Mirram then gestured, to her attendants, and the meeting was over.

No one spoke on the way home; as Jaora was fond of saying, every wall had a thousand ears—but once in their own quarters, Jaora assured Oraine that Mirram would do all that was necessary to achieve their aims—and this time, Lord Vardo would listen.

"For he must have sons." Jaora hugged Oraine. "And you, *breda,* have helped ensure this."

"I haven't done anything!" Oraine protested, but Jaora merely laughed.

"Oh, but you have, and you will. Now let us all prepare to receive our lord more than one night in a week! Oh, it was a blessed day when you came to us."

Oraine hoped so—but quickening was always a chancy business. She only hoped increased chances—and chances at the *right time*—would give the three of them what they desired so desperately.

Even I, Oraine realized in surprise. *Even I.*

~o0o~

Another year passed before Oraine realized that the silent battle she and her sister-wives fought had been won at last.

She could not remember, now, the last time she had gazed up at the sky yearning for the stars of home. She could not remember the last time that the sounds and scents of Daillon had seemed jarringly strange to her. She could not remember the day when she had begun to think of this place as home or the day she had first taken pride in what she did here.

The day she first came to love Jaora as a sister. Or Tallis.

As with so many things, enlightenment came as Oraine sat

alone in the sky-garden. She might be "only a woman", but she counted—and added—very well indeed. And after so many tendays, the sum of her reckoning was clear.

She was with child. She knew that as certainly as she knew the paths of the four moons across the sky. She was to give their lord his first child. His first son.

She was certain of it. Instinct? Laran? Or perhaps some more subtle sense that any woman might call upon to guide her when the need was greatest. My *child. My boy. And that means—*

It meant that she—the unwilling bride, the reluctant wife— *Oraine of Daillon* would rule Lord Vardo's household. *And Jaora and Tallis will quicken next, I know it, and why should they not? A lord needs daughters as well as sons. But my child will be his firstborn son.*

The son who would care for her, someday, as Jorik cared for Mirram.

Oraine folded her hands over her still-flat stomach and smiled. The copper chains that bound her wrists coiled softly about her fingers, but she didn't notice them anymore.

PEBBLES

by Rhondi Salsitz

Rhondi Salsitz writes, "I am a writer with both traditional and indie publications, and also a co-editor for the *Zombie Needs Brains Shattering the Glass Slipper* anthology. I live in sunny California (too sunny, really, we have drought again) with a blended family including one large English cream retriever, a brown tabby cat, and a white Turkish Van heart-stealer feline. Under seven pen names for Middle Grade, New Adult, and Adult audiences, I've published epic fantasy, space opera, thrillers, romance, urban fantasy, and cozy mysteries novels as well as numerous short stories. Check me out at *www.rhondiann.com*.

The chill hit Paulin. Years of poverty left him with little body fat on his twelve-year-old frame and he felt it arrowed into his very bones. The feeling shattered when Tyrmera reached out and caught up his hand, her own heat pouring into him, and Paulin shook himself. She *tsked* as she folded up the blanket they sat on, packaging him.

"I can't stay warm."

She leaned against him, affecting him as though she were a furnace herself until he stopped shivering. Tyrmera laughed softly. "It's your too-thin blood."

Her pale hand wrapped intimately about his darker one. He rubbed the back of his free hand across his nose. "I know. I'd help it if I could."

"Learn your stones! Then you won't need me to warm you."

She shouldn't know about them, but he'd told her everything as if it could help him understand things.

He looked at Tyrmera, her sleek black hair in contrast to her soft complexion and snapping brown eyes. She missed few details with those sharp glances. He wasn't tall, not yet, but she was even smaller. "I don't want to not need you."

She shoved him at that. "You're *Comyn*! I'm not. Sooner or later, they'll be telling us to stay apart anyway."

He tucked his blanket closer. The weather made his jaws ache. "I won't let them."

"You won't have any choice," Tyrmera answered with all her wisdom. "And I won't, either."

She let go of his hand and tapped his chest as if she could see the velvet bag hanging from its braided cord and tucked against his chest under layers of cloth. A spark of warmth flared against his bare skin as she did. Did the stone answer to her quicker than it did to him? Impossible. She did not have the heritage he did, although if he could give it to her, he would. She'd been one of the first to find him.

Tyrmera had sneaked into his dorm rooms when he was left alone, her presence still and quiet. Her dark-crowned head had cautiously peeked over his bed's edge. Then her touch had taken the feverish heat away, soothing him.

Paulin looked at her, awakening from his memories. "You heal me."

She made a face at him. "It's all you, within you and without you."

He couldn't deny her that. *Nedestro* in his background, a Darkovan grandmother and *Terranan* grandfather, his mother had told him, but without naming them. She showed no sign of her heritage at all but he...and his younger brother...both had brown skin. His was a soft *jaco*-colored caramel but his brother had looked as though he could disappear into a shadow without being seen. His brother had died when he could scarcely walk or talk. He had no actual names for relatives. If his mother had known, she'd never told Paulin. She'd brushed a kiss across his forehead, said, "I have to leave you so you can find yourself," and drifted away.

Laran hadn't come easily, felling him like one of the lord and ladies' estate's great trees, toppling him, and sending him into a fever-raging coma. He'd been found in an alleyway by Tyrmera and her Travelers, abandoned. When the cause of his illness became apparent, they gave him to the lords. The Comyn had taken him in, adopted him, and nursed him carefully. Healers murmured over him and that elixir of flowers had been brought in for him to sip although he didn't remember that part of it.

He blamed the *laran* for driving his mother away.

Paulin's eyes misted. She had told him he gathered up people as if they were pretty pebbles he could treasure and never wanted to let go. She told him to keep on doing it, that he would need his pebbles throughout his life, and then she'd gone. He didn't know if he did that—it seemed not a good thing, the way she put it— but he did value his friends. Some, he more than valued. He was certain he loved Tyrmera.

He touched a wing of her black hair. It glistened like a bird's wing in the thin light of the sun.

"See? You're the one who's ginger-headed."

He wrinkled his nose. "Burnt orange. And it's not smooth like yours, it has all these curls and kinks in it —"

"Stop complaining." Laughing, she pulled him to his feet and draped the blanket about his shoulders like a great and clumsy cloak. "We must move to keep you warm, and I've selling to do."

"Selling what?"

"Why, these fine blankets for Gidar! Come on, keep up."

And he moved after her, stiffly at first between his limbs didn't want to thaw but he trudged determinedly after. Tyrmera dragged him to a market stall draped with similar blankets and scarves and separate hoods. She took a stack off a display pole and draped them over his arms. "You will be my horse!" She danced away.

He did get warmer, trying to stay up with her, and she taught him to bellow "Blankets here! Fine blankets!" until he was nearly out of breath. He stopped her. "Say it like this," he said, a hot spot in the pit of his stomach that might be from exertion or the weight of the goods he carried or something more.

"Fine blankets to warm your child! A scarf for your love's slender neck! A hood against the storm! Gidar's finest here!"

She shrugged, dropping back to pace him as he called out the virtues of their wares, his young voice deepening as he did, and people stopping to listen. He could hardly be seen under all she'd piled upon him, but he could be heard. He extolled the expertise of the maker, the rich tone of the colors, the tightness of the weave for long wear, the virtues of being secure and warm, and before long, he had only his original blanket left.

Tyrmera weighed her purse in her hand after. "How did you do that?"

Paulin blinked. He began to feel a chill again. "I just…did."

They'd circled the market and neared Gidar's booth. The weaver looked up from some yarn and thread she sorted. Aged but not yet old, her eyes widened as Tyrmera dropped the purse in her lap. "What is this?"

"We sold all we took. Except that one, and we bought that earlier."

Gidar had one eye that almost always squinted shut, but it had opened nearly as much as its mate. "Avarra's blessing. I needed those sales."

"We'll get more tomorrow. People will remember and ask."

Gidar opened the purse and took out tokens, grabbed up Tyrmera's hand, and said, "Your earnings."

Tyrmera dipped a curtsy. The weaver tilted her head and assessed Paulin. "Lordling. You wish a cut as well?"

He shook his head, suddenly without a voice.

"Then I offer my friendship, for whatever it is worth to one such as yourself." And the weaver bowed low.

Embarrassed, he felt Tyrmera hooking his elbow, dragging him out of the booth and away.

"Lessons! You don't want to be late." She guided him all the way to the estate gates and pushed him across the boundary.

As she stepped away, the wind grew colder in her absence. "And where will you be?"

Tyrmera tucked a strand of hair behind her ear, hesitating. "Thendara is not at peace. Gidar told me to get in before curfew. The Federation is," and she shrugged, "up to its usual troubles."

"Stay on the estate then. Work with our staff."

"I can't. She'll worry about where I've gone." Tyrmera

glanced at the skies. "It's getting too late to send a runner out with a note." She turned about, ready to dash away, her skirts swirling about her, her pants beneath tucked into the tops of her boots. Even so, he reflected, she wore less than half he did. Shivers threatened to overtake him. "Go. Go!" and she shooed him off.

Shrugging deeper into his blanket, Paulin trudged toward the estate gates, his nose going numb as he walked. He reached up now and then to rub it, wondering as he did how generations of Darkovans eventually got used to the cold. He wasn't. Would his children be warm someday? Or did it take *laran* to accomplish it? Or maybe—

A horse stomped right in front of him, and Paulin threw his head back, startled.

Against his chest, his stone reacted as well, and he clasped his hand over it, hoping to quell it, to squash a force he hadn't intended.

The *Terranan* liaison sat the mount confronting him. "Young Paulin, isn't it?" He looked down his nose.

"Yes." Paulin didn't like the man, had never, and didn't like the insult he heard now in the liaison's tone. Was it because the *Terranan* didn't like all Comyn even though they were now the invaders? Paulin knew that the man had supposedly been trained to be culturally sensitive, but it seemed manners could be easily forgotten.

As if in answer to Paulin's thoughts, Lord Sigarrio, his teacher, strode out of the gates as well. "Lord Paulin," his teacher corrected smoothly, his deep voice brisk and firm. "You forget yourself, Envoy."

"Ah. Yes. Forgive me." The liaison bowed slightly forward in his saddle and almost lost his balance. He jerked his hand around. The horse let out a whicker of pain and the instructor caught the reins.

"He is a creature, not a machine."

"Forgive me again." The Envoy's mouth tightened. "Curfew looms. I have no more time for lessons this evening. Lords Sigarrio and...Paulin." He leaned over, twisted the reins free of

Sigarrio's grasp, kicked his mount sharply and the two leapt away.

Sigarrio frowned after them. "Trouble, Paulin?"

"No. Not yet anyway." Paulin stretched his legs to catch up with his teacher as they walked.

"There will be. You stay clear of him."

Paulin looked up, examining his teacher's face. "You know that?"

Sigarrio's brows had knotted over his deep-set eyes. "It doesn't take *laran* to see a man who's on the wrong side of things or who fighting for balance."

"Oh."

"As for you, you're late."

"Not by much." Paulin hesitated as they passed the stable yard. He darted away from Sigarrio and found the stable boy, Narton, working on brushing down a fuzzy gelding. The smell of the stable enveloped him: wood chips, manure, feed, even the warmth of the equines. The horse kept stomping one hoof and then the other, but the groomer patiently murmured to it and worked with his curry comb. He didn't look up as Paulin closed on the two of them.

"You did the *Terranan's* mount?"

"I did, lord. Was he displeased?" Narton flicked up a quick glance, long enough to begin a frown before turning back to his job.

Paulin told him, "I doubt he even noticed, but I did. The horse was groomed, his tack polished, and he'd been freshly trimmed. The estate stables have a reputation and you met it." He searched his pockets and fetched out a token with his initial on it, proper, he'd been told, for rewards. "I thank you." He hoped his recitation was proper.

Narton's face lit up. His gratitude followed as Paulin ducked back to rejoin his teacher.

Sigarrio nodded. "Well done, lordling."

"I'm learning."

"Indeed."

He knew the hard work done by many in support of a few.

Now the Comyn were teaching him that the few worked as hard as the many, although in an entirely different manner. He'd seen the toll extracted and it frightened him a little. One day he'd have to step up, when his fevers settled, and they could determine exactly what ability his heritage portended. They hadn't discovered a place for him, yet. He understood that his mother had been a bastard and he, no different. That seemed to muddy all the waters. Not for him, but for them. And not for Tyrmera.

"Mmm-hmmm. As for your journey off-grounds. Gathering pebbles, I believe you once called it?"

"Visiting with friends."

"Your life is different now, Lord Paulin. Or it will be."

"I know." Paulin sighed heavily. "But I don't understand why."

"You are different."

"Not that different. I'm still me."

Sigarrio shook his head. "No. You have *laran*, and a talent deep within you that will show itself, we believe, strongly. Because of that, you need protection as well as training. You won't be allowed out of the gates for a while, until we know you're trained enough, and you have a guard accompanying you."

Paulin stopped in his tracks. "But—but you can't do that to me!"

"Not just I. You're a ward of the estate now, and the Lord and Lady have decided it's for the best. You're here now, and here you'll stay." Sigarrio scanned the edge of the estate, his face showing little expression, but Paulin knew that's when he was most unsettled.

"At least let me say goodbye—"

"And to whom would you bid farewell? To the Dry Towner mother who abandoned you in Thendara's alleys? The one we cannot locate?"

His chin jutted out. "She knew you'd find me."

"Did she? Before or after you froze to death? When, if she'd contacted any one of us in any House, we'd have come for you. Taken you in. Welcomed you. Welcomed her. Why didn't she do that, Paulin?" Sigarrio went down on one knee, so he could look into Paulin's eyes, his own dark hazel ones fierce with emotion.

"It wasn't like that. She broke when my brother died. She tried. It was like…like a bird with a shattered wing, trying to fly, trying to get around…and she couldn't."

"All she had to do was reach out. But that is no longer here or there. You were found, gathered up, and we have you in our hearts. We have a future for you."

Paulin looked away from his teacher, unable to match the fervor of his gaze or even to bear it. He knew only that he had to find a way to see Tyrmera again because she was the only being who could make him feel warm, as if he truly lived.

~oOo~

Envoy Rollins turned his horse over to the courtesy stables and stomped his feet upon the ground, trying to regain some sensibility in them. Barbarous way to travel, never mind the protocol. He would be happy to be shed of this planet, of the secrets and machinations of its inhabitants, not to mention Belfontaine and his echelon of officials. All, all of them, as treacherous as a *plyvoyan* mongoose in zero gravity. The thought of sharp fangs and sharper talons unnerved him.

He stepped into headquarters, de-activating his warm suit. A buzz of activity from the station washed over him as he stripped his gloves off and stowed them in an inner pocket. Getting off this dim and dull planet as soon as he could clanged in his thoughts. He'd lined his pockets as well as he could hope to, and better, more lucrative, assignments awaited. Belfontaine played with fire and Cottman IV might well go up in flames. Rollins did not want to be in place when it happened.

He hesitated as he passed the duty station belonging to Paul d'Sante. D'Sante was due to ship out even sooner than he was, in the next few days or so, and Rollins had no love or even respect for the senior officer. He was too straight-and-narrow. Be that as it may, the commander could be used to his advantage. Rollins thought he knew something that d'Sante wanted and it would not hurt to have the officer owing him. He paused long enough for the system to ID and announce him, and then stepped into the small office.

The stripped-down aspect of the office surprised him with an unexpected bareness compared to its usual state. The commander wasted no time, it seemed, in readying his departure. He stopped short of d'Sante's console as the officer looked up and assessed him.

"A little late to make acquaintance, Rollins."

"Not if I have some information you want." Rollins let his gaze scan the office leisurely but d'Sante refused to take the bait and returned to the stowing away of a few precious objects from his console. Rollins waited a few more long minutes and then continued, "I know why you asked for this duty post."

Something flickered in the older man's deep brown eyes and a brow dipped down slightly but nothing more than that, and it might have been a trick of the lighting rather than a tell. Rollins couldn't decide. All he knew was that his tactics did not seem to be working. He shifted his weight. When no comment came, he cleared his throat to say, "I can find what you want."

There. He'd laid it out. The other could either answer him or take his jump and leave Cottman IV behind, unfulfilled.

"You can?" A skeptical expression from d'Sante.

A rush hit Rollins. An answer at least. "Yes, I can."

D'Sante sat down, as though his attention had finally been caught. "You're a cultural liaison. Why is it you think you have the connections needed to provide what I'm looking for?"

Rollins wanted to sit down as well but had caught no signal that the commander would welcome it. So, he stayed on his feet. A tiny winking light in the corner informed him that 1) the sweeper was on, meaning that 2) a damper was probably also on, communications monitoring that the man had privatized. He didn't blame d'Sante for having a healthy sense of caution in Belfontaine's HQ, despite being due to jump off-planet in mere hours. The commander had been there long enough to recognize the signs of a troubled regime. Did he know how troubled? Rollins suddenly hoped not, for he was in over his head on this one and couldn't afford to have a man like d'Sante looking into his record as well.

He sat himself down, invited to do so or not, and leaned forward to convey his sincerity. The commander did not move a muscle, giving Rollins no clue how his action was being taken.

"I know these people," he began.

That brought a short laugh. "No one knows this world's people," d'Sante said. "They are a few thousand years removed from us. They've evolved a way to live on this unforgiving planet. No matter how you were trained, you don't know them."

"I know enough."

D'Sante sat back, rejecting his overture.

Rollins felt desperation creep up his throat and into his words. "One payment. I make the jump with you."

"No."

"But you don't know what I have to offer."

"That I do not. But you've failed to convince me that you have anything to offer." D'Sante reached over to his com board, hit a few tabs, and brought up a visual that he took in. "You're due to rotate out in a few spans yourself. Why the hurry? A sudden departure can't look good on your record."

Rollins sat very still a moment. Then he said, "Critical mass." He said nothing further, clamping his lips shut tightly. "And you're looking for blood."

When d'Sante finally stirred, it was only to tap a few more times on the board. "All right," he said. "You have till two nights to bring me whatever evidence you claim you have, and then I am gone."

Rollins shot to his feet. "Yes, sir."

And then he himself was gone, aware that d'Sante's gaze, both hard and thoughtful, stayed on him until the doors slammed between them.

The commander sat in his near-empty office, debating with himself, and then leaned forward. A subordinate with hair as fine as feathers answered the call. "Put a tracker on him."

"Yes, commander."

"One he can't wipe and that will transmit the bearings to me."

"Understood."

D'Sante stood up and began to gather up his own equipment.

~oOo~

Paulin looked up at his teacher. "That's as many as I can remember."

"You need to learn this, lad. The Hasturs and the Altons and all the others are your bread and butter now. You need to appreciate that."

He would have shrugged but that might slide the blanket off his shoulders, and he couldn't bear the finger of cold that would immediately slip in if it did. He only knew that while all the Comyn were important, he was not. The estate's attention centered on Marguerida Alton and her recent return to Darkover, and the chaos that seemingly followed in her footsteps. In her twenties, she dominated all the talk, thought, and actions of the others, even the elders. He'd been saved from starvation, yes, and brought back from threshold fever but then relatively forgotten—and he liked it that way. Forgotten, he could sneak out to see Tyrmera. She might not be blooded as he was supposed to be, but she brought true sunlight into his life. He hunched over, miserable, when Sigarrio reached out and snapped his chin up.

"Look at me when I talk to you!"

Startled, Paulin mumbled an apology, blinking rapidly, his pulse pounding.

"You're to stay away from her."

How did he know his thoughts? He wrenched his face away to stare down at his boot toes. Because of the *laran*, he supposed, that traitorous sense beyond other senses. "Yes," he agreed reluctantly.

"You question my authority."

His gaze flickered up then. "I do. What's wrong with me that I can't see her?"

"It's not you that has the wrongness." His teacher paced a step or two away and then returned. "You are Comyn and she is not. You've just passed through a very tough case of threshold sickness, and you have studies to begin. You're no longer just a boy—you've responsibilities now, and *laran* to master. Friendships of the past are gone as you face the future." Sigarrio picked up his left hand. Paulin's caramel skin contrasted with the paler and freckled complexion of the master, but he noticed in surprise that their hand size nearly matched. "Do you want to understand?"

He needed to understand something, anything. Paulin nodded.

"Take out your starstone."

Finally. Something he could do. Paulin thrust his hands up, underneath his blanket, and fumbled through his layers of shirts until he reached the soft, small bag that held his matrix and pulled it into his fingers, cupping it within his palm as he held it up for Sigarrio's inspection.

And, for the second time that day, he warmed.

Then it swept over him, a wave of heat that felt as if it could burn him from head to toe, peel off his skin, make a sun out of his insides and scorch all of him away except for that small bit that resided within the safety of his starstone. His ears rang with words and voices he could not shut out, though he tried both to understand and deafen them. Paulin managed a tiny cry before falling even deeper.

He woke, on his back, with a damp cloth over his eyes, his skin still feeling as though he'd been roasted over a fire, unsure if he preferred the usually ever-present chill to this state. Paulin's ears popped as though they too had awakened, and then he could hear the muted conversations in the hall nearby.

"He's a seer."

"Fevered mutterings during a threshold kickback."

"I think it's an ability we haven't seen before. He's...he's seeing the future but not with sight, with auditory senses. He's repeating what he's hearing."

"Improbable. You're grasping at nothing, Sigarrio, not even straws. Your boy rants uselessly in a fever, and there's nothing more to it than that."

"I heard two dialects. Two voices, if you will, being relayed. A smattering of another language, as well. You can't dismiss this out of hand. I heard a clear warning of betrayal against Lew Alton. The Senator should be warned."

The voices lowered and grew more intense, and he found he

even heard the smacking of a shoulder against the corridor wall. Paulin turned his head away.

They rose again. Sigarrio, his voice unmistakable, swore lowly before continuing, "Herm Aldaran needs to know about this one."

"Next you will suggest I contact the Senator and tell him— what? We have no evidence. He is fighting for our life, our independence, and he hardly needs to be alerted to the ravings of a child."

"You once posited that if it was *laran*, my lord, that it could not be nonsense, even if we did not immediately understand what was happening."

"Indeed. And you would have me reach off world to test my own statement?"

A scoffing noise. Could that be Regis Hastur himself? The gruff tones suggested it, and that meant trouble. Paulin settled the cloth back over his eyes, shutting out the noise, his stomach clenching. He didn't know what his teacher meant, but he could hear voices raising and lowering, the pace quickening as the words got tenser and, despite his uncomfortable warmth, he pulled the blanket under him up around his ears to muffle them. He was not welcome. He knew that. He was nothing, come from nothing, but he would gladly go back there if that meant he could be with Tyrmera. She believed in him.

The argument grew faint as the two men, or perhaps there were three in the hall, moved away and even the footfalls finally could not be heard.

That's when he sat up and determined to leave the estate, even if it meant they would not let him back in.

He reeled down hallways, hugged walls when he thought he could hear others moving about, and eventually made the back stairs to the kitchen. The ovens, always warm, glowed at him as he passed, banked for the evening until early, early in the morning.

The youngest cook, up to his elbows in dough, saw him leaning against a wall.

"Lord Paulin."

He put his hand to his mouth, asking for quiet. He and the cook got along well enough, Rodriges was often good company when Paulin could not sleep. He would stir when Rodriges tired. Another pebble, he supposed, in his pocket if one considered friendships so simply.

Rodriges eyed him. "Sneaking out."

He nodded.

"Must be a girl."

His face heated and the cook, handsome despite the blotches of flour here and there, laughed lowly. "Fortune to you then. I've some sweet breads in the basket. Take a few. A woman's lips are always tastier after a sweet bread."

Paulin dipped his hand in the basket as he passed and whispered his thanks as he took the back kitchen door out into the night. He almost didn't notice the cold as it slapped him in the face.

He trotted down to the city and past a pub where a familiar figure sat on a curb, drinking. Narton put a foot out into his path. "Lord!"

"Sssshhh." Paulin caught himself up from nearly sitting on the stable boy's lap.

Both said together, "What are you doing here?"

Narton saluted him with his mug. "I am drinking my *Terranan* tip." He winked at that. "And you?"

It was not for one of the stablemen to question the comings and goings of a Comyn lord, but he knew he'd earned it. "I am," he confessed, "looking for Tyrmera. Do you know her? She is a Traveler, I think. Works Gidar's blanket stall."

"Aye, the girl with the storm-dark hair? You fancy her?"

"She's a good friend."

Narton wiped a finger across his upper lip where foam and a bit of new mustache fuzz rested. "And you, lordling, have need of them." He stood. "Count me as one as well. If she works a stall, she probably rents a bed in one of the longhouses. Best place to begin looking. Stick close to the walls, though, as curfew walkers are about."

"Thank you, Narton!" They clasped one another by the wrist

before Paulin darted off toward the market lanes and dorms where many tradespeople stayed. Despite the curfew, people milled about, though sparsely compared to daytime. They stopped him from time to time, asking about the blankets he'd been hawking, and he obligingly told where Gidar's booth could be found. And he'd question them back: "Have you seen Tyrmera?"

Finally, he got an answer, the last longhouse at the edge of the market field, and he hurried in that direction. The sweet buns had cooled, stuffed in a shirt pocket, and he put a hand to his chest, seeking out his matrix for comfort because he might freeze in place if he didn't keep moving. A slight warmth answered him, sluggishly spreading, little more than a spark in the obsidian night. He had hoped for more.

A lanky, disapproving man with gray hair looking more like feathers fluffed about his head propped open a door for him. "She'll be in the back corner." He stabbed a knobby finger inward.

Some of the occupants had invested in glow baskets, but their light didn't cast far and shadows seemed to gobble it up. He trod carefully, thinking of a time in the past when he and mother and brother occupied such a shed, near the river Valeron but that river stretched through much of the known civilizations, so it did not place him, really. He couldn't remember his roots. As he moved carefully through, a Dry Town woman turned on her bunk, her chains tinkling faintly. Tyrmera wore no such chains, so he knew that she was no true Dry Towner. He'd come to decide she was more likely a Traveler. He'd never really asked. The two had found each other shortly after he'd been brought to Thendara and had been fast friends this past year. He felt as if he'd always known her and always would.

Moving cautiously through the dimness, he finally came to the corner described as hers. The bunk, blankets tossed aside, stood empty. A voice whispered deep inside his head: *Or she's dead.* Another followed: *She goes nowhere.* Bits of dialogue he could not remember or know what they would ultimately mean. But he thought of Tyrmera and worried. His skull hummed and his skin grew over-warm again.

~oOo~

Rollins snugged his warm suit tightly about his wrists and made sure his gloves overlapped. His face bore the brunt of a near-evening breeze, but he didn't intend to be out in the open Thendara streets long. He'd only seen the girl briefly but would recognize her. She'd be found in town, on the streets or, more likely, in the markets, laboring for whatever she could get. His lip pulled back at that. He would use her to draw the boy out. He understood far better than these children how life, alliances, and even betrayals worked. He'd spent half his education studying them.

The curfew walkers ignored him, as they should, and the few Darkovans he could accost were almost all too drunk to make use of. He took what sneers he could stand until he finally grabbed a young idiot by the neck and shook him. "A stall worker. Someone who hawks the goods. Where am I likely to find one?"

His captive rolled an eye, whites showing, and stammered out where the Travelers and others might be staked out. He collapsed to his knees when Rollins let go, and the envoy left him there. He could be pointed toward an ambush, but he had a blaster secured in his inner vest, a slight, needle-nosed gun that, although highly illegal out here in the streets, was also awfully effective. He had little worry.

Only shadows paced after him.

His long stride carried him where he wished to be, just as the last edges of sunlight faded from the sky. The moons, their light cast almost shyly, would do little to warm the city and reminded him how he despised this world.

He found her in the far corner, lying on her side on a meager mattress with a few blankets pulled over, probably staring at the shelter wall, and trying to fall asleep. She bolted upright as he halted next to her, and his hand shot out to stifle any cries.

"Do nothing we both regret."

She stared at him over the ridge of his hold, her face a long oval framed by straight, glossy hair, her bone structure and puberty beginning to stretch and carve her looks. Neither plain nor pretty but morphing into what she would become. Rollins considered her.

"I have no business with you, but I want the boy you're sometimes seen with."

She gave a hard swallow. He could feel it under his hand. He loosened his hold so she could murmur, "He's gone for the night. He's a—"

"A lordling. I know. If you send for him, he will come."

Her gaze moved back and forth, considering either his words or an escape. Finally, she gave a stiff nod.

He let go of her and moved back. "I wrote a note for you. Mark it with your sign. You have one? He can read, can he not?"

She nodded her head. When she'd finished the missive, she sat down on the edge of her bed, eyes wide and watching him.

He beckoned away. "We wait. Over there," and he indicated an empty bed against the far wall, away from the glow baskets and draped in shadow.

She seemed to pale further. His mouth curled. "I won't be touching you. But you will stay quiet."

They moved. She put off a heat all her own and Rollins opened the neck of his warm-suit and slid his hood down. Now all he had to do was be patient. The room steadily grew darker.

It took long enough that the girl had slumped off to the side and fallen asleep. Finally, Rollins saw the slender figure making its way hesitantly down the length of the sleep hall, only to stop by the empty bed. He grabbed the sleeper by the nape of her neck and hauled her to her feet. The boy turned but did not move further when he saw Rollins using her as a shield.

He let the title roll mockingly off his tongue. "Lordling."

"Liaison."

"Come with me if you wish her freed."

"I won't go anywhere with you. Not until you let her go." His eyes watched the girl though, and Rollins could feel her come awake in his hold, rather like feeling a bud open into a blossom.

Rollins gave a tight smile. "You will do as you're told."

The boy's chin jerked up and their gazes met, solidly, and he thought the other would back down but instead, he faced an obstinate, insolent stare. Boy that he was, he still stood almost tall enough to meet Rollins, one to one. *Lordling*, thought Rollins bitterly. He shook the girl slightly. "We have little time."

"Hurt her and you will have even less."

"Bark at me when you have bigger teeth."

The boy beckoned with his hand across the length of the sleeping dorm. "These are my teeth."

Hairs rose at the back of his neck as Rollins suddenly became aware that a good many of the sleepers had risen from their beds and stood, watching. Waiting. A tall lad who smelled of the stables called out, "I'm with you, Paulin."

A bent woman with only one good eye added, "And I. And all of us!"

But he still had the girl in hand. "We leave here, and you come with me without any trouble. Or she's dead."

The steady gaze defying him flickered. Then the boy inclined his chin. "Very well."

Paulin watched as Tyrmera dragged her feet as the *Terranan* pulled her inexorably toward the exit. His stomach clenched as he tried to determine what best to do. Did he truly have help? Or, because he was Comyn, would his struggles be his own? Or, perhaps, he would be aided because he was the lesser of the two evils. His lips went dry.

The blanket, fastened at his neck with a braided cord now, felt heavy and too warm, a cumbersome cloak he no longer needed. His starstone flared against his chest. Head up. Confident and steady breathing. He was not yet a man, but he was not a stripling child either and this envoy, this liaison, thought little of him. Better to be underestimated.

They made it as far as the entrance door, where two figures blocked the way out as the longhouse door flew open. A man with feathery hair stood silhouetted by a bright glow basket, and next to him, a tall and broad-shouldered man with skin the color of *jaco*. Like his, unlike anyone else he'd ever met.

The tall man spoke. "She goes nowhere."

Rollins dropped her.

Paulin went to one knee to catch Tyrmera as she let out a sob and then fell silent. He stared up at the man in the doorway as a sense of wonder filled him. His mother had described him, but he had not dared believe it.

"Commander."

"Envoy Rollins. Explain yourself."

"This is what you came to Cottman IV to find. This...this boy...is undoubtedly your grandson."

D'Sante looked at Paulin. It was not an unkindly look, but a deep assessing one, of the kind he had gotten many a time from the Comyn lords and his teachers and qualifiers. He met it back, relatively certain that he would not fail this exam any more than he had failed the others.

"And you base this upon..."

Rollins stammered a bit. "The...the...skin tones, the intense interest the Lords have in him, the, ah, native intelligence..."

"Stop trying to flatter me. Had you a DNA scan done?"

Rollins seemed on edge. "Not yet, sir."

"And what makes you think this one—name?"

"Paulin, sir."

"Paulin carries my blood."

"Because you lost a son here, sir, during re-contact, about twelve years ago. But not before he sired a child."

"I did. It gave me a good excuse to come here and examine the inner workings of the Federation HQ."

Rollins' jaw worked without sound for a few moments until he gave up entirely.

The commander leaned down to Rollins. "I came to root out corruption and failed, but I have a report I can deliver. You will be leaving here far earlier than you planned, because I cannot afford to leave you behind."

He bent to Paulin. He held his hand out for a shake and Paulin took it. In that moment, he felt a jolt, his starstone buzzed inside his shirt, and he looked at the man in shock. Voices. *He might have been my grandson, but he had his own destiny and I had to respect that.*

The commander seemed not to have felt that jolt. He helped

Tyrmera to her feet. She stood uncharacteristically quiet, before turning to Paulin. She gave him a nudge. "Go with him."

Had she felt it too? The bond that might have been familial? The blood link?

The commander shook his head slowly in denial. "I can't take you with me."

Stung, Paulin felt his feelings leap and knew that it showed in his eyes, despite his training, despite the Comyn way. "You don't want me."

"I would be proud to, but that's not your destiny." The commander leaned close. "They will need you here more than ever. There are those who will continue to build walls and citadels to shut people out. But you..." He paused and then drew a ring about the both of them. "You build circles to draw them in. Towers to watch over them. I believe that's the way it should be. I will not take tomorrow away from Darkover. You have this home in your heritage, both of you." He put his hand on Paulin's head. "There are no gingers in my family tree. Obviously, there are in yours. It seems to be common here." His gaze swept over Tyrmera. "Even in your hair, although it's well hidden among the black strands. In the sunlight, your hair must gleam like a bird's wing, auburn among the ebony."

Her mouth dropped open and she put a hand to her temple.

"I will make certain the curfew walkers don't bother you. Good fortune to you both, and my apologies for the actions of our envoy. There are those of us who hope to build a future with you someday, stone by stone. Pebble by pebble, if necessary." With that, the commander collared the unfortunate and cowering Rollins, hauling him out of the doorway, gone but leaving behind a thread, that Paulin would never lose or forget.

Tyrmera leaned against him. "We saved each other."

"We did." He put his hand out, his warm hand, and caught hers up. "If you think you're tough enough, you need to meet my teacher. And the testers."

"Tonight?"

He thought about it. "No. Tomorrow when the sun can gleam in your hair."

She laughed. He remembered and brought out his sweet buns to give her one while they walked toward the estate.

And Rodriges was right. The crumbs did sweeten the kiss.

BERRY-THORN, BERRY-THORN

by Leslie Fish

Leslie Fish was born and raised in a dull, boring suburb in dull, boring New Jersey, and when she escaped to college she swore she would live an adventurous life or die trying. She succeeded. She's worked as a professional folksinger, a science-fiction author, an industrial pirate, a yard clerk for the C & O Railroad, a Go-Go dancer, and an editor for a labor union newspaper. She has several books and albums of her science-fiction folk music available on Amazon, and several of her songs are posted on YouTube. She currently lives in a small farming town in Arizona, along with her husband, Rasty, three guitars, and a variable number of cats that she breeds for intelligence.

"I do not understand," said the Trailman elder. "Why are you angry at the Beautiful Ones?"

Toshan irritably shifted his weight on the padded branch and was alarmed to feel it shift under him. Gods of all Kyrri, how he hated being this far off the ground. With strained patience, he tried once more to explain. "The *Chieri*…" He would *not* use the Trailmen's term for them, not ever. "…have tricked and misused all of us: Trailmen, Cat-men, Kyrri, Ya-Men—even the Hyumans. They have used us and our ancestors for their benefit, and it is time we stopped them. Now they plan some great work of their own which will change all of Darkover. This they do without our knowledge or consent, and we must stop them. They are few, but we Underpeople—all of us not-so-beautiful people—are many, if we all stand together. We ask you to join with us, to come to Thendara where their 'great work' is planned, and help us put an end to it."

But already the elder was shaking his gray head in denial. "We have no quarrel with the Beautiful Ones," he said. "They have not misused us. Our legends say, and the Human scientists agree, that they raised up our ancestors from near-mindless beasts—the little Chikchuks—and gave us minds that can think beyond the next moment, mouths that can speak, memories and tales to guide us. They have never done us harm, and whatever work they plan will not harm us. We will not leave the forest, and we will not go to Thendara. Take your quarrel to them, if it pleases you, but we will not help."

Toshan had to bite his lip to keep from shouting: *You fool, they never shared their psychic powers with us! They never made us their equals!* If he said that, the elder might recall that the *Chieri* had shared their powers with Humans, and the Humans had never harmed the Trailmen either. Quite the contrary, in fact. No, best leave that line of argument for now. "I only ask you to think about these things," was the best he could do. "Now I must leave—" *Quickly, please!* "—and speak to the other Underpeople who have agreed to join us. They are very many." A l*ie, but he doesn't know it.* "…How do I get down from here?"

The elder only waved to two younger Trailmen, who pointed and led Toshan to the same ladder by which he had ascended an hour earlier. Toshan bowed formally, though he dearly wished he could wring the stupid elder's neck, and picked his way across the platform of interwoven branches to where the ladder waited.

Climbing down the vast tree trunk was infinitely worse than climbing up had been. Toshan had to keep his eyes fixed on the rough bark ahead of him to prevent him from looking down, and that meant feeling with his toes for the next rung of the ladder. It was a slow, strenuous, and frightening process, and he was aching in every joint before he finally reached the blessed solid ground.

Palu was there, wrapped up in a Human-made silvery camping blanket, waiting for him. "He said no," Toshan reported, stamping his feet on the ground just to feel its welcome solidity. "And there are no other Trailmen nests within useful distance. Let's see if Krensa and Bili have any better news."

"It will be a long walk back to Thendara," Palu gloomed. "For Ancestors' sake, let's use those stag-ponies I liberated."

"Are you mad?" Toshan hissed. "The sight of Kyrri riding saddled beasts will be remarked upon. Word might get back to the Hyumans, and they won't keep it secret."

"So take off the saddles," Palu snapped. "We can get close to Thendara before we have to walk again, and time is running short."

~oOo~

Back at their meeting place in the old Thendara house, the plotters met with worse news.

"There is simply no talking to the Ya-Men," Bili complained, clenching his furred hands. "It's dangerous even to get near them. We'll gain no allies there."

"The Cat-Men gave us no better," Krensa growled, fur standing up on her arms. "Even those few we could find laughed in our faces and threatened to *eat* us if we didn't go away, quickly. So we did."

"So, no allies." Morai scratched irritably at the fur on her chest. "Very well. This will be an uprising of the Kyrri alone. This is fitting, really; it should indeed fall to us to punish our arrogant descendants, who have altered all life on our world to suit themselves, who have warped and twisted what is natural and right—"

Knowing that Morai could go on for hours like this if not interrupted, Toshan quickly cut in: "But how many of us do we have in our ranks? How many must we have to disrupt the *Descendants*—" He almost spat the word. "—at their work? Do we even have further news about what the 'work' is, or when?"

Morai stopped in mid-tirade to favor him with a nasty smile. "We do indeed. While you were away, Yosheth got news from the Hyuman quarter; word is sent out to evacuate the city, and to remove as far as possible from the Hellers, before the equinox. There is a city of tents being raised out on the plains, and that is where the *Chieri* and their Hyuman allies are gathering. Some of them are bringing Kyrri servants..." She sneered at the term. "...and we can easily hide among them. Hyumans can't tell one Kyrri from another, and we all know the trick to deflect passing *laran* scans from our descendants, do we not?"

"Concentrate on The Song," Bili replied automatically. "If necessary, bite yourself and concentrate on the pain."

Sure enough, Krensa started singing: "Berry thorn, berry thorn, berry-berry-berry thorn..."

"So we must uproot ourselves again and follow the Hyumans out to this tent city, must we?" Toshan sighed. "How soon?"

"Tomorrow." Morai's tone brooked no argument.

~o0o~

The tent city out on the plain was impressive, as was the number of Humans and *Chieri* gathered there, and even a good two dozen Kyrri—most of whom worked in the food tents, Toshan noted. There was no difficulty fitting in with them, although Toshan recited the shielding Song until he grew heartily sick of it. This was not the entire population of Thendara, of course; other inhabitants had gone off to farms and other settlements outside the city, but the number of Humans gathered here was still surprising. Yes, the great 'work' was definitely afoot here.

The Humans had cleared a large patch of land where the starships took off and landed regularly. The *Chieri* were concentrated in an enormous central tent, and rarely seen outside of it. There was another huge tent beside it, where certain Humans scurried in and out but no one else was allowed inside, as Human guards made abundantly clear.

"I saw it being built and filled," Yosheth all but whispered, while he chopped vegetables for those privileged Humans' dinners. "That's where they keep their 'eelek-tronic' equipment. They use it to speak among themselves, and the ships, constantly."

"Whatever they are planning, it involves those ships," Morai considered, munching on a liberated carrot. "Could we slip some *shlatha* root into their food, do you think?"

"Oh no." Yohseth shook his head quickly. "We tried it, our first night here. Those guards carry implements that they sweep over the dishes, and which warned them. We also tried with the drink we took to the Descendants' tent, which was likewise prevented. The guards are, as they say, on 'high-security alert'."

"Could they be distracted?" Toshan asked, calculating

numbers. Only seven of the Kyrri in the tent-city were knowing Liberators. The rest couldn't be trusted.

"Not easily," Yosheth admitted. "We tried, with a fire in the food tent. The Hyumans were on it in seconds, and none of those guards shifted a foot away from their posts."

"There must be some way," Morai muttered, "To get the seven of us into the Descendants' tent. Are any of our kind allowed in there? We must watch for a chance at some greater distraction."

"No, none of us even pass the tent entrances," Yosheth sighed. "We deliver to the guards, and the *Chieri* come to take the approved dishes inside. Much the same is done at the Hyuman's eelek-tronic tent. We cannot get in there."

"Yet stay close," Morai whispered. "Stay close and watch. Some chance will come."

~oOo~

As equinox day approached, more ships took off than landed. Soon the landing field was empty, and the Humans seemed increasingly tense. All that the Liberator spies could learn were technical terms about "impact effects," "orbital correction," a frantic concern with "precision," and jargon-filled reports on "the course of the asteroid."

"It could be," Bili considered, during one of the Liberators' covert nightly gatherings, "that this asteroid is approaching Darkover, and the Great Work is to deflect it away. The whole matter could have nothing to do with us."

"Oh? Does your Hyuman education tell you that?" Toshan sneered. "Perhaps we'd best send you instead of Shleeth and Vintha to watch the electronics tent."

Bili flattened his ears and glared. "Even the *Chieri* would not want our world struck by an asteroid," he snarled. "And the Hyumans seem to want us to learn from them."

"The Hyumans care no more for us than the Descendants do," snapped Morai. "They'll certainly never give us the *laran* powers of the *Chieri*. It doesn't matter, really, what the Great Work is. It's only the best distraction for the Descendants that we're likely to have for a long time. It's at them we must strike, when the chance comes."

"That will most likely be on equinox day," Toshan concluded, "and during their Great Work."

"Then let us all be close to their tent that day, holding vessels of food and drink for excuse, but always ready to seize our chance."

~oOo~

And so it was that in the late morning of equinox day five Kyrri, dressed as servants, sat in an obedient line near the entrance to the *Chieri* tent holding covered dishes and flasks, waiting but not approaching. The guards glanced at them only occasionally. Palu, at the end of the line, was quietly singing: "Berry thorn, berry thorn, berry-berry-berry thorn..." Two more Kyrri, similarly occupied and mumbling the same song, sat near the electronics tent. They all managed to look bored, though the tension in the air was palpable. All the rest of the great tent city was hushed, waiting.

A screech of electronic noise made everyone flinch. It was followed by a staticky voice announcing: "She's raht on target, not a hayer off. ETA fahve minutes. Get ready."

"Get ready..." Morai echoed, but for what she didn't say.

"...Berry thorn, berry thorn..." Palu sang on.

"ETA one minute," buzzed the electronic voice.

A wave of warning—not heard but felt, yet in clear words—flared out of the *Chieri* tent. *Get down!* It roared silently.

Kyrri, guards, and everyone else in sight dropped flat to the ground.

"Countdown," shouted the staticky voice: "Thirty...twenty...ten, nine, eight—"

Bili, remembering what he'd heard of ship transmissions, shoved his dish and flask aside and wrapped his arms around his head.

"—five, four, three, two, one. Contact!" The voice abruptly shut off.

For a long instant, nothing happened.

Then the ground jumped.

Everyone felt it and heard the sound—like a deep gong

ringing far below. The sound stretched on and on, reverberating in the ground, then shaking, rippling away. A chaos of voices rattled from the electronics tent—and then a growing cheer in Human voices. Then came a sense of profound relief, so thick it could almost be touched, spreading everywhere.

Morai raised her head and saw that the guards were still lying flat.

"Now!" she snapped to the other Liberators. "Go in now!"

She thought to pick up her dish and flask, and the others copied her. Morai darted into the *Chieri* tent's entrance, the other Kyrri following in a line, and the guards didn't think to stop them. Inside lay a short cloth-walled corridor, where the Liberators dropped their bowls and flasks and pulled out assorted blades and bludgeons. They burst out of the cloth corridor and into a vast room...

...whose walls were lined with what the oldest Kyrri recognized as matrix screens, all filled with astronomic displays, tended by assorted *Chieri* who were just rising to their feet. In the center was a thickly padded chair, and in it sat a motionless pale-eyed *Chieri* with long silver-white hair. Beside that one, a young red-haired Human woman—Comyn, by the look of her—stood up, clenching a glowing blue stone, and frowned at the inrushing Liberators. Morai, Toshan, and Krensa dashed toward the pair, knives first, long-cherished slogans ready on their lips.

"Oh, enough!" shouted the Human girl.

Shock.

Darkness.

~o0o~

Toshan came up to dizziness, then waking, and pulled his eyes open to see that he was still inside the tent, in that central room. So were the other Liberators, in a line, just sitting up, facing the young Human and the *Chieri*. Their assorted weapons lay scattered on the floor, ignored. Toshan sat up slowly, wondering if he should try to dart for a knife. Morai was already ranting about ungrateful descendants and oppression and withholding gifts and—

"Oh, be still," snapped the Human girl. Light flared briefly in her closed hand.

Sure enough, Morai stopped in mid-word and Toshan found that he couldn't move. It occurred to him that he'd tied his fate to a vengeful fool who couldn't keep quiet to save her life.

"What were you thinking?" the girl insisted. "Did you want us to miss our mark? Do you want our world to die, just so you could be avenged for imagined slights, envy, and your own shortcomings?"

Imagined?! Toshan bristled, remembering countless unfavorable comparisons between Kyrri and *Chieri. You are The Beautiful Ones, and we are...*

Then it struck him that he had never heard such denigrating comparisons from the *Chieri* themselves. Such had always come from...other Kyrri, such as the Liberators. The word 'envy' stuck like a thorn in his ear.

Then the pale-eyed *Chieri* in the chair moved for the first time—only to raise a hand slightly, but enough to draw everyone's attention. Toshan got the impression that this one was in female phase, and very old...immensely old.

"We are not your descendants," he heard her say clearly, though he could see that her lips didn't move. "We are rather your cousins, sprung from the same root-stock long ago. Our kind had the gene for *laran,* and yours did not. Yes, we saw that your ancestors had potential for intelligence, and yes, we manipulated your ancestors' breeding to develop that—yes, just as we did with the Trailmen and the Cat-men and the Ya-men— but we could not, and we cannot, enhance what you do not have. I'm sorry."

You gave it to the Humans, Toshan thought resentfully, looking at the Human girl with her red hair and six-fingered hands and the obvious matrix crystal held in her fist.

"We did not precisely give *laran* to the Humans," the old *Chieri* went on as if she'd heard his thought. "They already had the potential for it, and we interbred with them to increase it. As for intelligence, they already had that when we found them."

—berry thorn, berry thorn, berry-berry-berry thorn... Toshan thought fiercely to smother the obvious next conclusion. The

Chieri had given his kind intelligence, and the Kyrri had not been grateful but had wanted more. Who were the true ingrates?

He scrambled for another thought, came up with a question, and concentrated on it. *What is the Great Work?*

The ancient creature heaved an immense sigh of almost ecstatic satisfaction. "Restoring the orbit," she replied silently. Accompanying that came two images: the blood-red sun rising on an equinox dawn, precisely filling the space between two familiar mountain peaks, and the same sun on another equinox dawn with space between the peaks and itself—as if the sun had shrunk.

Toshan understood none of it.

Now it was the girl who sighed, and with impatience. "Thousands of years ago," she said aloud, "For reasons we're not certain about, this planet became unbalanced, and its orbit began to spiral outward, away from the sun. The change was tiny—just a few handspans every year—but over the ages the distance grew, and the average annual temperature dropped. That brought on other changes..." There was a quick thought of *reduced fertility*, and then the girl went on. "Our ancestors sought many solutions, but the best of them was to bring the Humans here— for the Humans had starships."

Now it was the old *Chieri* who sent an added note. "The clever ships of Vainwal, their precise measurements, their ability to herd and drive asteroids..." An image of a vast stone flying through the night sky. "They could do what we could not, not in thousands of years."

And Toshan saw that even the Beautiful Ones could feel envy, and envy of a species who had little or no *laran*. It was unthinkable.

He concentrated on the image of that great flying stone. *Asteroid...?*

"The Humans' ships spent years searching for a sky-stone of just the right mass," the girl went on, "Then another year driving it into just the right position, at just the right speed, to strike just the right spot..." An image of the snow-covered central mountains of the Hellers. "...At just the right time. Just enough to push the world into an inward-spiraling orbit. Just a few handsbreadths each year, but enough to save us." The girl actually chuckled. "Perhaps in another ten thousand years we'll need to shove the planet again to make it stay in its ideal orbit, but that will be work for another generation."

With a jolt, Toshan realized what had caused the ground to jump and ring just a few moments ago. *They wanted to move the world!* ...And the *Chieri* might have guided the Work, but they themselves had not done it. Humans had.

"I daresay the weather will be very harsh for the next few days, especially near the Hellers," the girl laughed, "But we can endure that. We can all endure it. Our world is safe."

At that point, the ancient woman sat up straight and looked out at the image-laden screens, and beyond. She drew a deep breath and announced, aloud: "I am Larshkenye, and I have helped to save my people and my world. The purpose of my life is fulfilled."

Then she sank back, limp, into the cushions of the chair.

"Great-grandmother!" the girl cried out in concern. She clutched Larshkenye's near wrist with one hand while the other swept the blue stone over the old *chieri*'s body.

Toshan felt the invisible grip on him loosen, and for a moment he wondered what he should do with his freedom. Then he saw Morai lunge toward one of the forgotten knives on the floor.

He started to shout, *No, no, you fool! Not now!* but before he could breathe a word the invisible grasp closed on him again, and on Morai too, who fell bonelessly to the floor. Through a corner of his eye, Toshan saw another of the *chieri* attendants watching the clutch of Liberators with a disgusted expression. This one time, he knew, that scorn was deserved.

But the ancient Larshkenye revived, sat up straighter, and pulled another deep breath. Toshan felt her trickle of amusement sweep the room. "Now as to your complaint..." she said, again without moving her lips, "You wish to live without Gifted beings lording it over you, correct?"

Toshan knew how all the Liberators would answer, what he

would answer if he could speak. In spite of all he'd learned in the past fragment of an hour, the resentment—the envy—was still there.

"So be it." Larshkenye flicked her eyes toward another of the matrix screens, which changed its image to a different astronomical display. "In the ages when we searched for a solution, we found ways to move ourselves—and other beings— to different worlds, worlds where they could survive and possibly thrive. We have moved other creatures of Darkover to different worlds for safekeeping, including your folk. We have a world for you, much warmer, inhabited by none but Kyrri—and Humans, of a sort you may find familiar. I believe the Humans call it 'Wolf.' May you be content there. ...Oh, and take your silly weapons with you."

Toshan felt the grasp on him shift, lifting him up, even dropping the knife back into his tunic. He could move his head enough to see that the other Liberators were rising also, and not of their own will. He saw the other *Chieri* move to encircle them, and one of the matrix screens flashing in rapid pulses. He could hear Morai snarling curses, and devoutly wished he could have kicked the fool. Then one of the flashes from the screen covered him—or he was pulled into it.

An instant of darkness, and then a solid thump of landing on what felt like sand.

Toshan opened his eyes on a different color of light, heard the silence of a vast, empty space, smelled a different—dusty—scent of air, felt a subtly different pull of gravity on him and unusual warmth in the air, in the ground. He blinked and sat up, and saw the other Liberators doing the same. They were on a great rolling plain of empty sand, near to a crude stone well etched with markings, under a featureless bright orange sky with a yellow blob of sun low in one corner. For once, Morai had nothing to say.

"This must be the world called Wolf," Yosheth muttered. "Does anyone know anything of it?"

"I think so," Bili coughed. "Part of the Terran Empire, settled for more than a thousand standard years, mostly desert and grassland with a few cities. Industries: herding, mining, metalworking, some fishing, and a little farming. No inhabitants except Humans...and Kyrri."

"At last!" Morai lunged to her feet. "A world without the Descendants, where no one has *laran,* and no one can claim to be better than us! A world where we can be free! A world—"

Toshan closed his ears to the developing rant, feeling for the knife in his tunic. Right now this was also a world with only one immediate source of water, and no food visible anywhere.

Ah, but over there—just coming over a low ridge—was an unmistakable Human. He was riding on a creature that resembled a Terran beast called a 'camel' and leading a string of others that were covered with lumpish packs. He was clearly coming toward the well. Even Morai shut up to watch him approach. As he drew closer it grew apparent that the man wore a scabbarded sword belted to his waist, and had some manner of rifle slung over his shoulder. He looked very much like a Darkovan Dry Towner, and Toshan began to wonder just how long Humans had been traveling in this part of the galaxy.

The man reined in his mount beside the well and ran his gaze over the line of Liberators. He shouted out a recognizable Dry Town challenge in Terran Standard, so thickly accented that it was almost incomprehensible. The Kyrri looked at him, looked at each other, and wondered how to react. Bili thought to make the usual standard bow, and the others copied him.

"What luck!" the man crowed. "Masterless Kyrri!" He pulled out his sword and waved it ceremoniously over their heads. "Then I am your master now: I, Sayeed Manborg. Drink your fill, and I will give you food. Then you will follow me to the city of New Purity, where you will serve me and my clan. Move sharply, now!"

The Liberators looked at each other, saying nothing, knowing that they had no other choice at the moment. Yes, they would follow the Human with the food, go to the nearest city, and work as servants again while they plotted rebellion, again. They were indeed free of the *chieri,* and had no one now to envy. It was indeed an improvement, Toshan understood. The Liberators had what they had wished for.

Even Morai would be pleased, for she would still have someone to resent.

NOTES ON THE STORIES

Golden Eyes, by Marella Sands

I remember seeing something about how settlers moving into the American West caused the extinction of the Rocky Mountain locust (last seen in 1902; declared extinct in 2014). When considering what to write for this anthology, I thought of the Rocky Mountain locust and wondered what had happened to similar creatures on Darkover. I'm sorry these little Darkover insects appear to be extinct by later centuries, because I think they'd be an interesting part of the landscape. Though....maybe a few still exist somewhere between Neskaya and Nevarsin? One never knows.

Little Mouse, by Shariann Lewitt

Shariann has been so inundated with university registration software misbehavior, we are grateful to have a story from her, with or without notes.

Avarra's Scion, by Evey Brett.

"Avarra's Scion" began in response to a series of tragedies at Evey's day job. So often, authors take their deepest pain and spin it into the gold of stories that touch the hearts of many readers.

Finders Keepers, by Deborah Millitello

At a convention, I heard an editor mention that she wasn't receiving stories with older protagonists. I decided I wanted to write a story with a main character who was my age but was still capable of taking care of herself, not rich or noble, but an ordinary woman.

A Cold, Bleak Day in the Hellers, by Barb Caffrey.

My thought was that during the Ages of Chaos, people still

had to get married, and some of them—the better types of nobles—would do so because they were worried about others rather than wanting to make a love-match for themselves. (Historically, if people fell in love while making a dynastic marriage, all well and good. Most didn't but learned how to tolerate each other.)

For my purposes, I wanted two unusual people to fall in love during a crisis. The female half, Cynthia, was a swordswoman— one of the Sisterhood of Swords—and a good one. The male half, Donal, was a scholar at Nevarsin and had been roundly mocked by much of his family due to his scholasticism. That said, he was close to one sister, who'd been shipped off to Temora to make a different dynastic marriage...and who'd stopped writing to him a few years earlier.

Cynthia was not used to men allowing her to take the lead in her private life. But she was the last member of her clan, besides her father; she'd been called home to make a marriage with someone she didn't know and didn't love because it was the only way to save both clans from extinction.

Donal, being who he was, saw Cynthia's gifts as valid, and while he gave counsel, she was the one who led the attempt to take over both kingdoms while she and Donal were celebrating their marriage.

In so doing, they discovered they worked well together, and that their aims in living a good life and doing right by those who followed them (the smallholders, or yeoman farmer-types) were often the same. They also were both literate and were reading the same book (unbeknownst to them!), and, finally, Cynthia was touched by Donal's love for his lost sister. (The story explains what happened to her, but I need to leave some suspense for the reader, elsewise they might not want to read the actual story.)

I titled the story "A Cold, Bleak Day in the Hellers" because that's what both Donal and Cynthia had thought about either one of them ever being married. (They married as freemates, not *di catenas*, which was also something both wanted but didn't realize until after they married. Psychologically, I believed both understood that any marriage under these circumstances would be for life, or at least until both clans were integrated due to the marriage, but I left that unsaid.) However, I could've called it "An Alliance of Equals," because that is exactly what it turns out to be.

That Cynthia has a sworn swordsister who comes with her, while Donal arrives alone, also was important to me—something I realized as I was writing the story. Best friends are important, but oft-times, solitary, scholastically inclined men don't always meet people as well as others.

I dedicate this story, as I have dedicated all of my stories, to my late husband, Michael. He was exactly that solitary type of scholar, and while I was not a swordswoman, we certainly did read the same sorts of books (but not realize it until we got together), and we had complementary skills. He was the person who made me believe that love could indeed be an alliance of equals and that all of your talents—whether they sometimes seemed strange or weird or whatever—were worth cultivating.

Field Work, by Margaret L. Carter and Leslie Roy Carter

We wanted to explore a slightly unusual use of *laran*, and I (Margaret) didn't recall animal empathy and control appearing often in past anthologies. We also wanted to play with the tension between Darkovan and Earth worldviews. We envision this story as set relatively soon after re-contact, when Terrans had little in-depth knowledge of Darkover, being restricted in their travel outside their own base and their interactions with the local people away from Thendara. Margaret devised the plot and wrote most of the first draft; Les wrote the fight scenes and added other incidental material.

To Reach for the Stars, by Lillian Csernica

As soon as I heard this anthology's theme, I knew I wanted to write about a jewel heist. I grew up watching Peter Sellers in *The Pink Panther* movies and Michael Caine in *The Italian Job*. I got to thinking about smuggling off-world jewels and matrix crystals. The key to a good heist story is to keep raising the stakes. At the heart of my story is Cherilly's Law. All it would take is one criminal clever enough to smuggle one matrix crystal off of Darkover. The efforts of Terran Empire scientists to duplicate the matrix crystal could break Cherilly's Law and destroy everything. None of the main characters in *Reach For The Stars* have reason to know Cherilly's Law, but the Comyn Council know very well the danger averted thanks to Maya, Dalia, and their sister Renunciates. They didn't just save the day. They might well have saved the entire universe.

Fire Seed, by Diana L. Paxson

After a College Creative Writing class focused on "literary fiction" had discouraged me from writing at all, reading the Darkover books showed that it was possible to write stories that people like me actually enjoyed. Marion was the first to treat in SF topics of great importance to under-represented populations, from psychic experience to same-sex relationships to feminism. I feel sure she would be exploring gender issues if she were writing today. "Fire Seed," is my latest in a series of "Forbidden Guildhouse" stories exploring this area. I am particularly interested in what happens when the new generation of social radicals clashes with the old.

Nor Iron Bars A Cage, by Rosemary and India Edghill

One of the joys of Darkover is its intriguing mix of species and cultures. The Domains get most of the attention, but the Dry Towns have a fascinating life of their own. It's easy to write the Dry Towns off as a brutal, misogynistic place without any redeeming social characteristics. But Marion herself hinted in *The Shattered Chain* that there may be more to the Dry Towns than that when Rohana says that Jaelle's mother *could* have found happiness "even in chains." So "Nor Iron Bars A Cage" is another story spun off that line. Because no culture is completely one-sided; cultures are woven of many threads, some bright, some dark. And just as the Domains have their downsides—isn't it possible that the Dry Towns have some upsides as well?

NOTES ON THE STORIES

Pebbles, by Rhondi Salsitz

Writing for a Darkover anthology is always a welcome challenge. While meeting the theme, I also try to find a niche in the history that hasn't been explored too much. Paulin's story takes place in the strife-filled years when the Darkovans re-establish contact with *Terranan*. His *laran* comes from a House all but lost to the Comyn and he may be an auditory seer. I enjoyed writing his story and hope the reader enjoys reading it.

Berry-thorn, Berry-thorn, by Leslie Fish

In all the years that I've been happily reading and writing Darkover stories, I've been fascinated by both the different intelligent native creatures on the planet and its interesting astrometrics. Seeing that its star logically has to be a red dwarf, and the planet has to have been stable long enough for those intelligent species to evolve, the cold climate doesn't make sense unless at some time Darkover was nudged out of its original orbit and has been drifting further from its sun ever since. At the latest point in its history, the Darkovan humans have driven off the Terran Empire and allied with other rebels in the nearest solar system as well as the native *chieri*. I could see all of them getting together in a plan to correct the planet's orbit, and I wondered what the other intelligent species on Darkover would think about this alliance. I also wondered how to explain the presence of the kyrri species on both Darkover and Wolf. This is my attempt to tie up all those loose ends.

ABOUT THE EDITOR

Deborah J. Ross is an award-nominated author of fantasy and science fiction. She's written over a dozen traditionally published novels and six dozen pieces of short fiction. After her debut sale in 1983 to the first volume of Marion Zimmer Bradley's *Sword and Sorceress*, her short fiction has appeared in *The Magazine of Fantasy and Science Fiction, Asimov's, Star Wars: Tales from Jabba's Palace, Realms of Fantasy, Sisters of the Night, Marion Zimmer Bradley's Fantasy Magazine*, and other anthologies and magazines. Her recent releases include Darkover novels *The Laran Gambit* and *The Children of Kings* (with Marion Zimmer Bradley); *Collaborators*, a Lambda Literary Award Finalist/James Tiptree, Jr. Award recommended list; and *The Seven-Petaled Shield*, an epic fantasy trilogy based on her "Azkhantian Tales" in the *Sword and Sorceress* series. Deborah made her editorial debut in 2008 with *Lace and Blade*, followed by *Lace and Blade 2, Stars of Darkover* (with Elisabeth Waters), *Gifts of Darkover, Realms of Darkover*, and other anthologies. When she's not writing, she knits for charity, plays classical piano, and hikes in the redwoods.

For the latest news about her projects, videos of readings, plus recipes and photos of her cats, sign up for her free newsletter *here* or at http://eepurl.com/dmg0-b

THE DARKOVER® ANTHOLOGIES

Edited by Marion Zimmer Bradley:
THE KEEPER'S PRICE, 1980
SWORD OF CHAOS, 1982
FREE AMAZONS OF DARKOVER, 1985
OTHER SIDE OF THE MIRROR, 1987
RED SUN OF DARKOVER, 1987
FOUR MOONS OF DARKOVER, 1988
DOMAINS OF DARKOVER, 1990
RENUNCIATES OF DARKOVER, 1991
LERONI OF DARKOVER, 1991
TOWERS OF DARKOVER, 1993
MARION ZIMMER BRADLEY'S DARKOVER, 1993
SNOWS OF DARKOVER, 1994
Edited by Elisabeth Waters:
MUSIC OF DARKOVER, 2013
Edited by Elisabeth Waters and Deborah J. Ross:
STARS OF DARKOVER, 2014
Edited by Deborah J. Ross:
GIFTS OF DARKOVER, 2015
REALMS OF DARKOVER, 2016
MASQUES OF DARKOVER, 2017
CROSSROADS OF DARKOVER, 2018
CITADELS OF DARKOVER, 2019
JEWELS OF DARKOVER, 2023

Other anthologies edited by Deborah J. Ross

LACE AND BLADE
LACE AND BLADE 2
LACE AND BLADE 4
LACE AND BLADE 5

SWORD AND SORCERESS 33 (with Elisabeth Waters)

Darkover® novels by Marion Zimmer Bradley and Deborah J. Ross

THE FALL OF NESKAYA
ZANDRU'S FORGE
A FLAME IN HALI
THE ALTON GIFT
HASTUR LORD
THE CHILDREN OF KINGS
THUNDERLORD
THE LARAN GAMBIT
ARILINN (forthcoming)

Made in the USA
Las Vegas, NV
12 November 2024

11645528R00138